THE WOMEN IN WHITE

ALSO BY SARAH PEKKANEN

The Locked Ward

House of Glass

Gone Tonight

The Ever After

The Perfect Neighbors

Things You Won't Say

Catching Air

The Best of Us

These Girls

Skipping a Beat

The Opposite of Me

WITH GREER HENDRICKS

The Golden Couple

You Are Not Alone

An Anonymous Girl

The Wife Between Us

THE WOMEN IN WHITE

A NOVEL

SARAH PEKKANEN

ST. MARTIN'S PRESS
NEW YORK

This is a work of fiction. All of the characters, organizations, and events portrayed in this novel are either products of the author's imagination or are used fictitiously.

First published in the United States by St. Martin's Press,
an imprint of St. Martin's Publishing Group

EU Representative: Macmillan Publishers Ireland Ltd, 1st Floor, The Liffey Trust Centre,
117–126 Sheriff Street Upper, Dublin 1, D01 YC43

www.stmartins.com

The Library of Congress Cataloging-in-Publication Data is available upon request.

ISBN 978-1-250-34955-2 (hardcover)
ISBN 978-1-250-34956-9 (ebook)

First Edition: 2026

10 9 8 7 6 5 4 3 2 1

For Anthony Barbarino. You were worth the wait.

AUTHOR'S NOTE

Although this book is a work of fiction, the quotes that appear in front of Betty's chapters are all real and verifiable. Many of the cited journals and articles were kept in the Duke Parapsychology Laboratory, which existed as a distinguished part of the university from 1930 until 1965. Inside the laboratory, researchers conducted tests designed to measure the psychic abilities of college students and other volunteers.

This keen interest in parapsychology wasn't limited to just Duke's history: Others who explored it include academics at colleges across the country and internationally, some law enforcement officials, the CIA, and even an astronaut on the *Apollo 14* flight, who conducted experiments unbeknownst to NASA.

Many of the documents quoted in my novel are still stored at the Rhine Research Center in Durham, North Carolina, which is an outgrowth of the Duke Parapsychology Laboratory. The employees of Rhine, as well as Sally Feather Rhine—the daughter of the laboratory's founder, J. B. Rhine—could not have been more welcoming to me, allowing me to conduct research, interviews, and even test my own psychic abilities. But my characters and plot are purely fictional and are in no way based on any individual, living or dead.

THE WOMEN IN WHITE

CHAPTER ONE

RILEY, PRESENT DAY

Just before I knock on the door of the small brick house, I'm gripped by the skin-tingling sense I'm being watched.

But when I twist my head around, the only thing I see is a neglected stretch of yard. It must have been pretty once. The bones are there—brittle rosebushes lining the worn picket fence, gardens overrun by weeds, a graceful sugar maple tree being choked by vines.

I turn back, shaking off my unease, and knock so firmly my knuckles sting. Betty Sadler is eighty-one. Her hearing may be failing.

She's a sweet woman, but incredibly picky. You can't imagine how hard it has been to fill this position, said the social worker who tipped me off about the caretaker job.

As the front door opens, I lower my gaze to Betty, who uses a wheelchair. Her white hair is swept into an updo and she's wearing a pink dress and string of pearls. Her skin is so creamy and unlined it could belong to a woman half her age.

I aim for a confident, warm smile. "Hi, Mrs. Sadler. I'm Riley Bell."

"It's a pleasure to meet you." Betty's eyes travel over me and I'm aware of the small mustard stain on my sleeve from a recent fast-food dinner. I'm grateful I at least changed out of jeans and into a skirt.

"I've never heard the name Riley before. Is it Irish?" she asks.

"Yes, it's actually my mother's maiden name."

"That explains your lovely auburn hair. Please come in."

I follow her into the living room. It smells like lemon cleaner and the furniture looks old but well-kept. The heavy gold drapes are pulled back, allowing the fall sunlight to brighten the space.

Along with running errands, cooking, and helping Betty bathe and dress, the job requires light cleaning. But Betty's house is already spotless.

"What a lovely home," I tell Betty, wondering if I should sit down or wait for an invitation. "Have you lived here for a long time?"

"Sixty years," Betty replies. "Time truly does fly by."

Betty doesn't use email, so I've brought a copy of my résumé. I slip it out of my bag, hoping nerves haven't made my hands sweaty. Standing in a stranger's house with nothing to my name but the old Toyota I've been sleeping in for weeks is a place I never imagined I'd be at age thirty-two. But impulsively marrying a hilarious, handsome guy who hid a massive gambling addiction led me here.

"Would you care for some coffee, or perhaps tea?" Betty offers.

"I'd love some. Can I help?"

"You just make yourself comfortable. I'll be back in a jiffy." She wheels down the hallway into the kitchen, propelling herself swiftly with arms that must still be strong.

I look into the dining room where a table and chairs are framed by faded floral wallpaper. There's a pile of papers on the table, close enough that I can glimpse the top one. The formatting gives it away: It's a résumé.

My competition.

When my life imploded in a series of hard, fast blows—my discovery of Danny's enormous secret followed by our bankruptcy and divorce filings the same week—I began searching for a better-paying job than my current one as a nurse's aide at a hospital. I've applied for dozens, but with only two years of college, I rarely get to the interview stage. I've run out of options.

Betty is offering a generous salary, plus it's live-in. I'll do whatever it takes to get hired.

I hear the spurt of water running and clatter of dishes in the distance. Betty probably won't be back for a couple of minutes.

"I love the painting in your dining room," I say loudly as I step toward it. "Is it of the Grand Canyon?"

"Yes," Betty calls back. "I always dreamed of seeing it but we never made it there, so my husband bought me the painting as a birthday present."

"I've never been, either." I reach down for the pile of neatly stacked résumés, hoping to glean a way to set myself apart from the pack. My eyes widen as I scan them. They're from nurse practitioners, physical therapists, and nursing aides. People who speak multiple languages and have twice the experience as me. Why would Betty ever choose me over these candidates?

I walk back into the living room, feeling defeated. *It isn't over yet,* I remind myself. There must be something I can do to make myself stand out.

A moment later, Betty comes in with a tray balanced on the flat armrests of her chair. Atop it are two pink-and-white china teacups with matching saucers, a sugar bowl, and a small pitcher of cream.

She sets the tray on the coffee table and hands me a cup.

"I hope you like Earl Grey," she says.

"Oh, that's actually my favorite." My insomnia forced me to give up coffee, but on chilly fall days like today I crave hot, sweet black tea. She smiles, seemingly pleased by the coincidence that we both prefer the same beverage.

"Tell me a bit about yourself," she prompts.

"Well, I've been a health care aide at Union Memorial for the past five years and I really enjoy it," I say, launching into the little speech I prepared on the drive over. "I like being around people, and ever since I was a little girl, I've wanted to be a healer. I used to bring home wounded birds and try to nurse them back to health. It's just in my nature, I guess."

"What a nice quality. And do you have family nearby?" she asks.

"Not too far away. I grew up in Northern Virginia, and my parents still live in the house I was raised in. Although right now, they're on a bike tour around Italy, which my father has always wanted to do."

"Italy! My goodness gracious. Did they travel by airplane or ocean liner?"

I blink. "Um, they flew . . . I also have an older sister and brother who live in the DC suburbs. They're both married, with five kids between them."

Betty nods. "May I ask, why are you interested in a live-in position?"

I shift in my seat. "Unfortunately, my husband and I recently divorced and we sold our home." It's a partial truth; the bank repossessed it.

"Oh, dear," Betty says. "How long ago did this happen?"

"A month ago."

Betty pats my arm. Her hand feels as soft as talcum powder. "That's how long my Douglas has been gone, too."

"I'm so sorry," I tell her as sadness fills her eyes. "I can't imagine how hard it must be."

"It was very sudden. A heart attack. I called for an ambulance and they took him to the hospital, but it was already too late. He didn't suffer, so I take a bit of comfort from that."

Betty lifts her cup to her lips and I catch a familiar scent, one I've heard is among the five most identifiable aromas in the world.

Betty isn't drinking tea. I smell coffee. A glance into her cup confirms it.

How could she know I prefer tea? My mind scrambles to find a logical answer. Before I land on one, Betty says something that leaves me so stunned I'm momentarily speechless: "I'd like to offer you the job. How soon can you start?"

CHAPTER TWO

The investigation of extra-sensory perception at Duke University . . . has come to include well over ninety thousand trials.

—Dr. J. B. Rhine, PhD, head of the Duke Parapsychology Laboratory

BETTY, 1964

Betty Sadler applied a fresh coat of Revlon's Berry Bon-Bon lipstick as she hummed along to the Marvelettes record spinning on the turntable. The pot roast in the oven smelled fabulous, and she'd already set the Sears dining table with her pink-and-white wedding china.

Make your home a welcoming haven and make yourself as pretty as a picture when your husband walks in after a hard day's work! a recent article in *Women's Weekly* advised.

Betty was mixing two Manhattans in a silver shaker—*A cold drink is a sure way to warm your man's heart*—when she heard the front door open.

"Darling? I'm home." Those simple words from her husband—her husband!—sent Betty's heart fluttering as she rushed to greet Douglas. He dropped his briefcase and cradled her face in his hands. The way he drank her in as he stroked her cheekbones with his thumbs before leaning down to kiss her made her body go weak. They'd gotten married eight months ago, just after her nineteenth birthday, and Betty had never felt happier.

"What did you do today?" Douglas asked as they sat in the living room with their cocktails. The cabinet console turntable dropped the next record, playing the catchy notes of "Love Me Do" by The Beatles, one of Betty's favorite bands—especially since Douglas looked a bit like Paul McCartney, the handsomest Beatle.

"After class I met Marilyn and Babs for a sandwich, then popped into the market. I'm almost out of Ajax and tomorrow's my laundry day." She frowned. "Is your drink alright, darling?"

"It's perfect." Douglas finally took a sip. "I'm a bit distracted. Work was interesting today."

"Your work is always interesting." Betty smiled and stood up. "Why don't I give you a moment alone with your thoughts while I check on dinner?"

As she stirred the green beans on the stovetop, she glanced over at Douglas. The intent look on his face—his dark brows knitted together, his eyes faraway—was the same one he'd worn when they'd met the previous fall on the Marquis University campus. He'd been so lost in thought he'd bumped against her as they passed each other on a walking path.

"I'm sorry!" Betty had blurted instinctively.

"It was my fault. Forgive me," Douglas had replied.

The Virginia campus looked especially beautiful that afternoon, its blue-gray stone buildings adorned with gothic touches like arches, finials, and gargoyles. The surrounding trees were tipped with orange and crimson, and students milled about, the girls in pretty skirts and dresses, the boys in letterman sweaters and white button-down shirts with skinny ties.

A light wind swept around them, sending leaves swirling through the air. Like a scene from a movie, Betty had thought as she'd stared up at Douglas.

"Are you a college girl?" he'd asked.

She'd nodded. "I'm in my second year. And you?"

"I'm earning a PhD," he'd replied. "I work in the Trimble Institute." Everyone on campus knew that inside the Department of Psychology building, researchers were doing extraordinary work, testing the psychic capabilities of the human mind.

"You work with Dr. Trimble? How fascinating!"

He'd cleared his throat, looking the tiniest bit nervous. And Betty knew with a swift certainty that he was going to ask her out and change her life forever.

Now Betty turned down the heat on the green beans and returned to sit next to Douglas, quietly waiting until he was ready to converse again.

"I tested a volunteer who did well with the Zener cards today," he finally said. "But not well enough for Dr. Trimble's purposes."

"Zener cards? What are they?"

"They were developed right here at Marquis. Each card has one of five symbols. I held up the cards while the subject tried to intuit which symbols were on them."

"And people can actually do this well?"

"Some better than others. Dr. Trimble's theory is that certain extraordinary abilities exist naturally in a tiny section of the population. Like the musicality of Dean Charles, or a mint quarterback's arm, or the writing of a Fitzgerald. Dr. Trimble is seeking the cream of the crop, the chosen few who have innate psychical ability."

Betty reached for a Lucky Strike from her pack on the table and Douglas leaned forward, pulling his silver lighter out of his breast pocket. She inhaled as he lit her cigarette, then said, "Tell me, what are the symbols on the cards?"

Douglas smiled. "How about I show you instead?"

Inside his briefcase was a pack of twenty-five, each printed with either a circle, a cross, three wavy lines, a square, or a star. "What's interesting about these symbols is each has one more line than the other—the circle has one line, the cross has two, and so on."

"Clever," Betty replied.

Douglas shuffled the cards. "How about I test you?"

She batted her hand at him. "Don't be silly."

"Come on. It'll be fun." Douglas held up a card with its back to her.

"Okay, fine. Let's see . . . a circle?"

He flipped it over, revealing a square.

"Try again."

"A star?" It was a circle.

She giggled. "I'm hopeless."

"Let's call those practice," Douglas said. "Take a deep breath. We find subjects do better when they're completely relaxed and highly focused."

"Oh, Douglas, I'm not any good at this. Shall we go eat dinner?"

"Won't you try for me again? Close your eyes and take a moment before you answer this time."

He held up another card. Her eyes drifted shut as she let her mind play with the five possible symbols, imagining them lined up in a row. Her interior world tunneled into that singular focus.

"Wavy lines." She kept her eyes closed. "A star . . . a cross . . . a squa—no, another star."

"Are you peeking?"

Her eyes snapped open. "Of course not."

Douglas shuffled the remaining cards, then picked up the top one. "Keep going."

By the time she guessed the final card, the record had ended and the room was silent. The ashtray held a snake of gray from her forgotten cigarette, and it didn't look like Douglas had taken another sip of his drink.

"How did I do?" she asked.

"It's too soon to say." Douglas placed the Zener cards on the coffee table, tapping the edges to align the stack.

"Make sure to put those back in your briefcase," Betty said. "You don't want to forget them tomorrow."

Douglas was looking at her, but his mind seemed elsewhere again. "It could be luck." His voice was so quiet she could barely make out the words.

Betty reached for his hand and tugged him to his feet. "You're in for some luck, too. I made ambrosia salad for dessert."

She chatted gaily while they ate, trying to find a topic to engage Douglas, but none took hold. When she finished clearing the table and washing the dishes, she came into the living room to see Douglas on the couch again, shuffling the cards. She stopped short, a strange sense of foreboding gripping her.

"Betty, come here," Douglas instructed her. "I'd like to test you again."

CHAPTER THREE

RILEY, PRESENT DAY

A rush of relief softens the hard knot that has taken up permanent residence in my chest as Betty shows me the bedroom where I'll be staying.

The walls are painted pink and the simple room holds a plain bed, wooden dresser, and nightstand. Paradise compared to sleeping in my car.

"When can you move in?" Betty asks.

I look down at my feet. "Um, anytime really. Even today if you like."

"Oh, that's wonderful!" Betty claps her hands together. "The sooner the better."

It almost seems too good to be true.

"It won't take me long," I tell her. "My belongings are already in my car."

Betty tilts her head and a sharpness fills her pale blue eyes. My cheeks burn as I realize I've revealed too much. But all she says is, "It's almost as if you knew you were going to get this job."

"Well, I hoped." I'm too ashamed to tell Betty my belongings are always in my car. Creditors claimed everything of value from our home, including the furniture.

"Come find me in the kitchen when you're ready," Betty says.

"Thank you, Mrs. Sadler."

"Oh, please, you must call me Betty," she says. "Especially since we're going to be housemates!"

It takes me a half dozen trips to empty my Toyota. When I bring in the last bin of clothes, I see Betty has left a set of daisy-patterned sheets on my twin bed. I pick up the soft old plastic package, reading the copy: *Penn-Prest means you never iron!*

The design and fonts on the mattress label look as retro as the ones on the sheets, and the mattress is just as pristine. *Betty sure knows how to take care of her belongings,* I think as I wander into the kitchen, stopping short in the doorway.

The cabinets and counters are low. That I expected; Betty needs an accessible space. It's the colors that surprise me: turquoise counters and a matching stove with oversized round dials. A black-and-white checkerboard floor. Burnt orange paint coating the walls.

A designer would call it retro. But this isn't like a kitschy throwback diner. The worn spots on the floor and edges of the counters reveal the kitchen is old enough to have gone out of fashion, then—more than half a century later—edged back in.

Betty is at the sink filling an ice cube tray.

"Can I help you with that?" I offer.

"It's no trouble." Betty expertly maneuvers to slide the tray into the freezer. "Surely you haven't finished unpacking already?"

"No, I just brought in my things—and I found the sheets. Thank you . . . I was wondering, is there a daily schedule you'd like me to follow?"

"Oh, we'll figure it out as we go along," Betty replies. "But there is one thing I do need help with today. My refrigerator is nearly bare. I was hoping you could run to the grocery store."

"Absolutely," I tell her. "I can go right now if you like."

"I have a list on my desk. Let me fetch it for you."

I follow Betty back into the living room, taking in more details of my new home. There's a record player built into a wood console along with albums by Bobby Vinton, Elvis, The Beach Boys, and The

Supremes. A brass sunburst wall clock. Bookshelves full of thick volumes with worn edges—mostly psychology, history, and classics by Steinbeck, Faulkner, and Hemingway.

This house has the feel of my grandparents' place, the one they lived in for fifty years, but they had incorporated modern touches like a flat-panel TV, microwave, and cell phone.

There's nothing like that here. Every single thing I've seen in this house could come from the past century—including the string of pearls around Betty's neck.

"My husband shopped at a store called the Food Lion." Betty hands me a folded slip of paper. "I'll give you one of his maps so you can find your way."

I reach into my pocket and pull out my cell phone. "I can just google it. Could I get your Wi-Fi password?"

Betty is staring at me like I'm speaking a foreign language. "Password?"

"For the Internet," I clarify.

"Oh, we don't have one," she says vaguely, like she's trying to pretend she knows what I'm talking about.

She wheels closer to me and peers at my iPhone. "Isn't that a marvel?" she breathes.

My gaze falls on the telephone on Betty's roll-top desk with the rotary dial and long curly cord attaching the receiver to the base. Is it possible she has never seen a cell phone? The way she's staring at mine tells me it is.

My eyes widen as the realization slams into me: It isn't just the décor that's frozen in time. The music Betty listens to, the books she reads, her innocence about electronics, even her clothing and beehive hairstyle.

Betty is still living in the 1960s, too.

CHAPTER FOUR

> Capt. Edgar D. Mitchell Jr., the astronaut, said today that four persons on earth participated in the extrasensory perception experiment he conducted during the *Apollo 14* flight to the moon early in February.
>
> —*The New York Times*

BETTY, 1964

"Isn't it a bit late?" Betty protested as she sat beside Douglas, watching their headlights carve a path through the dark streets.

"Betty, if what I think is happening is actually happening, I have to bring you to Dr. Trimble."

"But surely he'll be home relaxing at this time of night." *Like we should be,* she thought.

Douglas gripped the Impala's steering wheel, peering at the road ahead. "Dr. Trimble is always working."

The psychology building rose up before them, its pale stone walls gleaming beneath the moonlight. With its leaded glass windows and tall pointed spires topping the roofline, it looked like a haunted house from a child's storybook.

"That's Dr. Trimble's Buick." Douglas pointed to a maroon car, the only one parked on the street.

Betty felt lightheaded. "Darling . . . I'm not sure about this."

He didn't seem to hear her. He climbed out of the car and hurried up the steps as she struggled to keep up with him.

Douglas unlocked the tall, arched door to the institute with a key on his chain. "Dr. Trimble?" His voice seemed to be swallowed up by the empty hallway. "Let's check his office."

Betty had come to the institute a few times before, but in this shadowy light, details took on an ominous dimension. A photograph on the wall of a college girl lying on a cot with her eyes closed while three men in dark suits stared down at her. Stacks of heavy books threatening to topple over on the floor of Dr. Trimble's office. And a peculiar blindfold, made from fabric straps and two halves of a Ping-Pong ball, resting on a small round table.

The director's dinner plate was on his desk: a chop, a baked potato congealing in a puddle of melted butter, a glass of milk, and a slice of chocolate cake. "His wife must have delivered it," Douglas explained in a whisper, like they were in a sacred space. The scent of cooked meat lingered in the air, but the meal was untouched.

Betty flinched when she caught sight of a barn owl perched on a table staring at her with round, unblinking eyes.

"It's stuffed," her husband whispered, but he was wrong. A stuffed animal was a sweet toy. This creature had been alive once. It was a trophy whose soul had been claimed by Dr. Trimble.

When the door flew open from the adjacent room, Betty started. Silas Trimble stood there blinking rapidly. In an instant, Betty understood why. The director had been in a small room that was completely dark. His eyes were now being assaulted by the light.

Betty peered beyond him into the room. The walls were painted black. There was nothing in it but a recliner chair. No artwork. No windows. It was worse than a jail cell. She couldn't imagine why anyone would voluntarily seal themselves inside.

"Why did you bring her here?" Dr. Trimble asked, frowning, as he looked over Betty's head to address Douglas.

"I've been testing her with Zener cards for the past few hours. Her average is eleven. My own wife! Who would ever have thought what you've been searching for could be right under my nose!"

Douglas's cheeks were flushed and excitement rang through his voice. She could envision him as a boy, bringing home a perfect report card to his father. Delivering a prize.

Betty knew he respected Dr. Trimble. Now she understood it was more than that—Douglas revered him.

Betty tried to smile pleasantly as she took in Dr. Trimble's graying beard and fringe of darker hair above his ears, his broad shoulders and slightly curved back. He was a large man, perhaps six feet two, and he carried extra weight in his belly.

"She may as well sit down."

Betty sank into the chair opposite his desk, with Douglas standing by her side. Dr. Trimble packed fresh tobacco into his wood pipe and lit it, then exhaled blue-gray smoke that smelled like burnt vanilla. He pushed aside his dinner plate and reached for a deck of cards identical to the one Douglas had shown her.

"I'm going to hold up the first card. Tell me the symbol when you're ready."

What began as fun in her living room carried a deep undercurrent of tension here. Her body clenched as she closed her eyes. The sweet smoke tickled her nostrils and she became aware of Douglas's breathing hitching faster than normal.

"A square," she finally said, because she had to say something.

She called out symbol after symbol, desperate to get this over with. To return to their cozy home and lay together in bed, their hands entwined as they drifted off to sleep.

"Five," Dr. Trimble announced. "Exactly what chance would allow. Are you sure you didn't let your wife see the cards, Douglas?"

Betty's eyes flew open at the rebuke in Dr. Trimble's voice.

Douglas stared at her, his whole face flushed now. She'd embarrassed him.

Betty had followed all the rules for young married girls, the ones she'd learned from experts like Suzy Wagner and Betty Crocker: She applied makeup and did her hair before Douglas awoke. She'd perfected seven recipes, one for each day of the week. She spritzed on jasmine perfume every morning before she greeted Douglas, and she did her facial saving exercises every night to keep her youthful appearance.

Her job as a married woman was to keep her husband happy. She had to fix this.

She took a deep breath, hoping her voice wouldn't shake.

"I was nervous. I know I can do better. Can I please try again, sir?"

She closed her eyes as Dr. Trimble held up the first card.

CHAPTER FIVE

RILEY, PRESENT DAY

Two things happen as I drive past the closest neighbor's house: A shaggy brown dog charges the fence, barking frantically and wagging his tail just as furiously, and my phone signal kicks in.

I pull over and email my boss at the hospital to give my immediate notice. She won't be happy with me, since I'm scheduled to work a shift in two days, but Betty won't know that because she didn't ask for references.

My fingers stop typing. Why wouldn't Betty check out a stranger she just invited to move into her home?

Maybe she did, I reassure myself. The social worker at the hospital, who I've known casually for a couple of years and who was assigned to help Betty after Douglas died, could have vouched for me. Perhaps Betty also knows that nursing aides can't work in hospitals if they've been convicted of violent crimes.

I finish my email and hit send. A whooshing sound indicates my resignation is on the way. I brace for a pinch of guilt that never arrives—maybe because I'm in survival mode, with no room to focus on anything other than how to claw my way out of what feels like a dark pit.

No one knows how bad things got these past few months. I lied to my family and friends, isolating myself because I was too embarrassed to reveal the truth: Danny desired the rush of gambling more than he desired me. Logically I know addiction is complex, with snarled psychological and physiological roots, but Danny's betrayal reinforced the secret shame I've carried around for most of my life: I'm not good enough.

I never had to look far to find evidence—my older brother and sister were straight-A students who earned master's degrees, but I have a mild form of dyslexia and school never came easily to me, which is why I dropped out of college. When I'm with my successful siblings and their perfect spouses and beautiful children, and my father and mother who paid off their house and are now spending their retirement years traveling, growing organic vegetables in their garden, and volunteering, there's a low hum of disappointment surrounding me, even if on a frequency only I can hear.

Knock off the pity party, I order myself as I pull into the Food Lion parking lot. An Ed Sheeran melody plays softly from overhead speakers as I steer a cart through the aisles, collecting eggs and cottage cheese, canned pears and iceberg lettuce, spaghetti and Jell-O. In the cleaning section, I find Bon Ami and Brillo scrubbing pads. The last two items written in Betty's spidery cursive are a can of salted peanuts and English muffins.

I look longingly at the dark chocolate caramel bars in the checkout aisle—my kryptonite. *After I get my first paycheck, I'll splurge on one*, I promise myself.

When I pull back up to the house, Betty is waiting on the wooden porch.

"You found the store!" she cries as I carry the bags up the steps. "You can just set those on the kitchen counter."

She shoos me away when I start to put away the groceries. "I'll take care of all this," she insists, tucking the perishables into the small fridge that's also bright teal. "Why don't you finish unpacking, then we can chat awhile?"

For someone who requires an aide, Betty sure seems independent, I think as I reach for my bedroom doorknob and try to twist it. It's locked.

Betty must be planning to give me a key. I'm about to ask her for one when I realize I'm at the wrong door. My bedroom is the next one down.

Something makes me tilt my head closer to the locked door, listening. I swear I can sense something within—not a presence. It's more ephemeral, like a mild electric current. Goosebumps rise on my skin.

I back away from the door, breaking the spell. I think I know what's going on; my mind is playing tricks on me. I'm bracing for the next bad thing, conjuring problems where none exist. I saw this happen with patients I treated at the hospital who'd endured traumas, their panicked eyes always seeming to ask, *What's next?*

I dive into my antidote for anxiety—organizing my surroundings. I neatly fold my clothes into the dresser drawers and stack my bins in the closet. The bathroom I'll share with Betty is at the end of the hall. I open that door to another 1960s color explosion: The walls, pentagon-shaped floor tiles, and even the toilet are canary yellow. There's a walk-in shower with accessible bars and a special chair with rubber grippers on its legs.

After tucking my toiletries bag in the cabinet beneath the sink, I check my reflection in the mirror. Even though I made an effort this morning with concealer and mascara, I look tired. I scrape my hair into a ponytail, then head back to the kitchen, where the rattle of ice against metal greets me. Betty is mixing a drink in a silver shaker.

"Douglas and I always had a cocktail before dinner. Would you care to join me? I'm making old-fashioneds tonight."

"I'd love to. I've never tried one."

She pours brown liquid into two highball glasses and touches her glass to mine. "Bottoms up."

My eyes water as I taste a sip. "The bitters take some getting used to," Betty tells me.

"It's good," I insist, hoping she doesn't see through my fib.

She picks up the jar of maraschino cherries off the counter and pours a splash of juice into my glass.

"That was my old trick to sweeten the taste, but over time, I learned to enjoy the flavor," Betty says.

I settle onto a counter stool. It's low enough that Betty and I are at eye level, and the seat fabric is worn. If it's strange to see me in what must have been her husband's spot, Betty conceals it.

I know from caring for elderly patients that they feel as if time is erasing them, and they want to be seen—not just as they are now, but as they were in their more vibrant years. So I ask, "How did you and Douglas meet?"

"At Marquis University," Betty replies, naming a college about seventy-five miles away. "He was my first and only love, and I his."

"Do you have any pictures of the two of you?"

"Our wedding picture is in my bedroom," Betty says. "I'd love to show you. Let me get it."

She wheels away and comes back with a sepia photograph in a silver frame. Betty is in a white satin gown with a sweetheart neckline and elbow-length gloves. She looks tiny next to her tall, lanky husband. He's classically handsome, with a square jaw and a shock of straight chestnut hair. They're both staring at the camera, unsmiling, as if the photographer had instructed them to strike a serious pose. But his arm is around her waist, and her hand covers his.

"You look wonderful together," I tell her truthfully. "Did you have a honeymoon?"

"We did, at a nice hotel right here in Virginia. That's why I was marveling at your parents' adventurous journey to Italy. I've never traveled."

"Outside of the United States?" I try to clarify.

"Or inside. I was born in Virginia. I've lived here all my life. My family did go to the shore every summer until I was sixteen, but just for a night. Of course, my parents are gone by now. My sisters, too. And Douglas and I never had children . . . We'd hoped to, but after the accident . . ." Her voice trails off. "Douglas bought this house and had everything arranged for me by the time I was out of the hospital."

"He sounds like such a good man," I say gently. I'm curious about the accident—all the social worker told me about Betty's injury was that she'd been paralyzed from the waist down—but I don't want to pry this early in our relationship.

A bubbling sound draws my eyes to the turquoise stove, where water in a big enamel pot with a floral pattern comes to a boil.

Betty wheels over and slides spaghetti noodles into the water, then stirs the sauce in a smaller matching pot. I hadn't even noticed she'd started dinner.

I jump up. "Can I make a salad? Or set the table?"

"Oh no, dear. You just relax. I enjoy cooking."

Betty doesn't need me to cook or clean. Given her bathroom setup, she can probably shower independently, too.

I can't ignore the question: Why did she hire me to move in?

CHAPTER SIX

Project Stargate was a multimillion-dollar program launched by the CIA at the height of the Cold War to try to get ahead of the Soviet Union on powers of the mind . . .

—WarHistoryOnline.com

BETTY, 1964

Time was blotted out within the walls of the Trimble Institute's testing spaces. Drapes covered the windows and no clocks were visible.

Betty's stomach was painfully twisted from the tension of performing test after test for Dr. Trimble. Betty suspected she'd done much better the second time with the card game; she'd reclaimed the clarity of mind she'd experienced at home with Douglas.

"Am I doing well, sir?" she asked.

For the first time, Dr. Trimble looked her in the eye and spoke to her instead of addressing her husband. "You may have potential." As he lifted his pipe to his lips again, she noticed his hands were shaking.

For the next experiment, Betty was told to relax and name any images that floated into her mind. Dr. Trimble and Douglas explained they would stand behind her and look at a series of photographs. Her job would be to try to pick up what they were seeing.

As Douglas passed behind her chair, he briefly touched her shoulder, and she found comfort in the warm, citrusy scent of the Shulton's Old Spice she'd given him for Christmas.

She'd get through this, then they'd go home, she reassured herself. Tomorrow she'd vacuum and do laundry and serve a chicken casserole or meatloaf for dinner. Douglas just loved it when she added a can of Hunt's tomato sauce and a few slices of American cheese to her meat loaf.

She named the final image that popped into her consciousness—an automobile—then looked over her shoulder to see Dr. Trimble jotting something on a notepad.

"Have there been peculiar experiences in your life you can't explain, Betty?" he asked.

Betty smoothed her plaid skirt. "I'm not certain I understand, sir." But she did; he wasn't through probing her brain.

"There are four branches of abilities I am exploring in my laboratory. One phenomenon is precognition. That's dreaming of or seeing events that will happen in the future. Then there's telepathy—the ability to communicate with someone else's mind. To see what they are thinking or viewing. Psychokinesis is the ability to influence matter with your mind. Moving an object without touching it, that sort of thing. The fourth ability is clairvoyance. That's perceiving information about something happening in a distant place. Have you ever experienced anything along one or more of those lines, Betty?"

Betty swallowed hard. "I-I'm not certain."

Dr. Trimble moved closer to her. She couldn't tell whether he believed her. "We're at the forefront of a revolution. Right here at Marquis, we've established the premier parapsychology institute in the world. We've conducted thousands of trials like the ones you just experienced. We're being watched by the entire world. And they're doing their own experiments in Boston, in England—it's catching on like wildfire. Distinguished people believe in what we are doing. Sigmund Freud, for example. Margaret Mead. Sir Arthur Conan Doyle. Albert Einstein and Alexander Graham Bell were believers, too."

He wasn't speaking to her anymore. It was as if he were onstage, addressing a captive audience.

"Our research has been thoroughly examined by the American Psychological Association," he said, pride ringing through his sonorous voice. "We are legitimate. We are scientists. We are trailblazers."

Douglas was watching Dr. Trimble in the same way her girlfriends watched Elvis on the silver screen.

"Bring her back tomorrow at nine AM," Dr. Trimble instructed Douglas, who instantly nodded.

Betty's chest constricted. She stood up and held her handbag against her stomach. Then she did what was expected of her.

"Thank you, Dr. Trimble. I'll see you in the morning."

He jotted something down in his notebook. She glimpsed her name at the top of the page, and just one digit next to it. It was heavily circled in black ink.

Betty was Girl Four.

CHAPTER SEVEN

RILEY, PRESENT DAY

Maybe Betty secretly craves companionship, not help. This small house probably feels vast and hollow without her husband. If that's the case, I need to be the most pleasant, engaging version of myself.

As we eat spaghetti, I ask Betty about her childhood and she describes growing up in a time when a milkman in a white cap delivered bottles to doorsteps every week, when her favorite playthings were paper dolls, and when some of her parents' friends scoffed at the notion of a girl attending college.

I'm about to follow up with more questions, but Betty beats me to it.

"If it's not too personal, may I ask why you and your husband divorced?"

My fork gently chimes the rim of the china plate as I set it down. I see no judgment in her expression. I owe her the truth.

"Danny was addicted to gambling. Mostly online but he went to casinos, too. It got really bad. He worked as a real estate agent so he had crazy hours and I sometimes worked the night shift at the hospital, so I never suspected a thing."

A lump forms in my throat. "Because we shared credit cards and bought the house together, I'm responsible for his debts, too."

Certain memories will always linger in my mind: the first time I saw Danny's easy smile. The warmth of his hand when he walked me to my car after our first date at a Thai restaurant. The furtive look on his face as he tucked an envelope into his pocket as he sorted through the mail.

An old girlfriend, I'd thought. Or worse, a current one.

It was even more devastating: The letter announced the imminent foreclosure on our little split-level home, the one I'd sunk every penny of my savings into and dreamed of filling with a couple of kids and a dog.

I rein in my spiraling thoughts. Betty is my boss, not a therapist.

"He never told you about his problem?" Betty asks.

I shake my head. "I had no idea. He handled all the finances."

Betty nods. "Men always do." I don't bother correcting her.

"Love is complicated," she continues. "Husbands try to hide things from wives to protect us, but sometimes it's better if we know."

"I would've helped him," I blurt. "If he'd wanted, I would've done anything. Gotten him into counseling. Worked with creditors."

If he'd wanted. Sometimes I almost hate Danny, but more often, I fantasize about him finding me and begging me to come back, saying he can live without his addiction but not without me. The worst part of my fantasy is when, instead of closing the door in his face, I step into his arms.

Betty puts her delicate, bony hand over mine. I'm surprised by how comforting it feels.

"Do you have close girlfriends to talk to?" Betty asks.

I nod. "A few. They're married, though, and most of them are starting families. Their lives are busy, you know?"

Plus they don't know the extent of what happened. I think my brother suspected, though. He was the one who gave me his old Toyota, claiming they didn't use it anymore.

"I'm glad you have friends to confide in." Betty's eyes grow faraway. "Do you know what I loved most about college? Being with my girlfriends. There were four of us who were very close. Sisters, in a way. We traded recipes and went to football games and ate lunch together almost every single day."

"Are you still in touch with them?" I ask.

"No, I haven't seen them since Douglas and I left Marquis."

"Oh my gosh, that must be—sixty years ago?"

Betty nods. "Sixty-one."

"And you haven't spoken to them since?" I ask.

I regret my question when I see the sheen of tears in Betty's eyes as she shakes her head.

I change the subject and we chat until Betty grows visibly fatigued and I manage to convince her to let me wash the dinner dishes. As I suspected, she's perfectly capable of changing and maneuvering into her bed on her own. Once she's settled, I bring her a glass of water for her nightstand and ask if she'd like the bedroom window open for some fresh air.

She hesitates, an emotion I can't identify playing across her face.

"Douglas and I always slept with the windows locked. But I think I would enjoy that."

I unlatch the brass lock and crack the window an inch, letting cool October air seep into the room.

"I'll keep my bedroom door open," I tell Betty. "Just call out if you need anything. I'm a light sleeper."

"It's nice to have you here, Riley," she says, her voice drowsy. "This house has felt so empty since Douglas died."

"I'm really happy to be here." She's a small, frail figure beneath the covers, and it makes my heart ache for her when I see she's sleeping to one side of the bed, leaving the other half empty.

I pause in her doorway. "Would you mind if I went for a short walk to stretch my legs? I won't be long."

"Of course not."

I hesitate. "I don't have a key."

"Oh." In the shadowy light, I see Betty's brow crease. "I just have one copy. You can borrow it; it's on the little dish on top of my dresser."

There's only one key to this house? It's another odd detail I don't question. *I'm lucky to be here*, I remind myself.

I find the silver key and tuck it into my pocket. "I'll be back soon."

I throw on my coat and head toward the neighbor's house, checking my phone as a signal kicks in. There are a half dozen emails from creditors that I immediately delete. The only one I read is from my boss. It's so kind it brings tears to my eyes.

We'll figure it out. Stop in and say hi sometime, Riley. Good luck.

I walk a bit farther, curious about my new neighborhood. I see a playset in one yard and a car up on blocks in another driveway. I'm about to turn back when a woman in a plaid jacket approaches, walking the brown dog I drove past earlier.

The dog makes a beeline for me and begins sniffing my legs.

"He's friendly!" the woman calls. "Felix, knock it off."

"It's okay. I love dogs." I bend to pet him and I'm rewarded with a soft lick on my hand.

"Do you live nearby?" the woman asks. She has deep-set brown eyes and a silver bob. "I thought I knew everyone on my street."

"I'm Riley. I just moved in with Betty Sadler to help care for her."

The woman's smile drops away.

"You're living in that house?"

"I mean—just as of today . . . Do you know Betty?"

They live a hundred yards apart. Surely they've crossed paths countless times.

She looks at me for a long moment. "No one does."

Maybe it's the darkness, or the chill in the October air. But her tone sounds ominous. I wrap my arms around myself. "What do you mean?"

"I baked them a pecan pie once," she says. "Almost twenty-five years ago. I remember because it was shortly after I moved in, and I gave them to all the neighbors for the holidays. The husband answered the door and kept me standing on the porch. He wouldn't accept it. He was quite rude, actually."

I must be gaping at the woman, because she elaborates.

"No one in our neighborhood ever sees them. They keep the porch light off on Halloween so kids don't trick or treat. We have a block party every Fourth of July at the neighborhood park. They've never once come. I've never even seen a delivery truck stop at their house."

She peers at me like I'm a curiosity. "I've seen a bunch of people at her door lately. Now it makes sense; maybe they were interviewing for the job. But she talked to them all on the porch and they left quickly. You're the only one."

"The only one?" I echo.

"I've never seen another soul go inside that house."

CHAPTER EIGHT

> [In] a typical Ganzfeld experiment translucent Ping-Pong ball halves are taped over their eyes . . . These measures are taken to reduce external noise and place participants in a comfortable, dreamy state of awareness.
>
> —The British Psychological Society

BETTY, 1964

Betty had seen the girl on campus before, walking arm-in-arm with her husband. They were impossible to miss, with their sleek blond hair, bright smiles, and gorgeous faces. Everyone called them the Pepsi-Cola kids, because they looked like they could be models in the advertisements.

And now the girl was here at the Trimble Institute, seated across from Betty in the main testing room. She was even more stunning up close, like a platinum-blond Ann-Margret.

Dr. Trimble made the introduction. "Betty, this is Kathleen. She's another volunteer."

The fear gnawing at Betty abated. If Kathleen—the gold standard for girls for looks and poise—was a part of this, it might be fine, after all. Bad things didn't seem to happen as often to beautiful people.

Kathleen beamed. "Your dress is so smart!"

Kathleen's tweed shift was more stylish, of course. She was being generous. Betty liked her instantly.

While she chatted with Kathleen, Betty observed two men coming into the testing room. Both had on dark-framed glasses and short-sleeved dress shirts, but only one of them made Betty smile: Douglas.

"That's my husband," she whispered to Kathleen.

"Ooh, you lucky duck! He's dishy!"

Betty tilted her head closer to Kathleen. "So is yours. I've seen you two walking around campus."

They burst into giggles. Then Dr. Trimble cleared his throat, and their laughter stopped. "Shall we begin?"

It wasn't bad at all, with Kathleen seated across from her and Douglas observing. They played dozens of rounds of the Zener card game. When it was time for the next test, Dr. Trimble exhaled burnt vanilla air from his ever-present pipe.

"I want you to look at these pictures," he instructed Betty, handing her a file. "Keep your mind absolutely focused on what you see and try to transmit the images to Kathleen."

"Yes, Dr. Trimble," she said.

Then Douglas took Kathleen to the far side of the room so Betty couldn't see or hear her. Betty turned to the first image—of a single pink flower on a white background—and studied it until her eyes burned. Then she turned to the next image. Dr. Trimble kept adding more images, stretching out the test until Betty's body began to feel weary, even though she was seated.

"I'd like to intensify this experiment," Dr. Trimble announced. He instructed everyone to follow him. Douglas's face was blank; it was as if he had been ordered to remain expressionless. Betty tried to catch his eye but couldn't. A strange new distance seemed to be edging its way between them.

When Dr. Trimble walked toward an interior door in his office, Betty knew what would come next: the blackout room.

As Betty glimpsed the lone recliner in the ink-black space, she heard Kathleen's breath catch. She stole a quick glance. Kathleen had gone so pale she looked like she might faint.

"Dr. Trimble, would it be possible for us to have a lunch break first?" Betty blurted. "I didn't pack one because I wasn't sure how long you'd need me."

Dr. Trimble was visibly annoyed, but he finally said, "Fine. But come straight back."

Kathleen reached for Betty's hand and squeezed it. Betty didn't need another test to know Kathleen was sending her a silent message: *Thank you.*

Kathleen knew the best place in town for a ladies' lunch special, a small diner on the outskirts of campus. They took Kathleen's car, a snappy red Sunbeam Tiger. Even though the early fall day was cool, Kathleen drove with the top down after tying her hair back with a patterned silk scarf. She offered one to Betty, too.

"I always keep an extra in the glove compartment for my friends," she said, and Betty felt a warm glow despite the chill of the October day.

Kathleen wore chic leather driving gloves with cutouts on the back and drove with her right hand gripping the top of the wheel and her left one resting on the car frame. It looked so daring; Betty would have to remember to try it.

When they stopped at a red light, a carful of boys pulled up next to them, with one dangling half out the window.

"Hello, hot stuff!" the boy shouted.

Kathleen just threw back her head and laughed and roared off when the light turned green. Betty felt as if they were in a film as the little car hugged the curves of the road and the boys honked their horn, trying in vain to catch up.

Once they were seated across from each other in a booth, Kathleen smoothed out her hair. "Oh, Bets, I must look a sight!"

Betty shook her head. "Not at all! The scarf saved your hair."

They chatted about inconsequential things until the waitress delivered their lunches—cottage cheese on beds of iceberg lettuce ringed by canned peach slices. No wonder Kathleen stayed so trim, Betty thought.

Afterward, Kathleen took out a pack of Chesterfields and offered one to Betty. They lit their cigarettes, sharing the single ashtray on the table.

"It's silly, I know. But I'm scared of the dark. I've been like that ever since I was a girl." Kathleen paused to smile up at the waitress in the pink uniform who came to remove their plates. "I know Dr. Trimble is going to put me in that room again and I just hate it. It's where he does the Ganzfeld experiment. He makes me wear this blindfold made out of halves of Ping-Pong balls. I have to keep my eyes open and it's just so strange, like I'm in the middle of a snow blizzard, almost blinded by the whiteness. He told me the blindfold is a necessary part of the experiment because it creates a dreamlike state for the mind but "—she gave a little shudder—"I get so unnerved I can't see much of anything beyond these strange flashes of lights."

"Dr. Trimble is so serious. But he's such an important man," Betty said.

Kathleen nodded. "My husband, Ronald, is proud I'm doing this, even though sometimes dinner is late because I've spent so many hours in the institute. I have to find a way to get through it. The other tests aren't bad."

"I'll do everything I can to help you," Betty promised. "Right after you get out of the dark room, we'll pretend we need some fresh air and we'll go outside together."

Kathleen's face tightened. "Just don't leave me. I might be able to do it if I know you're on the other side of the door, Bets."

"I'll be right there."

She was so focused on Kathleen's palpable fear that she never once considered the other possible scenario.

When they returned to the lab, Dr. Trimble beckoned to Betty.

She was the one he wanted to isolate in the blackout room.

CHAPTER NINE

KATHLEEN, 1962

Only one in thirty girls who applied to United Airlines' six-week stewardess training course in Chicago were invited to attend the rigorous classes on how to serve meals, do hair and makeup, and learn the classiest way to smoke a cigarette. Kathleen was overjoyed when she learned she'd been accepted.

Stewardesses—or air hostesses, as they were sometimes called—were required to be between twenty and twenty-seven years old, between five-two and five-nine with a slender, well-proportioned figure, unmarried, have a pleasing, unblemished face, and to retire at the age of twenty-seven.

Kathleen knew her chances were good when one of the interviewers had nodded approvingly as she'd walked into the room, commenting, "When hard-working businessmen get on our planes, they're going to like being served by this girl."

Uniforms were carefully tailored to each girl's body, and caps and gloves had to remain snowy white. Weekly weigh-ins were mandatory, as were girdles.

Infractions were dealt with severely. A scrape on a leg meant a girl might not fly that day. A few extra pounds meant she might not ever fly again.

Kathleen had spent six months working as a waitress and saving every penny for a bus ticket from her hometown in Minnesota to Chicago for the interview. She knew it was the best investment she could make in her future. She'd see the country, meet interesting people, and most important, leave the dead-end town where her mother had slept with so many men she wasn't sure which one was Kathleen's father.

Kathleen might not have gone to college or come from money, but she had a sense about people and could accurately read their intentions. She knew the red-headed stewardess who always went into the cockpit to serve a certain captain would have her heart broken, and she was proven right when the captain showed up one day with a gold wedding ring glinting on his finger while the stewardess cried in the lavatory. She could tell the businessman in seat 1A was a complainer, so after she spread a linen cloth over his serving table she complimented him on his smart suit and made sure his whiskey glass was always full. She turned down the group of girls she'd met at training who suggested they all rent a place together near their base of Chicago, knowing the apartment would be too rowdy and too many men would be coming and going, tainting all the girls' reputations.

She wanted to be the opposite of her mother in every way possible.

The flying life was as spectacular as she'd dreamed. Kathleen had been instructed to greet passengers like dear friends who'd come to visit, and passengers were always well-dressed and in festive moods, excited for the glamorous experience. Kathleen was given a Polaroid camera to snap pictures of first-timers so they could cherish the memory. She served gourmet meals, topped off champagne glasses, and charmed children.

Above the clouds, hurtling toward a different city nearly every day of the week, Kathleen felt a sense of freedom so vast and exhilarating it sometimes stole away her breath.

Then one day, Ronald stepped onto her plane, and her heart stuttered. He was traveling to California with his mother, father, and younger sister for an oceanfront vacation.

Their family didn't just look perfect; they *were* perfect. The gracious mother in heels and tasteful jewelry; the father who listened attentively as she spoke instead of spreading a newspaper in front of his face; the younger sister who smiled easily and remembered Kathleen's name when she requested a ginger ale. And Ronald, who, as she lit cherries jubilee for their dessert, stared at her face, illuminated by the burst of fire, as if she were the true object of wonder.

"You've taken such wonderful care of us," Ronald's mother said as she bid them goodbye.

"Come back and see us soon, Mrs. Moore!" Kathleen replied. She shook hands with each of them, feeling Ronald's strong fingers close around hers, then he disappeared. Kathleen was walking through the terminal with her neat rolling bag when Ronald reappeared. He was out of breath, like he'd been running to find her.

"I would love to take you to dinner tonight," he said as she stared up at him, so handsome in his dark suit and crisp white shirt. "Please say yes."

"But your family . . . don't you have plans?"

"They'll understand."

She agreed to meet him, and was grateful for every minute of her training when he took her to a French restaurant where he tasted the wine before approving it and her place was set with four forks. She knew how to walk across the room with poise, cross her legs elegantly, and converse gaily.

Six months later, they were engaged. She left her job, as was required once a ring was on her finger, and moved to Virginia so Ronald could attend law school at Marquis University. That brief chapter of her life was forever closed, though she kept a Polaroid photo another stewardess had taken of her on her first flight and looked at it sometimes to reminisce.

It felt bittersweet, like most endings. She'd have liked to have flown another year or two, but then there would be no Ronald. And their golden life together was just beginning.

CHAPTER TEN

"The Ganzfeld effect happens when your brain is starved of visual stimulation and fills in the blanks on its own . . . You might hear someone speaking to you or telling you to do certain things. . . . . You might feel that bugs are crawling on your skin or that your internal organs are moving around."

—Healthline.com

BETTY, 1964

Maybe Kathleen's fear was contagious, because Betty felt a stab of unease as she stepped into the blackout room. She looked back at Douglas, who gave her the slightest nod. She exhaled, willing her body to relax. She *had* to do this.

"I'll stay right here," Kathleen whispered.

Dr. Trimble handed Betty earplugs, then held up the strange blindfold. "The half Ping-Pong balls prevent light from leaking in," he explained as he tied the blindfold around Betty's head.

"Keep your eyes open," he instructed. "The field of white creates an unstructured and uniform visual field. Kathleen will be studying images and transmitting them to you. When visions come to you, describe them aloud."

It wasn't awful. Not at first, anyway. The recliner felt soft and welcoming and after a few moments, Betty seemed to be melting into it.

In the absence of external stimuli, it was hard to discern the contours of her own body.

She hadn't slept well last night, and as the minutes ticked by, she grew drowsy. She saw strange flashes of red and orange light. Then something changed. Images began to form, like scenes from a film. She spoke them aloud as they floated through her mind: a sailboat riding the ocean waves, a vase of dying flowers, a train chugging down a windy track.

Then a different sort of vision intruded. It was of Silas Trimble. He was standing on the other side of the door, his face twisted with greed. His fingers were outstretched, like they yearned to reach into her brain, tracing its wrinkles and curves.

She couldn't repress a shudder.

Dr. Trimble was Douglas's mentor. He was a highly respected scientist, a legend on campus. She knew she shouldn't entertain such thoughts, let alone speak them aloud.

Betty grew completely disoriented. Were her eyes open or shut? She couldn't tell. Her breath hitched faster. She was about to open her mouth and call out when she felt a hand clamp down on her shoulder.

She gave a little scream, but it was just Dr. Trimble, here to untie her blindfold and end the experiment.

"You can come out now, Betty," he said.

She blinked at the light searing her eyes. She couldn't see Douglas or Kathleen; Dr. Trimble's tall, broad form blocked her line of view.

He must have had a device in the room to hear her answers. Perhaps it was hidden beneath the recliner. Or maybe he'd had his ear pressed to the door the whole time. Or maybe—and this was the worst thought of all—he'd snuck back in, and hovered by her in the darkness.

"Thank you, sir," she replied.

He led her out of the room, and she felt lightheaded with relief when she saw Douglas and Kathleen. Dr. Trimble hadn't banished them; they'd stayed close to her.

"How was the experience for you, Betty?" Dr. Trimble asked.

She knew what he wanted her to say. He didn't need permission to plumb her psyche, but he wanted her full cooperation.

She pretended to misunderstand.

"Oh, I enjoyed it, but it would be difficult to do every day." She gave a little laugh. "What with taking care of our home and my classes."

His compressed lips revealed it wasn't the answer he wanted.

"I'll speak to your professors," he told her. "They won't have any complaint about you missing classes."

He was claiming her.

That night, Betty made their little home especially welcoming. She drew the floral curtains her mother had sewn, plumped the sofa cushions, and put together a chicken casserole. *Good Housekeeping* had taught Betty to layer the edges of the dish with biscuit dough that turned golden brown as the casserole cooked. It made their home smell as mouthwatering as a bakery.

She had to rush to get ready, but by the time Douglas walked through the door she was freshly bathed, wearing his favorite belted blue dress, and mixing cocktails.

Always before, he'd greeted her with a kiss that felt like love. Tonight was different. The thing that had sprung up between them at the lab had followed him home. He kissed her, but gingerly. Like they no longer knew each other as intimately.

She kept up a light chatter during dinner, avoiding the topic of Dr. Trimble's lab. It wasn't until they lay down in bed together and he reached for her that Betty said what had been on her mind all evening.

"My prescription will run out next week." He knew what she was talking about; she only had one, for birth control pills, which she'd been allowed to get once she was a married woman.

"I thought maybe I shouldn't refill it."

In the darkness of their bedroom, she couldn't make out the expression on his face. He wanted children; of course he did. They'd settled on three or four. After she graduated, they'd begin trying. That was their plan.

Gripped by an urgency she couldn't articulate, Betty felt desperate to start trying right away. This very night.

"It's too soon," Douglas said.

She scratched her nails lightly over his bare arm in the way she knew he loved.

"We could have a little one in time for the holidays next year," she whispered. "A strong, healthy boy who looks just like you. Or a sweet baby girl with ringlets."

Douglas sat up in bed.

"Of course we will, we'll have both! But not right now, Betty." Douglas's voice rose. "Dr. Trimble believes you have the gift, Betty. He's going to rewrite history. And we get to be a part of it!"

She'd only heard that kind of passion in Douglas's voice once before, when he'd proposed marriage.

Tears sprang to her eyes.

"I know how important your work is," she whispered. "But I could do everything for the baby. You'd go to work every day, like always."

She waited while he thought it through. Douglas never made decisions rashly; his logical mind needed to sort through every variable.

"What if being pregnant affects your ability to be tested?" Douglas said. It was the worst answer he could have given. He must have felt dampness on his arm because he flicked on the nightstand lamp. "Sweetheart, are you crying?"

She couldn't speak; great wrenching sobs clogged her throat.

Douglas hurried out of bed. When he returned, he was holding a glass of brandy and two aspirin.

"This will help, Bets," he told her. "Things always look brighter in the morning."

He wrapped his arm around her and fell asleep quickly, but Betty lay awake beside him for hours.

His decision was made. Betty belonged to Dr. Trimble.

CHAPTER ELEVEN

RILEY, PRESENT DAY

I barely sleep, even with the luxury of stretching out in a real bed instead of curling up in my car. I know I tossed and turned because of the first-night effect, which I learned about on a podcast. In unfamiliar surroundings, one hemisphere of the human brain stays partially awake. It's essentially keeping guard.

But there's another, more disturbing reason for my fractured rest: *I've never seen another soul go inside that house.*

Surely the neighbor was exaggerating. Betty and her husband couldn't have been sequestered alone for decades. That sort of confinement could make someone go nuts.

The thought makes me feel a little claustrophobic, so I convince Betty to let me tackle the garden this morning. I've always loved being in nature, but even the satisfaction of yanking out stubborn weeds and feeling damp, cool soil in my hands doesn't relax me.

At one point I straighten up and see Betty on the porch, watching me with an expression I can't decipher. When she catches me noticing, she calls out, "Ready to break for lunch?"

"Sure," I shout back, wondering how long she has been there.

Over a tuna melt—which I've never eaten before but is surprisingly tasty—I ask Betty to tell me more about Douglas.

"Oh, he was brilliant," she says, her face lighting up. "He loved to read and listen to classical music. He could identify a composer from just a few notes of a melody. And he was always so calm and decisive. He had a wonderful temperament."

I'm about to ask if he played any musical instruments, but Betty changes course.

"One of the things we enjoyed doing was having dinner parties with our friends. Kathleen and Ivy would bring their husbands—Helen wasn't married yet—and us girls would gather in the kitchen while the men conversed in the living room. Once for my birthday, Kathleen and Helen made the most delicious pineapple upside-down cake."

"Were those the friends you mentioned before? The ones you were so close to in college?" I ask.

She nods eagerly. "Yes. Kathleen was the sort of girl who did everything gracefully and made it look easy. Helen was shy and sweet. And Ivy—well, she was a ray of pure sunshine."

I ask if she has pictures of them.

"We never took any. I guess we always thought we'd have lots of time together . . ." Sadness draws down her features as she falls silent. I have the sense she's waiting for me to solve a problem she hasn't yet divulged. But I can't figure out what it is. Once again, Betty shoos me away when I try to do the dishes and she tells me she doesn't have any errands for me to run today.

I return to the garden, and by the time the sun is sinking into the horizon, I've deadheaded the last rosebush lining the fence. I head inside to wash up and at 5 PM sharp, as I'm walking into the kitchen, I hear the rattle of Betty's cocktail shaker.

"I'm making sidecars tonight. They have brandy and orange liqueur in them. I think you'll like them." She pours the concoction into two coupe glass.

I thank her and sink down onto Douglas's chair, still thinking about what Betty really wants. Companionship, yes. But my gut tells me there's something more—something specific. I take a stab at guessing it: "I was wondering, would you like to go out somewhere tomorrow? We could see a movie if you'd like, or just go for a drive."

"Hmm . . . that's an interesting thought. I think I'd prefer to stay in the house."

I suggest we play cards or listen to music together after dinner, but Betty says she's tired and wants to go to bed early. "It takes me a little time to shower and change," she explains.

"Can I help—" I start to ask, but she's already shaking her head.

After I clean the kitchen, wiping down already spotless appliances and sweeping the few crumbs from the floor, I go into the living room, looking around for something to do. I'm so used to losing myself in streaming a series or mindlessly scrolling reels that my hands are fidgety; I keep instinctively reaching for my phone, then remembering I don't have service.

I finally climb between sixty-year-old sheets, my eyes gritty and my body aching to rest, but my old friend insomnia followed me here. It takes forever to fall asleep.

The next morning I take a quick hot shower and by the time I walk into the kitchen, Betty is waiting there, wearing a mint-green dress, her hair in a chignon as usual. I immediately sense a shift in her energy. She looks nervous but determined. This is it: She's finally going to reveal the thing that's been on her mind.

"Would you care for some tea?" she offers.

"I've love some, thanks," I say. By now I know better than to try to help.

She twists the dial beneath the old kettle on her stove. "All our talking about my old college friends made me wonder . . ." She clears her throat and starts again. "If it isn't too much of an imposition, would you be able to drive to Marquis and try to track down my old friends? I would really love to talk to them again."

Relief washes through me. That's all she wants?

"Oh, I don't think I'll need to drive all the way there to look up your friends." I pull out my phone. "I can try to search for them online if you give me their full names."

Her whole face lights up. "Really?"

She reaches for a pad of paper and writes. Her fingers are trembling, I notice.

I stare down at the paper. Betty identified the women by their husbands' names: *Mrs. David Lennox (Ivy), Mrs. Ronald Moore (Kathleen), Ms. Helen Hopkins.*

"I can go check right now," I tell her. "I'll just need to walk down the street to get my phone connected."

From the look on Betty's face, it's like she's been waiting her whole life for this moment.

I don't even bother to grab a warm coat; that's how confident I am that I'll be back inside soon.

It's usually easy to find someone online if you have a few specific details. But social media searches and Google dives only turn up a few women with the same names as Betty's friends who are nowhere close to the right age.

I head back to the house, dreading the thought of watching the hope drain from Betty's face. Maybe she won't even want me to stay around now.

I straighten my posture; I can't let that happen.

I make sure my voice is bright and confident when I reenter the kitchen. "It was a little tricky to do the online search, so I think your original idea is the best one. I can drive to Marquis."

College campuses have old yearbooks, student newspaper archives, and alumni offices. There have to be clues leading to the women. I won't come back until I've got some tangible news for Betty.

Betty hands me a cup of tea and I thank her and sip it, feeling some of the chill leave my body.

"When do you think you might be able to go?" Betty asks.

For once, I know exactly what she wants. "I can leave this morning if you'd like."

Betty's eyes are shining; she looks younger and fully alive. It's from the anticipation of reconnecting with dear friends. None of this computes with what the neighbor told me about Betty and her husband being rude and standoffish.

"You may need to spend the night." Betty gets her purse and extracts some cash she presses into my hand. "This should cover the cost of a motel."

I quickly pack an overnight bag while Betty hovers just outside my room.

"I'll be back tomorrow and I'll do my best to bring some good news with me," I promise.

Her smile drops away. "Just promise me you'll be careful, Riley."

I'm struck by the feeling that she isn't talking about my driving.

CHAPTER TWELVE

Since the 1960s, more than 2,200 children from across the world have described apparent recollections from a previous life, all documented in a database maintained by . . . the University of Virginia School of Medicine.

—*The Washington Post*

BETTY, 1950

After months of anticipation, the fair had come to their town in Virginia. Posters were taped to storekeepers' windows and stapled onto telephone poles, and crowds gathered on Main Street to watch the caravan of tractors and trucks roll by. *County Fair Opens Today!* blared the headline of the newspaper crinkling in Betty's father's hands at the breakfast table.

Betty skipped down the sidewalk, transfixed by the wonders that lay just ahead.

"Slow down, peaches!" her mother called, but Betty couldn't. Riotous music crackled through giant speakers, rides spun and bounced, and cotton candy and roasted nuts perfumed the air. She felt like a character from a storybook stepping into an enchanted land.

Betty's father had given her six nickels to spend. She'd been entrusted to carry them wrapped in a handkerchief in her skirt pocket. With every skip, the little knot bounced lightly off her leg.

She waited impatiently until her mother caught up to her at the entrance gate. Then they stepped inside.

Her head spun as she took in a juggler entertaining onlookers, two 4-H club boys leading cows to the newly erected barn, and a row of booths selling everything from pickles to knitted socks.

"You couldn't hit the side of a barn from two feet away, sonny!" someone shouted so loudly that Betty flinched. She spun around and saw a man with shiny jet-black hair parted down the middle, sitting in a chair raised above a tank of water.

Betty's eyes widened as a teenaged boy from the neighborhood named Rusty threw a baseball at a red target next to the barrel and missed.

"You throw like a girl!" the man hooted.

Rusty's cheeks reddened. He picked up another baseball and hurled it harder. This time he hit the target. A buzzer sounded and the man splashed down into the water.

The man popped up a second later, his black-and-white-striped suit soaking wet, and shook himself like a dog. Rusty's friends cheered and he collected his prize, a bright yellow yo-yo, as the man climbed back into the chair.

"Betcha can't do it again!" he shouted, but Rusty was already walking away.

Betty reached for her mother's hand and tugged it, pulling her toward the line for the merry-go-round.

When it was her turn, she handed one of her precious nickels to the man at the booth. She picked a purple horse with a curly white mane and her mother boosted her onto its back. Betty held onto a strap while the music played and her horse began to move up and down, making Betty's stomach tickle. The faces in the crowds blurred as she spun past them, laughing. All too soon it was over.

"Do you want to ride again?" Betty's mother asked, but she shook her head. There were too many other things to do.

She bought a cotton candy, pinching off bits that melted in her mouth and turned her fingertips sticky and pink, then walked by the row of carnie booths. You could throw a ball through a net or toss a plastic ring over the neck of a soda bottle or try to guess the number of brightly wrapped sweets in a giant glass jar. If you were the closest, you'd win the whole jar. It was enough candy to last a year, even if Betty shared it with her family.

"Get your guesses in! We're picking today's winner in an hour!" the carnie shouted.

It cost a nickel for a chance. Betty's mother was a few feet away, examining an apron for sale at one of the booths, so Betty printed her full name on the slip of paper, as instructed, then eyed the jar before carefully selecting a number. The carnie folded up her slip and put it into a basket filled with other guesses.

"What's next?" her mother asked, coming up to stand beside Betty.

Next was a visit to see the baby lambs in the barn, then Betty ate a corndog and watched the apple pie judging contest. She couldn't resist buying a colorful pinwheel and blowing on it.

Betty saved her final nickel for the grand finale: a ride on the Ferris wheel. As they soared high above the ground, Betty stared down at the tiny people and buildings. She didn't have the exact word for what she felt but later, when she thought back on the day, she'd realize it was this one: *alive*.

Her mother was tired, though. Betty could tell because she was limping slightly, like she always did when the heavy blue veins in her legs ached.

"Ready to go?"

"But the candy contest," Betty protested. She led her mother back to the booth.

As they reached it, she caught sight of the man behind the counter. "Is Betty Sadler here?" he was calling. "Betty Sadler?"

"That's me!" Betty cried.

He stared at her in a way that made goosebumps rise on her arms.

"Little girl, you are very lucky!" His voice was loud and people turned to stare.

"Two thousand six hundred and forty-two candies are in this jar. Do you know how close you were?"

Betty did know—she'd written down the number, after all—but she shook her head.

"You got it exactly right! First time it's ever happened. You're the winner!"

The crowd applauded as the carnie reached out and shook Betty's hand. His felt rough and dry as it swallowed up her small fingers.

Then the carnie lifted the glass jug and put it into her mother's arms. Betty's mother staggered under the weight.

"Could my husband pick it up when he gets off work?" she asked, sliding it back onto the counter.

"Sure thing."

A man in a short-sleeved white shirt crowded close to Betty. "Skip Rappaport from the *Daily* paper. How'd you know the exact amount?"

Betty looked up at her mother, unsure of what to say. But her mother's eyes gave no clues. Her arms were folded and her mouth was a tight line, as if she wasn't happy at all that Betty had won.

"I guessed," Betty finally told the reporter, who scribbled down her answer with a pencil.

"You're the luckiest girl in town," he said. He asked Betty to pose next to the glass jar as a camera flashed, then Betty's mother tugged her away saying, "It's dinnertime."

They were almost at the gate when Betty's mother ran into some friends from their Catholic church. While the women chatted, Betty watched the Ferris wheel spin in slow circles. Then she looked at the pinwheel still in her hand. You had to blow on it to make it move—it was a windless day, so the points were still—but somehow, the pinwheel began to spin all on its own. Betty stared at it, delighted, as the points moved faster and faster and the colors blurred.

"Look at that ankle biter!" A clown with giant shoes and a painted face was pointing at Betty. "How are you doing that?"

Betty looked up to see her mother's mouth falling open. The two women from the church were staring at her. One began backing away, crossing herself. Others gathered, drawn by the clown's shout.

All the noise and movement around her seemed to stop. No one was applauding or taking her picture, like they'd done when she won the candy.

She had the sinking feeling she'd done something terribly wrong.

The next thing she knew, she felt a sharp pain in her arm. Her mother was yanking her away, dragging her out the gates as her pinwheel lay on the ground, crushed.

"Don't ever do anything like that again!"

Her mother kept repeating it, her voice trembling, as she marched Betty home.

"I won't!" Betty promised as tears ran down her cheeks. She didn't understand what had just happened; she hadn't meant to do anything. But one thing was clear. Her mother was scared of something. Maybe even of her.

CHAPTER THIRTEEN

I am not one of those who dismiss a priori the study of so-called occult psychic phenomena as unscientific, discreditable, or even as dangerous. If I were at the beginning rather than at the end of a scientific career., I might possibly choose just this field of research . . .

—Dr. Sigmund Freud

BETTY, 1964

The meaning of the number four circled after her name became clear to Betty the very next day.

"My final girl is here," Dr. Trimble said to someone on the phone as he opened the door for Betty and pointed her toward a testing room.

Kathleen and two other girls Betty had never seen were gathered there.

Kathleen stood up and hugged Betty. "He's been on the phone awhile," she whispered. "You might as well get comfortable."

Betty sat down next to a girl with bouncy dark curls who was so pregnant she could rest her folded hands atop the shelf of her belly. The woman smiled, revealing deep dimples, and put down the yellow blanket she was knitting.

"I'm Ivy," she whispered. "Are you a new volunteer?"

Betty nodded. "You, too?"

Ivy shook her head. "I've been volunteering with Dr. Trimble for a few months now, ever since my husband was hired as a Marquis football coach."

That was reassuring. Ivy seemed robustly healthy and full of good cheer. Nothing troubling could be in store.

Belatedly, Betty reminded herself that of course nothing untoward could exist, since Douglas was intimately involved in the work at the institute.

"And I'm Helen," said the last woman, whose wispy blond hair was swept into a high ponytail. Helen looked the youngest of all—maybe eighteen. She wore a plaid skirt and saddle shoes that were twins of the ones Betty had in her closet, and she seemed shy; she kept her gaze downcast, occasionally flicking up her eyes to meet Betty's. "I've been volunteering here for about four months."

"I'm Betty. My husband, Douglas, works with Dr. Trimble."

"Oh! I know him!" Helen exclaimed. She seemed to have the kind of fair complexion that easily turned pink; spots of color bloomed on her cheeks. "I mean . . . he's given me lots of tests here."

Dr. Trimble entered the room and the women fell silent.

"Collective energy is exponentially more powerful," he told them, as if he were in the middle of a conversation. He paced back and forth, looking at each of them in turn. "I've been waiting for this day for a long, long time."

Ivy and Helen stared at him, wide-eyed. Betty flicked her gaze to Kathleen. She was nibbling one of her perfect fingernails.

"We are on the cusp of something very special. But in order for my work to be effective, you girls must trust me completely. And I must be able to trust you."

Betty found herself nodding along with the others. "Of course, Dr. Trimble," Ivy said.

"I need your cooperation with a few things." He handed them each a document. "First, sign these. You will be legally bound to never disclose what takes place inside my lab. Not with your husbands, mothers, or friends. Certainly not with newspaper reporters or researchers at other institutes who are trying to mimic my trailblazing work."

Of course they all signed the papers; he was a man of authority.

"You four girls will be working together during my next phase of experiments. In order for my hypothesis to be tested, I need your minds to be in sync. To that end, your experiences need to be as uniform as possible while you are my subjects. Starting today, you will be served lunch here so that you consume identical meals. You will arrive and leave at the same time. I also want you girls to dress alike so that you don't fuss about or compare clothing. You'll wear all white. As with the Ganzfeld experiment, the white canvas will create a uniform field, enhancing your untapped gifts."

Out of the corner of her eye, Betty saw Kathleen wrinkle her nose.

"Sir, I don't have anything in all-white that's suitable for fall," Kathleen protested.

Dr. Trimble massaged his beard with his thumb and forefinger. "My wife will make your uniforms then. It'll be better that way; your dresses will truly be identical. I'll instruct her to have them ready by tomorrow."

Gathering material and sewing four dresses would take at least a few days, even for an accomplished seamstress, Betty thought. But she didn't dare speak up. Dr. Trimble was pacing now, looking at each of them in turn.

"Fear," he said loudly. Betty flinched as his voice seemed to boom around the room. "The human mind is the greatest undiscovered terrain in every realm of every world. But fear is its mortal enemy. People used to burn witches at the stake. In some religions, visions are considered the work of the devil. I need you four to be unafraid. To embrace the unknown. To *covet* it."

He leaned against the edge of his desk and lit his pipe.

"I know each of you holds secrets. You hide them because of the reactions you fear. Or because you're frightened of your own capabilities."

Betty jerked away her eyes, but she still felt utterly exposed, like he could see through her.

Helen cleared her throat. "I'm not sure what you mean, sir."

"I think I do." Ivy sat up straighter as she spoke. "When the phone rings, sometimes I know who is calling before I answer. It's been that way since I was a child. But my parents forbade me to speak of it. So I don't."

"Yes." Dr. Trimble leaned closer to her. "But that isn't all. Tell me more."

Ivy's voice quavered. "A year ago I was longing to visit my sister, and my husband, David, took me to the train station to buy me a ticket. I was holding my suitcase, about to board, when all of a sudden I knew I could not get on that train. David was so impatient with me, but I just cried and told him I felt unwell. He took me home and I went straight to bed. The next morning we learned the train had crashed and six people on it had died."

Dr. Trimble nodded. He leaned even closer, his eyes burning with intensity.

"It was commonly believed the world was flat until Aristotle revolutionized that assumption. People used to postulate that the stars in the sky were gods. That the sun went around the earth. Now we're on the cusp of another great scientific leap. But our exploration will be the most complex and meaningful one yet. Our discoveries will transform not just the way we see the world, but the lives of every single person in it."

He leaned even closer to them. "I am a pioneer of the human mind."

Betty felt as if a shudder were running through her soul. *And we're your laboratory animals*, she thought.

CHAPTER FOURTEEN

IVY, 1964

Ivy hadn't ever wanted to move out of California. She loved their sunny little apartment, her neighborhood knitting group, and the briny smell of the ocean that beckoned from just a few blocks away.

But when David was offered the position of assistant coach for the Marquis University football team all the way across the country, she knew she had no choice. Always the sunny-side-up girl, as her friends called her, she focused on the positives. When David received the offer letter seemingly out of the blue, he'd come home and picked her up, twirling her around. He hadn't been in such a good mood for ages; usually David only wanted the evening paper and a stiff drink and silence after work.

"It'll be a wonderful adventure," Ivy told him—and herself. She even wrote those exact words in the diary she faithfully kept.

The job meant a promotion for David. He was currently the assistant defensive coach for a team that never seemed to deliver on its promise, but now he'd be helping oversee an entire team. And Marquis had won a slew of championships.

The move was a good thing, Ivy mentally repeated as she packed up their daisy-patterned wedding china and the big glass bowl she used for sherbet punch. She pushed away the ominous feeling that threatened to suffocate her, telling herself she was simply experiencing the unease of a big change. And when the edge of a newspaper sheet sliced through the tender pad of her index finger, drawing a drop of blood, she refused to see it as a sign, wrapping a Band-Aid around the paper cut and continuing to pack.

They arrived at the Marquis campus on a chilly February afternoon and the very next night, a reception was held for them at the college president's home.

"Appetizers and cocktails," David told her as he slicked his hair back with Brylcreem, making it smooth and shiny. "All to celebrate *me*!"

Ivy changed twice before David approved of her outfit, a lavender dress with a matching jacket. She sprayed on her favorite perfume, Shalimar, which smelled like jasmine and citrus. She reached for her only warm coat, made of black wool.

"That doesn't compliment your dress," David commented. He was right, of course, so Ivy shivered during the walk from their new faculty housing apartment to the president's home.

When the door opened, a dark-haired woman in a mint-green suit with a boxy jacket, the kind former first lady Jackie Kennedy favored, smiled at them.

"You must be our guests of honor!" she cried, her southern accent making her words sound even more special.

Ivy squeezed David's arm. A dozen or so people were gathered in the grand living room around the crackling fire in the stone hearth. A waiter in a white shirt and black tie passed trays of pigs in blankets, stuffed celery sticks, and deviled eggs while classical music played. All in honor of her husband! She stood up straighter, proud to be by his side.

"Come in out of the cold! Quickly, darling, get them a drink," a distinguished-looking man said as he strode toward him. He extended his hand to David. "I'm Rudolph Sherman. Welcome."

The president of Marquis!

David shook his hand vigorously. "Thank you for having me, sir. This is my wife, Ivy."

President Sherman nodded at Ivy, and she smiled and thanked him for his hospitality and waited for the men to drift away. She knew

President Sherman's wife would come collect her and introduce her to the women. The women would be invaluable to Ivy; they'd tell her where the best department store and cobbler and bakery were located.

But then the strangest thing happened. President Sherman extended his hand to Ivy and looked at her as if she were a guest of honor, too.

"It's a real pleasure, Ivy," he said.

She felt her cheeks heat up. Then, remembering her manners, she gushed, "What a lovely home you have, President Sherman!"

Luckily President Sherman's wife returned with the drinks before Ivy could do anything to embarrass David. She waited, again, for the men to walk away. Again she was surprised.

"There's someone I'd like you to meet, Ivy."

President Sherman turned and beckoned to a tall, broad-shouldered man.

"Silas?" President Sherman called. "Mr. and Mrs. Lennox have arrived."

The tall man folded his half-eaten appetizer into a napkin and hurried over. He stared at Ivy for a long minute, not even looking at David. "I'm Dr. Trimble," he finally said. "I understand you were a volunteer in some of California University's psychical tests. I'd like to talk to you."

He took Ivy's arm and began to lead her away, with President Sherman following them.

Ivy turned to look at David and saw him standing there alone, his eyes narrowing.

They both knew, in that moment, David wasn't the real reason they'd been enticed to come to Marquis. But of course, Ivy could never speak of it.

All she could do was try to get David to forgive her.

The whole mess began because they needed money.

Ivy couldn't tell David the $15 a week allowance he gave her didn't cover the cost of their household supplies; he'd already complained that she was far less diligent about cutting coupons than his mother. "We're not the Rockefellers," he was fond of saying.

The sign, taped to a telephone pole on the campus of the California college, beckoned to her: *Volunteers needed at The Institute of Psychical Studies, $5 payment.* She tore off a little tag of paper at the bottom containing a phone number and made the call that very afternoon. And the next morning, in a flowered shift dress with bows on the shoulders she'd sewn from a McCall's pattern, she appeared at the research center.

She was breaking a decades-old promise to her mother, who forbade her to speak about the strange knowings that gripped her from time to time, but she was a married woman now, which meant her allegiance must be to her husband. And it was David's birthday next month. She wanted to surprise him with a special gift, maybe cologne or even cuff links. This was the only way she could afford it.

Besides, attitudes were different in sophisticated cities than in the town where Ivy had grown up. The university had an entire branch of the psychology department devoted to the study of psychical ability; nobody there would shun her if they knew what she could do.

"We'll start with a simple test," the skinny male researcher in thick black glasses told Ivy. "I'll look at a series of photographs and you'll sit over there with your eyes closed and tell me if any images come to your mind."

She nodded and they began.

By the end of the first hour, two other researchers were clustered around Ivy, watching. They begged her to come back after that first day, so she did. And when they told her they were writing about her abilities, she wasn't bothered. No one who knew her would ever read an obscure academic journal. The tests grew stranger, but more lucrative. Once she answered the phone to hear a new researcher inviting her to take place in what he called a double-blind test. Ivy was told to go to a certain coffee shop and sit in the last booth on the left, where she'd find a deck of Zener cards waiting. She was to administer the card test to herself, touching the top one and speaking aloud the symbol that came to her, then continuing with the next card.

Even though she attracted a few curious stares from other customers, Ivy agreed to do it because she earned $40—the most she'd ever made in a single test. It was a windfall for such a small amount of work.

She bought David a beautiful pair of gold cuff links, which he adored. But how strange that the very thing she'd sought out to sweeten her marriage would become the source of its downfall.

CHAPTER FIFTEEN

RILEY, PRESENT DAY

Is Betty delusional? There's no evidence her three girlfriends attended Marquis. I'm sitting in the campus library, flipping through a 1964 yearbook. Their names are missing from the alphabetical listing of students beneath black-and-white thumbnail pictures.

Even more disturbing: Betty didn't attend the school in 1964, either. Her name doesn't exist in the yearbook.

Why would she create such a strange fabrication and send me on this wild goose chase?

I close the yearbook and rub my temples, pushing back against the headache gathering in my skull. This library existed sixty years ago; the architectural bones are the same, as are many of the volumes on the shelves. Change the clothing and hairstyles of the students, and it could be 1964. Betty might've sat right where I am now . . . if she was ever actually here.

A loud thump makes my head jerk toward the noise. A woman has just dropped a heavy textbook on the communal table in the center of the room.

I take in the other students: A guy is resting his head on his folded arms, presumably sleeping, next to a student who is furiously typing on his laptop, which is covered with stickers. There's a woman in puffy boots and leggings with at least six piercings on each ear who seems to be tutoring another woman with a math textbook, calculator, and graph paper spread out on the table.

I must be missing something. Betty seems cogent. But perhaps she got a detail wrong. I'm about to go check the 1965 yearbook when a couple passes me, holding hands.

I watch them as they exit, still holding hands as they awkwardly navigate through the door together. Then I open the yearbook again. I searched for Betty's friends, but I didn't check for their other halves. Helen wasn't married, but Betty said the husbands attended or worked at Marquis.

I strike out with Betty's husband, Douglas, then Kathleen's. That leaves Ivy Lennox.

I find her husband on page 47.

David Lennox was the defensive coach of Marquis University's football team. In the picture, he appears short and bulky, and he's unsmiling.

I don't need to check with Betty to know what I should do next. This time the search on my phone yields results.

David Lennox helped coach several championship teams during his four decades at Marquis, according to his obituary. It says he was wed to a woman named Mary in 1966, who predeceased him, but there's no mention of Ivy. The final line of his obituary jumps out at me: *He is survived by two children, a son, David Jr., and a daughter named Sandra.*

I dig deeper. They're not hard to find; thankfully, it's not a terribly common last name.

In the images that spring onto my phone, David Jr. looks just like his father. He recently retired from the Navy and lives in Hawaii with his family.

But Sandra Lennox still lives in Virginia, not far from campus. She looks younger than her sixty-two years, with her dimples and headful of bouncy curls. She's a therapist who specializes in mental health disorders and acute grief.

Loss is an inevitable part of life, her website states. *Grief doesn't follow one particular path or adhere to a set of rules. I walk with my patients through the rocky terrain of loss, letting them know they are not alone.*

There's a link to a local newspaper article that details her volunteer work with runaway teens, drug-addicted individuals, and the houseless population.

In other words, she helps save outsiders.

I've never met anyone as dedicated as Sandra Lennox, a fellow therapist was quoted as saying in the article. *She lives for her patients.*

I step outside the library and reach for my phone and dial Sandra's office number, planning the brief message I'll leave.

I nearly drop my phone when she answers. Maybe she's taking a lunch break, too.

I fumble with my words: "Hi, my name is Riley Bell . . . I'm calling about someone from long ago . . ."

"I understand." Sandra's voice is warm and encouraging.

"Oh, I'm not a prospective client—I'm trying to help someone locate an old friend. She has the same last name as you so I thought you might be related."

"Who is the friend?"

"Ivy Lennox."

For a long moment, all I can hear is Sandra's breathing. She has dedicated herself to helping others through grief, but right now I swear she's experiencing it; I can feel the weight of her emotions through the phone line.

Then she says, "Ivy was my mother."

CHAPTER SIXTEEN

> The deputy director of the CIA revealed that over thirty universities and institutions were involved in an 'extensive testing and experimentation' program which included covert drug tests on unwitting citizens.
>
> —a US Senate hearing report

BETTY, 1964

"I need this recipe, Bets!" Ivy cried. "It's divine."

Betty turned as she stirred the gravy on the Chambers stovetop to see Ivy dragging a pretzel stick through the cheese porcupine appetizer.

"Just five ingredients, too. All you do is blend cream cheese with beer and shape it, then add black olives for eyes and pretzel sticks for quills," Betty said.

"I better not have any more," Ivy moaned. "I've already put on sixteen pounds and I'm not due for a month!" She shook a cigarette out of her pack and lit it. "It's a good thing smoking helps curb my appetite."

"Is the recipe from *Good Housekeeping*?" Helen asked.

Betty nodded. "I clip all their best recipes, so let me know if you'd ever like to look through them."

Betty knew Helen didn't have a boyfriend, but at eighteen, she still had time for someone to propose, and it wouldn't hurt to have a few crackerjack meals up her sleeve. After all, everyone knew the quickest way to a man's heart.

"Your dinette table is real classy," Ivy told Betty. "Is it from Sears?"

Betty nodded, feeling a swell of pride.

"Sweetheart? Is dinner almost ready?" Douglas called from the living room.

"Almost! Do you gentlemen need your drinks freshened?" Betty asked as she hurried to the living room with the martini shaker.

"I could use a top-up," said David Lennox, Ivy's husband. He made Betty vaguely uncomfortable, even though he'd never done anything wrong. She felt his eyes trace the curve of her behind as she bent over to refill his drink, but that was the sort of thing a lot of red-blooded men did.

"I wouldn't mind one either. Thank you, Betty," Ronald said, giving her a warm smile. He was the male version of Kathleen—kind, confident, and a total dreamboat.

In the living room, the men talked about the usual things: the stock market, the winning streak of the Richmond Tigers football team, their excitement over a new car called the Ford Mustang.

But for the four women in the kitchen, it was different. Ever since they'd signed Dr. Trimble's privacy agreements, an invisible boundary had encircled the four, cinching them together.

Douglas knew some of what was going on, of course. But even he wasn't privy to all of Dr. Trimble's latest experiments and theories. Dr. Trimble was slightly paranoid, Betty had come to believe. Or maybe he was being prudent. After all, competitors were working around the world. Dr. Trimble had showed the women a journal from the Society for Psychical Research, printed just last June. Tests in places like Boston and London were producing impressive results, with subjects able to transmit thoughts of specific images and predict unsettling events.

Dr. Trimble responded by demanding more of their time. Already they saw him five days a week. Now he was stretching the lengths of those days, and calling them in on some Saturdays, too. Every day, when the women showed up at the laboratory, they found the stiff, white dresses his wife had sewn waiting for them. *She must come collect them in the evenings and launder them*, Betty thought, because the dresses were always crisp and snowy, smelling faintly of bleach. They'd only seen Mrs. Trimble a few times when she'd come to deliver their lunches: usually simple meals like cheese sandwiches on white bread with a side of potato salad.

Mrs. Trimble wasn't an old woman, but her face was devoid of color and her body sagged, like the life was being slowly leached out of her. It was hard to discern her age, but she could be anywhere from thirty to forty-five. She always gave a little nod of her head to Dr. Trimble as she silently exited, but he didn't acknowledge her.

Dr. Trimble seemed to have a special interest in Betty. Most subjects, he told her, excelled in one arena. Kathleen was very strong in telepathy, Ivy excelled at precognition, and Helen was exceptional in clairvoyance.

"But you, Betty, are highly gifted in every single category," he'd said just this afternoon. "What are the chances? Infinitesimal. And somehow you were drawn to me, as if following a path determined long before either of us knew the other existed."

Betty had clenched her hands nervously. She hadn't been drawn to him—if anything, being in his presence made her feel trapped. But she hadn't dared breathe a word of protest.

Instead of bringing her closer to her husband, her work with Dr. Trimble was having the opposite effect. Betty could barely bring herself to identify what was happening, because it sounded so awful. But the truth was, sometimes Douglas acted like a petulant child.

"What did you talk about with Dr. Trimble today?" he might ask.

"He told me about a new experiment they're trying in Boston," she'd say. Or "Nothing, really, I just spent more time in Testing Room 1 with the girls."

No matter what she said, it was never the right answer.

Douglas would turn away from her, his body rigid. At night, he reached for her far less frequently.

Tonight she hoped to undo some of the tension between them. Even though it was Saturday and she'd spent all day working with Dr. Trimble, she'd stayed up late the previous evening vacuuming and polishing and scrubbing. She wanted Douglas to feel proud of her hostessing abilities.

Now Betty opened the oven to check on the roast, releasing a delicious-smelling puff of hot air. "I won't be returning to school next semester," she told the other women. She hoped the flush in her cheeks was seen as an effect of heat from the oven.

Ivy clapped her hands and squealed, clearly thinking Betty was about to make an announcement, but she had it all wrong. "Dr. Trimble talked to my professors and they agreed it would be best if I focused on helping him," Betty explained.

Helen and Ivy nodded. Only Kathleen, chic as always in a peach dress and matching wide headband with the back of her hair teased high, regarded Betty with a concerned look.

"You're already in the lab every day," Kathleen pointed out. "We all are lately. It doesn't matter as much for the rest of us—we weren't doing anything important—but I thought you wanted to earn your degree."

"It's fine," Betty said quickly. "It's not like I was going to be a career girl. Douglas and I want a family soon."

Kathleen nodded. "That's good, then. I swear, if it wasn't for the three of you, I'd have quit long ago. But the truth is, Ronald is so busy studying all the time these days that I don't know what I'd do to occupy myself. And I'd miss you three too much if I left. I just wish . . ."

Betty knew what Kathleen was about to say. She felt it, too. Kathleen wished Dr. Trimble wasn't demanding so much of them. These past few weeks, the women had no free time because every spare minute was spent at the institute. They were all feeling run-down.

Stretched too thin. You could see it in the dark shadows under Ivy's eyes, the way Kathleen had grown even thinner, and in how Helen kept hiding a yawn behind her hand.

But Kathleen never got to finish her sentence.

"Feel this!" Ivy grabbed Betty's hand and held it against her stomach. Betty felt a tiny foot or elbow press back.

"Hi, little one," Betty cooed.

"She must love the cheese dip, too," Ivy said.

"She?" Kathleen asked.

"David insists we're having a boy, but I know she's a girl." Ivy lowered her voice. "I already sewed a pink dress for when we bring her home from the hospital."

While the other women touched Ivy's swollen belly, Betty pulled the roast out of the oven. It looked perfect, as did the carrots and potatoes surrounding it.

Douglas would have to be pleased.

She opened her mouth to call Douglas in to carve just as the phone rang.

Douglas was closest, so he answered. She heard the happy boom of his voice, then winced as it deflated.

"It's for you," he called to Betty.

She walked into the living room and took the receiver from his hand, stretching the curling cord a few feet away.

It didn't matter that it was six-thirty on a Saturday night. Dr. Trimble wanted to talk to her.

"I need you girls tomorrow," he said. "Come at noon and prepare to stay overnight."

It was a Sunday. Her sole day off to do the shopping and ironing and get her hair done.

Betty had planned to spend time with Douglas. To try to patch the new hole in her marriage. But there was only one answer.

"Of course, Dr. Trimble."

CHAPTER SEVENTEEN

RILEY, PRESENT DAY

Sandra Lennox opens her front door, her smile revealing deep dimples. She runs a hand through her salt-and-pepper curls, making them even more unruly. "It's been a day. Join me in a glass of wine? It'll be heroic of you, since then I won't have to drink alone."

I like her instantly. "I've always been selfless that way," I joke.

I follow her to the kitchen, where something delicious is simmering in a Crock-Pot. The kitchen looks as inviting as it smells, with its butcher-board counters, deep window seat lined with orange and blue pillows, and copper pans hanging from a ceiling rack. Sandra turns down the volume on her iPhone, softening Sheryl Crow's ballad.

"I love your house," I tell her.

"Thanks! I just bought it last year," Sandra says. "I used to live in the city, but I guess I'm more of a country girl at heart. Being surrounded by the woods feels so peaceful. I've never slept as well as I do here."

A black lab with a grizzled gray muzzle appears and nudges my thigh. I reach down to stroke his head.

"Hank pretends he's never been loved or fed before," Sandra tells me as she uncorks a bottle of Sancerre. "Don't fall for it."

"He's a sweetheart." I scratch the soft fur behind his ears.

"I adopted him a couple years ago. It's harder for old dogs to find a home, but I wanted a senior because he's so calm around my patients. I swear he helps them open up. So we both got lucky."

"Do you see patients at your house?"

She nods. "Sometimes. I have an office a few miles away, but certain patients prefer a homey environment."

Sandra pours us each a generous glass, then touches hers to mine.

"Thank you for finding me." Her voice thickens. "When you called . . . it was the first time in years anyone had spoken my mother's name. Decades, really. It's worse than feeling like she's forgotten. Sometimes it's almost as if she never existed."

I know a little bit of what that's like, I think. The erasure of my life, the crashing realization that everything I'd built and become was gone in a matter of days, was something I hadn't yet fully processed or grieved.

I wasn't a wife any longer. I might not ever become a mother like I'd hoped. Danny made me feel whole. He was my person. Learning the depth of his betrayal didn't just break my heart. It shattered my ability to trust my own instincts and decimated my sense of self.

I usually fight to keep my thoughts from going down this track; my energy is focused on forward motion. It must be Sandra who is conjuring the emotions I've become good at suppressing. She's a psychiatrist; she inspires confidence.

But I'm not going to share mine with her. I'm not here for myself. I need answers for Betty.

"I'd love to hear more about your mother," I say.

Sandra sips deeply from her glass and curls up onto the window seat, gesturing for me to do the same. "She was confined to a psychiatric institution shortly after I was born. My father divorced her soon afterwards and quickly remarried. She died when I was four. Her diagnosis was schizophrenia. Back then, the treatments were nothing like they are today. They often did more harm than good."

Sandra reaches into her wallet and pulls out a picture. "This is the only photo of her that I have."

In the sepia-hued image, I see a version of Sandra. The same smile, those curls. Even in the worn, creased picture, Ivy looks vibrant and kind.

"You look just like her," I say.

Sandra nods. "My father hated that. And my stepmother hated it even more."

So Sandra was an outsider in her family, too.

"Sometimes I wonder if it was actually severe postpartum depression. Maybe she was misdiagnosed. With the right medication, my mother might still be here."

Her face twists, like she's about to burst into tears, then she regains control. "Tell me more about Betty. Is she your grandmother?"

"I'm her caretaker. I haven't been working with her for long, so I don't know her very well."

"Why is she looking for my mother now, after all these years?" Sandra asks.

"Her husband passed away recently. She seems lonely. She really wanted to reconnect with your mom and a few other college friends. She said they were as close as sisters."

Sandra nods. "There were four of them."

I blink in surprise. "How do you know that?"

"My mother kept diaries from the time she was a young girl," Sandra explains. "I inherited them along with a box of her things. For so many years, I couldn't bring myself to look through any of it." She half smiles. "Ironic, I know. As a mental health professional I'm all about getting people to confront their demons. I never truly appreciated how much courage that takes. But I keep her diaries in my nightstand now. I've practically got them memorized. It's the only way I can feel close to her."

Sandra wraps her arms around her knees and suddenly I see her as a girl, grieving the mother she never knew. Her accomplishments are impressive: Her private practice appears to be thriving, and her Tudor-style home is surrounded by what looks like ten acres of wooded land. She received an award from the mayor because of her volunteer work with the city's homeless population. But I sense there's a hole inside her that nothing can fill, just like the one that exists inside me.

"You don't happen to know how I can find the other women, do you?" I ask. "Assuming they're still alive."

Sandra shakes her head. "I've never tried. My mother wrote about the girls of the institute all the time, but then her entries abruptly stopped a few weeks before she was sent away to the psychiatric hospital."

"The institute?"

"Didn't you know that's how they met?" Sandra's eyebrows knit together. "The Trimble Institute was an offshoot of the psych department at Marquis University. It was run by Dr. Silas Trimble back in the sixties. The four of them were volunteers."

At least I now know the women were real.

"Dr. Trimble's grandson might know where the other women are," Sandra tells me. "He tracked me down a couple of years ago. He wanted to write a book about his grandfather's work. Nice enough guy, but he was a little all over the place."

"Do you know his first name?" I ask.

She frowns. "Give me a second . . . it started with an *S*, too, but it wasn't Silas. Steven? No, wait. Samuel. That's it. He's local, or at least he was when he reached out to me, so he should be pretty easy to find. Can you believe he had the nerve to ask me to give him my mother's diaries? He wanted to write a book about his grandfather's work and he thought they'd be a good source of information."

A sound comes from her phone—a trio of high, staccato notes—and when Sandra looks down at the screen, her dimples pop again.

"There's a man I've been seeing—it's new-ish, but promising. He just texted that he finished work and he's on his way over for dinner. He's a carpenter and I met him when I hired him to build this bookshelf."

She gestures to a beautiful set of shelves filled with books that look well-loved. Scattered among the volumes are healthy green plants and colorful knickknacks.

"It's gorgeous," I tell her.

She stands up. "I don't mean to rush you out," she says. "You're welcome to stay and meet him." The last thing I want to do is intrude on Sandra's date. Plus, I can tell she wants me to go; she wouldn't have stood up otherwise.

As I drive down the long private road and Sandra's house recedes in my rearview mirror, I feel the faint stirrings of an emotion it takes me a moment to identify. It's hope.

Sandra's early life couldn't have been easy, but she has channeled her loss into helping others. Into building a legacy of her own.

For the first time, I wonder if there's a way I can find new meaning in my life, too. If a fresh start could be possible.

CHAPTER EIGHTEEN

IVY, 1957

Ivy knew from a young age she was luckier than most. It wasn't because she possessed a beautiful face; Ivy's thick curls refused to be tamed no matter how much Aqua Net she used and her lips were overly full, although decades later those very attributes would be coveted by many women.

She didn't come from a wealthy family, either. Ivy's father worked at a furniture store, selling Danish modern coffee tables and tripod lamps, and groused about the manager who'd been promoted over him.

"He's slick, that one," Ivy's father would ruminate, downing his second whiskey sour before dinner. "But he'll get his comeuppance someday."

Unlike her father, Ivy had been granted the gift of a sunny disposition. She woke up every morning cheerful, as if it were her default setting. She brushed aside rudeness and petty slights. Her smile was a reflex.

And she did have one other advantage in life: She was often lucky. Sometimes she'd feel compelled to change an answer on a school test at the last minute or touch up her appearance. Small decisions that made her life take a turn for the better. Because the new test answer was always the right one, and when she instinctively freshened her lipstick and smoothed her hair, she often ran into someone she knew and felt a higher level of confidence.

Once, Ivy was drawn to pause and peer into a storefront window she'd passed countless times before. She didn't question the compulsion. She'd learned not to. Seconds later, the driver of an idling Chevrolet lurched forward, smashing into the space where Ivy would have been walking.

The elderly driver climbed out, clearly shaken, looking at his fender crumpled against the side of the building. And Ivy took his arm and helped him to a bench, reassuring him that no real harm had been done.

Ivy was uncommonly bright, but that quality wasn't yet prized in girls either. She concealed her intelligence, just as she learned to hide the strange happenings that marked her life. Her parents forbade Ivy to guess who was calling when the phone rang or to talk about dreams she'd had that seemed to foretell future events, though she secretly recorded the events in a diary she hid beneath her mattress.

"She's plump and homely. She's going to have a hard enough time catching a husband without being the town freak," Ivy overheard her father tell her mother once. Those words seared into Ivy, as scarring as a brand.

After years of silence, Ivy broke the dream rule only once, when she was a senior in high school.

There was a quiet, shy boy named Charlie in her class whose home life must have been terrible. He was small and wiry, and he often came to school without lunch, but with bruises on his arms and legs or a black eye he blamed on a farming mishap. His father was known for having a volatile temper, especially when he drank. Most people in town gave the man a wide berth.

Charlie missed school fairly often—Ivy couldn't bear to think about why—but because he was brilliant, his marks put him at the top of their class. Other kids mostly ignored him, even the bullies. Maybe they recognized there was nothing they could do to Charlie that was worse than what he endured at home.

Charlie ran the several miles from his family's farm to and from school every day because the bus followed a meandering route that took longer, and his time was precious. Ivy had heard he rose before dawn to complete farm chores, too.

One clear image surfaced in Ivy's mind whenever she thought about Charlie: One morning a praying mantis flew in through a classroom window. Girls screamed and boys batted at it, but Charlie just put out his hand and caught it, cupping it as tenderly as if it were a rose. "Crush it!" someone shouted, but Charlie released the stick bug back out the window. As he watched it wing away, Ivy felt certain he wanted nothing more than to do the same. The sadness embedded in his eyes broke her heart.

The dream came to her during a cold snap in late January of their senior year.

Charlie was running alongside a shiny black sedan, his legs moving so quickly they blurred. He and the sedan disappeared over the horizon into the warmth of a golden sky.

She awoke abruptly at twenty-one minutes past midnight and was unable to fall back asleep.

The dream meant something.

But what?

It wasn't until the last class period of the day that Ivy looked out the window and spotted the black sedan from her dream pulling into the parking lot. A tall man in a plaid sports coat got out, walking purposefully toward the school entrance. Then Ivy lost sight of him.

As soon as the final bell rang, she scrambled to find Charlie. She caught him on the sidewalk outside the school lacing his beat-up work boots in preparation to run home.

"Please wait, Charlie. Don't go yet." She gripped his scrawny arm. He turned to her, startled.

"Just a little longer," she pleaded.

"Why?" he asked.

She couldn't answer. But something in her expression must've convinced him.

Five minutes passed. Other students streamed by, walking home. The school bus started up and rumbled down the street. She could feel Charlie's rising agitation.

"I have to get home," Charlie whispered.

"Trust me," she begged.

Agonizing minutes ticked by. Finally the man in the suit came out of the school.

"As soon as that black car goes, run alongside it," Ivy instructed. "Run like the wind, Charlie. Faster than you've ever gone before."

The car's engine turned over. Its wheels began to move, slowly at first, then picking up speed as the vehicle turned out of the parking lot and onto the long, narrow road.

Without a word, Charlie took off, his legs churning. Ivy's heart leapt into her throat as she hurried behind him, trying to see what was happening. For a moment she worried Charlie wouldn't catch up to the car; it had too big of a head start.

Then Charlie seemed to find another gear.

His arms and legs whirled so fast they blurred; he moved like a sleek, efficient machine. It was a gorgeous thing to watch Charlie run. He caught up to the car. Then he passed it.

After a moment, the car drew up and kept pace with Charlie. Then the driver honked his horn furiously until Charlie stopped. The door opened and the man in the plaid sport coat slowly climbed out.

Ivy was out of breath, and still far behind them, but the man's booming voice carried to her.

"Son, do you know who I am?"

Charlie shook his head.

"I'm the basketball scout for the University of Virginia."

Ivy's heart sank. Charlie didn't play basketball. Maybe her dream had meant something else. Perhaps Charlie would've been hit by a car had he left earlier, or maybe by delaying him, she'd helped him avoid a violent encounter with his father. This moment could just have been a precursor to the main event.

The man looked at Charlie's worn boots and heavy backpack.

"Twenty-one miles per hour," the scout said in his loud, clear voice. "I clocked it on my odometer."

Ivy stopped cold. Twenty-one. The precise number in her dream; she'd documented it in her diary.

"Son, our track coach is going to want to talk to you."

Charlie ended up getting a full scholarship to UVA, where he won dozens of medals and trophies. He was used to a grueling work schedule; he handled the blend of athletics and academics easily. "And I get three squares a day in the cafeteria," he told Ivy in a phone call.

He could have trained for the Olympics, but he decided to focus on a career. He married his college sweetheart, had four children, and enjoyed success as an engineer.

When he tried to thank Ivy, she asked for only one thing: that he never speak of it again.

CHAPTER NINETEEN

RILEY, PRESENT DAY

My cell phone shrills a little after 8 PM as I'm about to pull into a motel on the outskirts of the Marquis campus. *Unknown caller* flashes on my screen.

"Hi there, Riley." I jolt at the sound of the man's gravelly, familiar voice. I used my maiden name to get a new phone number. But somehow he found me.

I speak the eleven-word phrase I've committed to memory: "Please cease and desist all calls and contact with me immediately."

The man laughs. "Are you trying to disappear, Riley?" His words carry an invisible menace.

He isn't a collector for the credit card or utility companies; those places usually adhere to debt collection laws that prohibit harassment, calls late at night, or threats.

This guy is associated with the casino Danny used to frequent when I worked overnight shifts at the hospital.

I don't even know his name, but he knows everything about me.

"Seen Danny lately?" he asks.

"We're divorced," I remind the collector. "I don't talk to him anymore."

"That's interesting, since he's the one who gave me your new number."

My breath catches in my throat. What did they do to him to get it? It isn't hard to imagine. Shortly before everything fell apart, I was sipping a glass of chardonnay on our couch and thinking about painting our living room walls maroon when I heard a noise outside the front door. I thought it was a cat.

When I looked out the peephole, I saw Danny crouched over, holding his ribs with one hand and trying to fit his key into the lock with the other. I opened the door and he fell inside, collapsing on the hall rug.

At first I thought he was drunk. Then I saw his bruised and swollen face.

"I got jumped," he said, trying to smile through his split lip. "They took my wallet."

Seeing him so hurt broke my heart. I wanted to call the police—I was desperate to punish whoever was responsible for the attack—but Danny convinced me it would be better if he w ent to the station in person in the morning. I brough him Advil and ice packs and gently rubbed his back while he slept, thinking that it could have been worse—I could have lost him forever.

By now I've put the pieces together. Danny wasn't the victim of a random attack. He was beaten up as punishment, and he had claimed his wallet was stolen so I wouldn't question the arrival of new credit cards.

"You understand how this works, right?" the collector asks now. "We've gotta get the money from somewhere."

I close my eyes and think about Danny on our wedding night, tears in his eyes as he told me how much he loved me. I have to believe it was true. More than that, I still love him.

"I can start paying you at the end of the month," I say.

"I'm counting on it." He hangs up.

I pull into the lot and turn off my car. It's only a dozen yards to the motel entrance, but every shadow feels like a threat. The debt collector excels at finding people; he may already know where I am.

I half run toward the entrance and when I burst inside, the short, bearded man behind the desk looks startled.

"Whoa, there, everything okay?" he asks.

I try to smile. "I just pushed the door too hard."

He gives me a room on the fourth floor. It smells like artificial floral cleaner and the carpet is stained, but there's a chair I can prop beneath the door handle and the lone window locks.

So much for putting my life back together, I think as I sit down heavily on the bed. I'm still trying to save Danny's.

CHAPTER TWENTY

Shortly before he was assassinated, President Abraham Lincoln was said to have recounted this dream: "There seemed to be this death-like stillness about me. Then I heard subdued sobs, as if a number of people were weeping . . ." According to the account, he heard a guard say that the president had been assassinated.

—Smithsonian Channel

BETTY, 1964

Betty jolted awake from a dream so vivid and terrifying her vocal chords felt frozen. Her brain seemed bifurcated, with half lingering in a surreal world where she was trying to snatch the yellow baby blanket out of the road before a truck drove over it.

She turned her head and saw Ivy lying on a twin bed, staring at the ceiling with a haunted expression. Kathleen and Helen were lined up in matching beds, too.

Slowly, she became oriented: It was Monday morning, and they were in the basement of the college's library, a cavernous space with a cement floor that was mostly used for storage and to house the giant furnace, boiler, and water tank.

Now this subterranean space was Dr. Trimble's newest testing ground.

He'd made them sleep here, in identical cots, in matching stiff white nightgowns Ms. Trimble had sewn.

A gentle bell sounded, then repeated a moment later more loudly.

Dr. Trimble's instructions from the previous night came back to Betty: He would awaken them at 5:30 AM. Before they spoke or stood up, they were to take the notebooks and pens on the floor next to them and write down everything they could remember about their dreams.

Yellow blanket, Betty wrote in cursive. Then she snuck another peek at Ivy.

Ivy wasn't looking particularly well. None of them were. Even beautiful Kathleen looked drawn and her lips were slightly chapped. But Ivy was suffering the most. She was always squirming in her testing chair, trying to get comfortable, and she had to use the ladies' room every hour. Sleeping on that tiny bed with a thin mattress at seven and a half months pregnant had to have been an ordeal.

But there was more. Ivy had confided in Betty that her husband, David, wasn't happy that her work with the institute meant she sometimes couldn't get a hot dinner on the table when he came home.

"It's natural for him to be a little jealous," Betty had whispered to Ivy, squeezing her hand. "They're used to having us all to themselves." Ivy had nodded, but her natural buoyancy hadn't returned.

Now Betty watched as a tear slowly crept down Ivy's cheek before being absorbed by her pillow. David had surely given Ivy a hard time about being away overnight.

Before she could change her mind, Betty quickly finished the sentence on her notepad. Dr. Trimble entered the room a moment later, still in his dark pants and white shirt from the evening before. His shirt was wrinkled and the ring of hair above his ears was sticking up on one side. *Had he slept here, too?* Betty wondered. She shivered at the thought of him slipping into the room, looming over them in the middle of the night.

"Tell me about your dreams," Dr. Trimble ordered.

Helen spoke of a beautiful bridge she'd seen that was located twenty miles away, the giant steel structure arcing over a body of water. "It's a real bridge; I saw it when I first came here," she added.

Kathleen described playing baseball with her husband, swinging the bat at his pitch. "I have no idea what that's about," she commented when Dr. Trimble pressed her for more details. "My husband plays on a league one night a week, but obviously it's men only. I've never even touched a bat."

Ivy was more subdued. "All I could see was a window, but it was covered with a dark screen. I kept staring out the window, but I couldn't see a thing. I have no idea where it was."

When it was Betty's turn, she read aloud from the note she'd hastily jotted: *There was a park with a yellow blanket and a picnic on it with food spread out. It was a beautiful, sunny day and birds were singing. A butterfly danced nearby.*

If I don't write down what I saw, she thought, *maybe it won't come true.* But she was only trying to fool herself; she knew it didn't work that way.

She had seen Ivy knitting a yellow baby blanket exactly like the one in her dream. Ivy kept it tucked in her bag and brought it out now and then to work on during lulls in her testing.

"It's for my baby," Ivy had said, stroking the soft skein of yarn.

"It's just gorgeous," Betty had replied. "Nicer than anything you could buy at a store."

Betty could barely let herself think about the implications of her dream. She, Betty, desperately trying to pick up the baby blanket. The vehicle blasting by, running over the blanket, leaving a thick black tire mark rolling through it.

She knew exactly what the symbolism meant.

Ivy's baby was going to die.

CHAPTER TWENTY-ONE

RILEY, PRESENT DAY

My restless night is punctuated by dreams so vivid they leave me sweaty and gasping. In one, Danny perches on a stool at Betty's kitchen counter while she serves him a plate of lasagna. Pots and pans clutter the counters, and shredded cheese is spilled everywhere, coating the floor like orange snow. The two of them are laughing like old friends.

"What are you doing here?" I ask in my dream.

Without looking at me, Danny replies, "What are *you* doing here?"

Then he turns and I glimpsed his ruined face. His teeth are knocked out and his eyes, blackened. "You shouldn't be here," Danny whispers.

I awaken with my pulse pounding between my ears.

Betty cooking in her kitchen, Danny looking roughed up—it was an amalgamation of details from my reality mixed with the surreal, like dreams always seem to be.

Even a warm shower and cup of coffee from the giant urn in the motel lobby don't allow me to mentally reset.

At least I have a clear mission. Sandra Lennox gave me the name of the Trimble Institute. My online research confirmed what Sandra told me, that it was an offshoot of the psych department devoted to exploring parapsychology until it was shuttered in the mid 1960s. I'm not a believer in that stuff, so it seems strange a prestigious university devoted so many resources to it for decades. Since it was once part of Marquis, the school's library should have more information.

A young guy with double hoop earrings and a name tag that identifies him as Benjy is manning the library's information desk when I arrive. I explain what I'm seeking, and he taps on a computer.

"We've got archives," he finally says. "But you have to look at them here. You can't take anything out."

"That's fine," I tell him.

"ID?"

I hesitate. "Do I need a student ID?"

He shakes his head. "We're open to the public." I show him my driver's license and he glances at it, then reaches for an iPad and spins it around so I can see it. "Type your name and address in the box here."

There are a few other names above mine, presumably of people who have looked at the Trimble Institute archives in the past. I type in my information and Benjy checks it against my ID before walking around the desk. "Follow me."

As he leads me down a flight of stairs, I catch the faint aroma of weed drifting from his clothes. We reach the bowels of the library and he swipes a card through an electronic lock to open a door. The floor is cement and the paint on the walls is chipped and faded. Stacks of shelves rise up like tall rows of corn, filling the center of the space, but the edges are bare.

Benjy stops at a shelf in the middle of the stacks and points to a row of large brown boxes. "Everything is in there," he says. "You want to look at it here, or . . . ?"

It's dank and silent in the basement, with no windows; I'd rather take the boxes upstairs. But they look heavy, and I don't want to press my luck by asking him to help me carry them.

"Here is fine," I say.

"When you're done, come back upstairs and sign out."

I wait until he disappears before I examine the boxes, which are all labeled by year. I choose the ones labeled *1963–64*, staggering as I pull the heavy boxes off the shelf.

They're full of folders which are in turn filled with strange papers—like something from a science fiction novel. The pages detail experiments designed to test psychic ability with handwritten notes and memos. There are black-and-white photographs of testing equipment and subjects, and hundreds of typewritten pages. The photos feel eerie, especially the one of a young woman wearing a blindfold made of halves of ping-pong balls. Luckily, the folders are neatly labeled.

There are dozens of folders labeled *1964*. But every single folder is empty.

I flip through the contents of the box, making sure the papers weren't misfiled. Then I muscle down other boxes, searching through every scrap of paper and double-checking dates until my fingertips are stained gray and my back is aching from being hunched over.

An eerie sense of déjà vu sweeps over me. Once again, it's as if Betty and her friends never existed.

CHAPTER TWENTY-TWO

HELEN, 1964

At age eighteen, Helen Hopkins could count on one hand the things she had going for her: a steady job, her own bedroom in a boarding house, trim ankles, and a neck so long it rivaled Audrey Hepburn's. Plus, she'd recently moved to Boston, which held possibilities, even if none ever seemed to present themselves to Helen.

Her only other choice would have been to remain in her widowed mother's tiny, run-down home on the outskirts of New Haven, Connecticut, where she wouldn't have a decent job *or* her own bedroom, let alone the prospect of romance.

In her fantasies, she bumped into a dashing stranger on the street who was enchanted by Helen, instantly understanding that she was special. She had the heart of a romantic, but the head of a realist. If she did happen to meet someone, how could she ever captivate him? She was usually clad in the blue cap and smock she wore to work in the Necco factory, where she slid colorful wafers into metal rows before they were wrapped in waxed paper. She earned 65 cents per hour—half the pay of her male colleagues who did the same job. Her salary didn't allow her to frequent nice restaurants or the theater, where the sort of distinguished man she dreamt about might be found.

But on a late spring evening in 1964, a tall, successful man found her.

"Miss Hopkins, is that you? You have a visitor," her landlady called as Helen came through the door from work.

Helen could hardly believe her ears. She never had visitors.

She hung her coat on the rack in the hallway, smoothed her hair, then stepped into the living room, where her landlady was serving coffee to a broad-shouldered man whose back was to her.

He stood up and turned around and extended his hand, saying, "I'm Dr. Silas Trimble."

After the landlady excused herself, Dr. Trimble removed a booklet from his briefcase and smoothed it open on the coffee table.

Helen recognized the article from the *American Society for Psychical Research* journal with the headline "Remote Viewing: A Case Study, October 1963." She had a copy of the article upstairs in her scrapbook. She knew every word of it intimately; it was written about her.

"Are there any inaccuracies or exaggerations in this report?" Dr. Trimble asked.

Helen shook her head. "Everything is true, just like I told the man who interviewed me."

Dr. Trimble asked her to recount the experience detailed in the article, and she did: A few months earlier, she'd been near the end of her shift at the wafer factory when the sudden, overpowering smell of mud filled her nose and lungs. She threw her arms over her head, fearing the building was about to tumble down atop her. Her breathing was rapid and shallow; she sensed a great wave—taller than any of the buildings in the city—was about to crest, then crash down. She could hear the screams of victims, then silence.

Her coworkers had gathered around her, and Helen realized she'd slipped off the stool and crumpled onto the floor.

She had told them of her vision, and her manager pointed to the window. "There's no storm," he said. "This building is made of steel; nothing could bring it down. Did you fall asleep on the job? Knock your head?"

Helen shook her head vigorously. "I was wide awake."

He shrugged and told her to get back to work. But the strong aroma of mud and dank water lingered in the air, even if no one else on the factory line could smell it.

Then news came from across the Atlantic: a landslide in Italy. Tumbling rock and mud, the Vajont Dam breaking, a great crescendoing wave that claimed thousands of lives in the Van Pola landslide at the same moment of Helen's experience.

Helen might've been dismissed as a hysterical woman, but there were half a dozen witnesses who verified her account of what she had seen, felt, and smelled.

"When I saw a newspaper advertisement that the psychical society was looking for such stories, I went in for an interview," Helen told Dr. Trimble. "You see, it wasn't the first time I'd had such a vision."

He smiled, which seemed jarring given the horror she'd just described. "I've been looking for you for quite some time," he said.

Dr. Trimble wasn't the man of her dreams. He was too old, too gruff, and besides, he not only had wiry gray hair sprouting from his ears, he was married.

But he was the first person who ever believed Helen was special.

Special enough to deserve to live in a brand-new city in the South, where the weather and pace were milder. To be given a free dorm room. Proper meals, rather than the toast and tea she made on the hotplate and in the kettle in her room.

Dr. Trimble had come all the way from Virginia to see Helen, and he wanted to bring her back with him.

"I've reached an agreement with the university president," he said while Helen pretended not to notice her landlady eavesdropping in the hallway. "We'll match your salary, and your room and board are free."

"How soon would you like me there?" she asked.

"I'm driving back tomorrow. Ideally, you would come with me," Dr. Trimble said.

It seemed too good to be true.

CHAPTER TWENTY-THREE

RILEY, PRESENT DAY

My head jerks up at a faint creaking sound. It's the door to the basement opening. Heavy footsteps thud, moving closer to me.

I leap up, wincing as sharp pins and needles assail my left leg. *I'm in a safe space*, I remind myself. No one can enter the archives unless they're an employee with a key card.

Still, I hold my breath until Benjy comes into view. "You've been down here for hours," he says. "Everything okay?"

There's nothing overtly threatening in his tone or manner, but I can't help thinking I'm in an isolated area with a strange man, and he's between me and the exit. I'm only five-four, and I'm a flighter, not a fighter. My anxiety soars again. Did he really come down here to check on me, or does he have a darker purpose?

"Just finishing up," I say, hating how high and squeaky my voice sounds.

"'Kay." He turns and I follow him as we ascend the steps to the main level and step into the lobby.

See? Nothing happened, I tell myself as the adrenaline ebbs from my veins.

I used to have good instincts about people. But after I learned what Danny had done, they evaporated. When I could no longer trust the man I considered my soul mate, I guess I stopped trusting everyone.

"Sign out here," Benjy says, spinning the iPad around again. "Don't forget to put in the time, too."

"Hey, some of the files were missing," I tell him. "I found folders labeled *1964*, but they were all empty."

Benjy frowns. "That's not good. I'll tell my boss."

He doesn't seem as bothered as he should be.

"I mean, you've got records of everyone who had access to the boxes right?" I say, indicating the names listed above mine in the iPad. "So it could have been one of them."

"Makes sense," Benjy says. His lack of initiative chafes me.

Maybe it's the frustration of running into another dead end, or my fear of returning to Betty without any good news, but the strangest thing happens; I seize an opportunity.

I scan the names on the iPad while pretending to labor over the keyboard. A man named Alex Finch came here four times recently to examine the Trimble files. The visitor prior to him came eight years ago.

Judging by the number of empty file folders, it would be difficult to sneak out all the papers. But if someone came four times, it could be possible.

I button up my coat as I leave the library, then get into my car and consider my choices.

I could go home and tell Betty her friend Ivy passed away long ago, and I can't locate Kathleen or Helen. Or I can stop acting helpless and meek. I can try to reclaim my life despite the hand I was dealt, like Sandra Lennox did.

A spark flickers inside me, and I sense I'm at a crossroads. The decision I make now will affect the next one, and the ones after that, like the first wobbling domino in a long row.

Someone is trying to erase evidence that Betty and her friends were part of Marquis. Which means I'm living with a woman who is essentially a ghost.

If I can find Alex Finch, maybe I can learn what happened to the missing files. More important, I could begin to understand the strange, mysterious woman who took me into her home.

CHAPTER TWENTY-FOUR

Psychic Dorothy Allison of Nutley, New Jersey, has assisted police in more than four thousand investigations and has received many letters from law enforcement agencies describing how she helped them.

—US Department of Justice

BETTY, 1964

It was a brilliant day for football. The early November afternoon shone clear and windless, with a sun so blindingly bright it appeared to be celebrating, too. Everyone at Marquis was rallying for the boys in red jerseys. All week long, signs had sprouted up in dorm room windows and on banners hung outside buildings: *Stomp 'em, Wolves!* and *Nip those Lions!* The marching band's trumpets and the roar of the crowd could be heard a block away from the stadium.

"We're going to be late!" Ivy cried, struggling to walk quickly in her kitten heels. Pregnancy had affected her center of balance.

"It'll be fine." Kathleen hooked her arm through Ivy's to steady her. "Nothing interesting ever happens in the first few minutes."

"But David . . ." Ivy cut herself off, falling silent. It wasn't the first time she'd struggled in discussing her husband.

When Betty and Kathleen talked about their men, it was with fondness or occasionally fond exasperation. Even Helen had shyly revealed details about a man she'd developed a crush on—he was tall, dark, and handsome, but he didn't seem to have the slightest romantic interest in Helen.

Ivy, the most outgoing of the four, was the opposite. Whenever she was asked about David, she tensed up, and her comments felt scripted.

David was the team's defensive coach; there was no way Ivy could miss the game even though she should be home with her feet up, since it was a rare day off from their work at the institute.

Silas Trimble didn't yield to the typical rhythms of eating and sleeping. He was a man of enormous appetites, but like a hibernating bear, he alternated feasting with famine. He wouldn't eat for a day or two, the meals his wife delivered for him congealing on his desk beneath a layer of waxed paper and ending up in the trash. Then sometimes, as if remembering he needed fuel to continue, he'd wolf down a dinner big enough to satisfy three men.

He never seemed to sleep, either. No matter how early or late they were instructed to come to the institute, he was there. But Douglas had revealed that every now and then, Dr. Trimble disappeared for twenty-four hours. He'd sleep for most of it, shower, then refuel for the next work marathon. He was taking one of those breaks now.

Betty couldn't help but think that Dr. Trimble was gaining strength while the four girls were losing it, almost as if he were siphoning it out of them. She was dreading the week ahead.

"Thank goodness we made it." Ivy sighed as she showed her ticket to the student manning the gate.

They began climbing the steps up the bleachers, with Ivy gripping the handrail tightly. Betty decided she'd buy some peanuts and cherry Cokes for the group. Ivy needed to keep her strength up, no matter what her scolding doctor said about her weight.

Cheerleaders in red swishing skirts twirled pom-poms as they chanted: "Give me an *M*! Give me an *A*! Give me an *R*! Give me a Q! Give me a *U*! Give me an *I*! Give me an *S*! What does that spell? Marquis!" Then the players ran onto the field, announced by the broadcaster, as the crowd erupted.

"Number forty-four is handsome." Kathleen nudged Helen. "But rumor has it he's engaged to a girl back in his hometown."

Helen gave a nervous laugh. "As if he'd be interested in me."

"Stop it," Kathleen ordered. "You're darling." She appraised Helen. "You know, I think it would suit you to try your hair a bit shorter. You've got such delicate features, like Mia Farrow. And how would you feel about tweezing your brows?"

"I never know how to do those things," Helen confessed.

"Next time we'll get together at my place. I'll fix you up in a flash," Kathleen promised. "The dreamboat you have a crush on will notice you, I can guarantee that."

Betty was listening with half an ear. She was so acutely aware of Ivy's discomfort she felt it as if it were her own. Ivy was shifting on the hard bench, occasionally reaching behind her to rub her knuckles into her lower back. Whenever the crowd shouted, Ivy cringed, as if the yells were reverberating inside her skull.

Even when Betty bought snacks for the group, Ivy didn't seem revived.

"Are you feeling unwell?" Betty whispered.

"Just tired," Ivy replied. She grimaced. "And I keep getting these twinges. My doctor told me they're false contractions and that I should have a cocktail to relax."

"Does that help?" Betty asked.

"Sometimes. But then I always feel like I have to go to the bathroom. I need to go right now, but the thought of all those stairs again—"

An explosion of groans and shouts interrupted her; the South Carolina Wolves had scored against Marquis.

"Oh no!" Ivy cried. She leaned forward as much as her stomach would allow as the field goal kicker lined up and made the extra point. "Damn!"

It was the first time Betty had heard Ivy swear. She lifted an eyebrow. "It's a long way to the finish. They'll make it up."

"David just hates it when we lose," Ivy muttered, almost to herself. "He gets all sulky."

She watched a little longer, then tapped Betty's arm. "I really have to go to the ladies' room now."

Betty stood up to let Ivy pass. As she watched Ivy begin to descend, she felt a sudden compulsion to accompany her. She stood up, squeezing past Helen and Kathleen and the rest of the row, frantically trying to reach Ivy.

Several people were in front of Betty and she couldn't push past them on the narrow flight of stairs.

"Ivy, wait!" she called.

But her voice was swallowed up in another roar from the crowd.

She gasped as she saw Ivy's ankle turn and her body drop down as her hand slipped off the railing. Ivy sprawled forward before catching herself on her hands and knees. Two male students hurried to help Ivy, guiding her onto the bleachers.

Blood was running down Ivy's shins from her scraped knees, and she was pale as a ghost by the time Betty reached her.

"Are you badly hurt?" Betty asked.

Ivy shook her head. "Just embarrassed. I hope I didn't miss an important play."

"Let's sit here a moment while you catch your breath," Betty said.

A boy passed Ivy a flask of whiskey and she took a sip. Someone else gave Betty a handkerchief, and she dabbed Ivy's legs with it, then wrapped her arm around Ivy's shoulders and felt the trembles racking her friend's body.

"I wish this was over," Ivy whispered, leaning her head on Betty's shoulder. "I'm just so tired."

Betty didn't have to ask what she meant because she knew Ivy meant all of it: the game, the uncomfortable last few weeks of pregnancy, and most of all, the experiments with Dr. Trimble.

CHAPTER TWENTY-FIVE

RILEY, PRESENT DAY

Alex Finch is easy to find. My only mistake was assuming Alex was male when, in fact, she's a young woman.

I stare at the pictures that pop up on my phone. She looks about twenty, and in her most recent Instagram photo, she's in a group with five other girls. All are social media gorgeous, with wavy hair, pouty lips, and sooty eyelashes.

I use my thumb and forefinger to zoom in on Alex, realizing that my first impression was wrong. She doesn't seem to quite fit in visually with the rest of the group, and not just because she's standing a bit apart on the end and is by far the tallest and curviest. Alex is in an awkward pose; she seems to be trying to hide her body behind the girl next to her, and although she's smiling, her expression looks strained.

I take in more details: Her brown hair doesn't look professionally styled or highlighted. The fingernails of the girl whose hand is draped over Alex's shoulder look like delicate works of art, and her makeup is wedding-day ready, but Alex looks more natural.

The words pop into my mind before I'm aware I'm forming the judgment: *She's another outsider.*

Alex also provided an easy way for me to find her. Her post is in front of the Tri Delt sorority house with the hashtag #sistersforever.

When I knock on the door of the grand, pillared sorority house a little later, a young woman in a sweatshirt so big it covers all but a sliver of her boxer shorts answers.

"Hi, I'm looking for Alex," I say.

She pulls her phone out of the pocket of her hoodie and thumbs a text at warp speed. The replying chime is almost instantaneous.

"She'll be down in a sec," the woman says. "You can wait in the living room if you want."

I'm surprised she doesn't even ask for my name before inviting me inside; I could be anyone. But when I walk into the cavernous living room and see a half dozen other girls lounging around, I realize they've got security in numbers.

One is dozing on the couch with her feet propped up in another's lap while other young women tap on their phones and sip Red Bull or coffee. The scent of pancakes and maple syrup floats through the air, making my stomach grumble.

Two girls are huddled in an oversized chair, their long, graceful legs stretched out on an ottoman, watching something on a phone screen.

"We were total chaos," one moans.

"My liver hurts," the other replies. "Wait, is that Syd dancing? She's holding that pledge by the tie like it's a dog leash!"

They burst into laughter.

"Are you looking for me?" Alex has materialized behind me. She's wearing exercise leggings and a big jacket. In person, the vibe I detected through her photos comes through even stronger. While the other young women are draped around nonchalantly, Alex radiates a stiff, anxious energy.

"Hi, yes, I'm Riley," I begin. "Is there somewhere we can talk privately for a moment?"

She shrugs. "I'm going for a walk. You can come if you want."

We step outside and she sets off at a brisk pace. I'm glad I'm wearing sneakers, too, so I can keep up.

"I know what this is about," she says. Her voice starts out defiant, but wavers and breaks on the final word.

I blink. "You do?"

"You're from the university, right? What are you, like, a counselor?"

"I'm sorry, I'm not tracking."

"I've heard what students are saying, the jokes they're making about me. There's a stupid meme going around on Snapchat. And yeah, fine, I was the one who came on to him. But he was all in!"

Something about Alex reminds me of an injured wild animal—she's acting tough, like she's ready to fight, but she desperately wants to curl up somewhere soft and safe.

I shake my head. "Alex, can you back up a little? I honestly don't know what you're talking about."

She wipes her nose with the back of her hand and starts walking even faster.

"A month ago I slept with my psych professor. All the girls think he's hot and I don't know . . . he said really nice stuff about the papers I wrote. That I was smart and insightful. I thought he liked me. But he's married and I guess he freaked out afterwards and decided I could get him in trouble. So he accused me of cheating on one of my papers, which I didn't. And now *I'm* the one in trouble. Everyone assumes I made up the sexual stuff to get back at him. Because why would a hot professor sleep with a girl who looks like me? Just ask anyone on Snapchat."

I feel myself bristle. I believe her; she can't be faking this kind of raw pain and anger. "Did you tell anyone about this?" I ask.

"I told everyone," she says. "My friends, my mom, my therapist—she thinks he's a narcissist, by the way. That's her professional opinion. No one can prove we slept together, but he apparently has proof I cheated. Which he manufactured."

"I'm so sorry that happened to you," I say.

She takes in a deep, shuddering breath and suddenly it's like I can see past her appearance, into her very soul. Her sneakers are brightly colored, with a designer logo, but the soles are worn, like she saved up to buy them and can't afford to replace them. Her clothes are plain and a little too tight, like she wishes she were a few sizes smaller. She's practically oozing a raw vulnerability. She's a scholarship kid, maybe, or someone who took out loans to go to college.

"If you're not a counselor, then who are you?" she asks.

"I'm here about something else," I say. "Can we slow down? It's hard to talk when I'm walking so fast."

"We're almost there," she replies.

A moment later she stops in the middle of the sidewalk and turns to face a row of townhouses. I shift so I can see her expression. Alex wears her heart on her sleeve, and I want to gauge her reaction to my words.

"I'm here about the Trimble Institute archives from the library."

Her face is blank. "What's a Trimble archive?"

"You went to the library four times over the past few months to research the Trimble Institute."

She shakes her head. She appears to have absolutely no idea what I'm talking about.

"Why would you say that?" she asks. "It's so random."

"Then someone used your student ID to sign into the library and access the files," I explain.

Her eyes widen. "It wasn't me. But guess what? My student ID went missing the day we slept together. That jerk must've—" She cuts herself off, her attention suddenly commanded by a guy coming out of a townhouse with a blue door.

I stare as the athletic-looking man with black hair locks the door behind him. "That's your professor?"

She nods and folds her arms. "I know what times he leaves for his seminars and I come here to show him I'm not going to disappear."

Despite her tough words, her lips are trembling. Then I notice something that breaks my heart: Her nails are bitten to the quick.

The man spots Alex and pivots, heading in the direction away from her. "Hi, Professor Woods!" she calls after him. She watches until he disappears around a corner.

"He pretends I don't exist now." Alex's eyes fill. "He must've taken my ID, too. Maybe to get me in trouble for something else."

CHAPTER TWENTY-SIX

Before David Berkowitz's arrest, [psychic Dorothy] Allison also was credited with giving an accurate description of the Son of Sam killer to a police artist and correctly predicting that he would be picked up on a traffic violation.

—*The Los Angeles Times*

BETTY, 1964

Two days after the football game, while the scrapes on Ivy's knees were still fresh, Dr. Trimble announced he had a new experiment for his girls. "Come to my car."

"Where are we going, sir?" Kathleen asked.

Dr. Trimble shook his head. "For the experiment to be pure, the only information you can have is what comes to you organically."

Betty looked at the other women, knowing their fatigue was reflected in her own countenance. By contrast, after his long sleep and greedy refueling, Dr. Trimble seemed larger and his color was heightened. His belly strained against his shirt buttons, and his cheeks were heavy and florid.

As she picked up her handbag and cardigan, Betty tried to catch Douglas's eye. He was administering the card test to a new volunteer, a pretty girl who smelled like roses and wore a blue sweater with a matching headband.

Dr. Trimble put on his long black coat and hat but before he led the women to the door, he did something peculiar. He stopped behind Douglas's shoulder, watching as the final few cards of the test were administered.

"Did you enjoy that, Emily?" he asked.

"It was fun, sir," Emily replied. She looked to be about eighteen, and had such perfect, creamy skin she could have been a Pond's Cold Cream model. "I hope I did well after you brought me all this way." Betty was surprised to hear that Emily had a British accent. It sounded so crisp and elegant.

Douglas pointed to something on his notepad while Dr. Trimble nodded.

"Excellent," Dr. Trimble said. "Continue with her."

Betty tried to catch Douglas's eye as she exited the building, but he ignored her.

Dr. Trimble led them to his maroon Buick Riviera. There was room for three in the back and one in front. Betty knew none of them wanted to sit next to Dr. Trimble but then Ivy said, "I guess I could use the extra room," and climbed into the passenger's seat.

Dr. Trimble drove slowly, hunched over his steering wheel. The silence felt thick and awkward, but Betty couldn't think of anything to say. She tried to take comfort in the feel of Helen's shoulder pressed against her own. At least she had the other girls; she didn't know if she could bear being sealed in the vehicle with just Dr. Trimble.

He'd always unnerved her. But lately, she felt almost afraid of him. The more he tried to command and harness her psyche, the more desperate she wanted to recoil.

After forty minutes or so, Dr. Trimble pulled to the side of the road. Betty looked around. They were in a rural area. In the distance was farmland, with spotted cows grazing atop rolling green fields. Thick clouds were creeping sideways toward the sun, threatening to blot out the warmth and light.

"You need to trust me completely," Dr. Trimble said. Then he handed them the ping-pong blindfolds. They tied them on, erasing their field of vision.

They drove a little longer, and Betty felt Helen's hand touch her own, feeling so small and delicate it could be a child's. She clutched it tightly, feeling her stomach churn, wishing this day were over.

The car stopped again and Betty heard Dr. Trimble grunt with the exertion of climbing out. One by one, he led the girls away from the car, guiding them by their elbows. Betty had no frame of reference; she could be anywhere.

When Dr. Trimble spoke again, his voice was so close to her ear that she flinched. "Each of you may have a different experience today, or you may have one unified vision. Whatever happens, you must remember every detail, even ones that seem insignificant. I'll come back to pick you up in due time."

He handed Betty earplugs and she dutifully inserted them, then he was gone.

At least, he seemed to be gone. He could be a few dozen yards away, watching to make sure they didn't remove their blindfolds or disobey his instructions.

This experiment was an escalation of the blackout room, Betty realized. Maybe the other girls weren't even nearby; Dr. Trimble could have led them to different locations.

She could be standing here all alone. She had rarely felt so vulnerable.

He would come back soon, she tried to reassure herself. And Dr. Trimble was a very reputable man; just yesterday, there was a photograph of him in the school newspaper along with the college's President Sherman at a celebration of a generous new donation to the institute.

Betty slowed her breathing and tucked her hands into her pockets for warmth. She felt her heels digging into the soft earth beneath her feet, so she slipped them off and stood in her nylons on the grass. At least she wasn't on a road; she could be on one of the rolling green hills she'd seen at their last stop. Maybe cows were grazing nearby. She found the image comforting, and tried to coax it forward.

As her breathing slowed, she counted the good things that lay ahead: She'd awoken extra early to begin dinner preparations, and tonight she planned to light candles and play "Bring It On Home to Me" by Sam Cooke, which had been their wedding song. Douglas hadn't mentioned it yet, but surely he'd come home with flowers or a gift. It was their one-year wedding anniversary. They would have a quiet, loving evening together.

She thought about how this very morning, she'd opened the oval plastic case containing twenty-one birth control pills, plus the seven sugar pills that she swallowed during her monthly curse.

She'd been tempted to throw the case into the trash, but she worried her husband would see it and there would be consequences for her rebellious act. Surely it wouldn't be too long before Douglas agreed it was time to make a baby.

Then the visions began—streaks that looked like lightning, followed by a light orange haze. She inhaled and smelled smoke. But not the vanilla aroma of Dr. Trimble's pipe.

This was a fire.

CHAPTER TWENTY-SEVEN

RILEY, PRESENT DAY

After Alex leaves, I stand on the sidewalk in front of her professor's house for a moment, unsure of what to do next. I'm about to walk to my Toyota when the door to the townhouse opens again.

A thirty-ish, petite woman steps out, the sun picking up the red and blond glints in her wavy brown hair. It must be the professor's wife.

Our eyes meet and she gives me a small wave. "Can I help you?" she calls, walking toward me. "You look a little lost."

"Just getting my bearings," I say. "Marquis is that way, right?" I point in the direction I came from.

"Sure is." She's just a couple of feet away from me now, close enough that I can see the small birthmark on her right cheekbone. She's staring intently at me, perhaps wondering what I'm doing lurking on her street. "Have a good day."

She turns back toward her car and I hear the chirp of the fob unlocking the door as I walk away.

She seemed a touch too interested in a stranger on her street. But maybe she's one of those people who is friendly to everyone.

Does she know what her husband is accused of doing? I wonder. Perhaps he is concealing everything. Maybe he's being extra sweet and solicitous, telling her to put her feet up while he cooks dinner, and holding her close at night while she marvels at her luck in marrying such a good man.

Or perhaps there's something nagging at her. Maybe she buries the unsettled feeling under the busyness of her days and spends her evenings scrolling through images of other people's lives rather than examining her own. She could be choosing a common form of myopia by avoiding seeing what's right in front of her.

Like I did.

My throat thickens as I finally acknowledge the signs *were* there all along: the way Danny always rushed to get the mail first. The time I asked him to get cash from an ATM and he claimed it was broken and not dispensing money. The phone calls at strange hours that he told me were business-related, which I reasoned was plausible since, as a real estate agent, he didn't have off hours.

I sensed very early on something was amiss in my marriage. But I quashed that fear, never wanting to disrupt the heady, romantic illusion of our lives.

No wonder I don't feel like I can trust anyone. Yes, Danny betrayed me. But even worse, I betrayed myself. And that's what really shattered my sense of safety.

To my right is the Marquis University library, where there must be plenty of information about Professor Joshua Woods. If Alex is telling the truth and he stole her student ID, he was likely the one who stole the Trimble Institute files. But why?

I turn to my right and begin walking quickly.

CHAPTER TWENTY-EIGHT

Penny Serra disappeared from Connecticut in 1971. Stymied by a lack of clues, the police brought in psychic Pascarella Downey. Downey had a vision of Serra's murder by a mechanic who smelled like oil and was wearing a name tag with the letter *E* . . . A mechanic named Edward Grant was connected to the crime and brought to justice.

—*Reader's Digest*

BETTY, 1964

Betty felt as if she were floating in a vast, hollow space, the only person around for miles. She couldn't even hear the sound of her own breathing.

She shivered, wrapping her arms around herself. The sun must have ducked behind a cloud, because the temperature was dropping. Time had grown blurry. She guessed she had been standing on the grass blindfolded for maybe twenty minutes, but it could have been longer. All she could do was hope Dr. Trimble released them soon.

She was anxious to leave. She'd picked up the scent of fire, and beneath that, a frantic desperation, like the distant scrabbling of creatures trying to escape a sealed container. Whatever it meant, it couldn't be good. She slipped back on her shoes, even though her calves ached. She didn't want this place to touch her.

Her stomach rumbled. *It must be close to noon by now,* she thought.

The girls' lunches were on the table just inside the front door of the Trimble Institute, where Dr. Trimble's wife left them each morning. Dr. Trimble hadn't suggested they bring along their midday meals today, and no one else had thought of it.

Betty hoped Ivy had some crackers or hard candies in her purse. Ivy hadn't looked well this morning. Her ankles were swollen and her foundation couldn't mask the darkening purple smudges beneath her eyes. Ivy was working practically around the clock. They all were, squeezing in household chores and ironing and cooking during their few spare moments. But it was especially hard on Ivy.

The wind brushed against Betty's face, feeling like the touch of fingers. An instant later, something compelled Betty to move. She stretched out her hands so she wouldn't smash into a wall or tree and stepped carefully. She didn't know where she was heading, but she felt an acute sense of urgency to walk to the left.

Then she heard Ivy calling. But the noise wasn't originating from a specific direction. It was as if the summons was coming from deep within her own mind.

Was this part of the experiment? she wondered.

"I'm coming, Ivy!" she yelled.

She stumbled over something—maybe a tree root—but caught her balance. She could hear Ivy whimpering in pain; it wasn't an actual noise, but more like the echo of one reverberating in her skull. Without hesitation, Betty ripped off her blindfold and earplugs. She blinked in the weak light. Helen and Kathleen were approaching, too, as if they'd received the same internal summons as Betty.

"Hurry!" Betty yelled. "Something happened to Ivy!"

Kathleen tore off her blindfold and began to run and after a moment, Helen did the same.

"There!" Kathleen shouted, pointing.

Ivy lay a few dozen yards away, beneath a tree. The girls ran to her side.

"Did you fall?" Betty asked, kneeling down.

Ivy's face looked gray. Her mouth was a grimace.

"The baby," she moaned. "Something's wrong."

Betty looked up to see Kathleen's and Helen's faces mirroring her shock.

"I'll go call for an ambulance," Helen said. She spun around in a circle, but they were surrounded by farmland. There wasn't a building in sight, other than an old barn. Dr. Trimble had deserted them.

"Which way?" Helen asked frantically.

"The road!" Betty pointed. "Flag down a car!"

As Helen took off running, Kathleen removed her sweater and tucked it over Ivy. Betty gripped Ivy's hand. "Just squeeze as hard as you need to. Help is coming."

"It's too early," Ivy panted. "She isn't due for a month."

The image of the ruined yellow blanket surfaced in Betty's mind, but she forced it away.

"You're both going to be just fine," she promised. She took off her sweater and draped it over Ivy's legs, feeling helpless.

In the distance, she could see Helen struggling up a hill in her heels, heading for the road.

Hurry, she willed the message to Helen.

For endless minutes, they stroked Ivy's brow and urged her to remain calm. When Ivy grew sweaty and restless, squirming and flinching as if ants were attacking her, they removed the sweaters and Kathleen prayed aloud.

At last, Betty heard a car rumbling toward them. Ivy's skirt had hitched above her knees, so Betty pulled it down to preserve her modesty. She looked up to see the familiar maroon Buick approaching, slowly maneuvering over the grass. Dr. Trimble was driving, with Helen beside him in the passenger's seat.

As soon as the car stopped, Helen leapt out. "Dr. Trimble was coming back for us. I waved him down on the road."

"Did you phone for an ambulance?" Betty asked.

Dr. Trimble hefted himself out of the vehicle in time to hear her question. "No. It'll be faster if I drive her to the hospital."

It took all three girls to get Ivy to her feet and help her to the car. They settled her in the passenger's seat, then climbed into the back.

"Tell me what happened," Dr. Trimble said as he began to bump the car over the grass toward the road, Ivy moaning with each jolt.

Kathleen cleared her throat. "After a while, I suddenly felt the need to find Ivy. It wasn't anything that happened externally. The urge came from within me."

"Me, too," said Helen.

"Betty?" Dr. Trimble prodded.

"It was the same for me. We all approached Ivy at the same time."

"Astonishing," Dr. Trimble said. He turned onto the road, but instead of speeding up, he slowed his car and twisted around to look at the three girls. "Describe the experience, please. And start at the beginning."

The car was practically crawling now. All Betty could do was rub Ivy's shoulder and hope they reached the hospital in time.

Their stories spilled out, divergent at first, then funneling together into a cohesive narrative: All three girls had felt a deep sense of unease on the land. Betty smelled smoke and channeled the need of some unknown beings trying to escape, Kathleen heard dozens of voices calling for help, and Helen saw a vision of a building consumed by fire against the night sky.

"Ivy, did you experience anything like this as well?" Dr. Trimble asked.

She whimpered in reply.

Betty caught sight of Dr. Trimble's heavy eyebrows drawing down into a frown. "Continue, girls."

They talked about hearing a summons from Ivy and finding their way to her despite their blindfolds.

"Extraordinary," Dr. Trimble whispered. He drifted to the side of the road and put the car in park while he lit his pipe. "The initial experiment was an unqualified success. I brought you to the site of a deadly fire that claimed the lives of twenty-two people a century ago. You sensed this, didn't you? But even more incredible, the *unplanned* experiment was the real triumph. That's the one that will command attention. This is the proof I've been seeking. My hypothesis is correct! Your gifts are magnified by your proximity to each other. I'll need all of you to stay late tonight. It's vital that we document everything while it is fresh in your minds."

Betty could feel Ivy's body shaking beneath her palm. The car still wasn't moving. Finally she could bear it no more. "Please hurry," Betty whispered. "Ivy needs medical attention right away."

Dr. Trimble's eyes widened, as if he had forgotten about the threat to Ivy and her baby.

It took an eternity to reach the hospital, and Ivy seemed half out of her mind from pain by the time nurses loaded her onto a gurney and wheeled her through the doors.

At least she's still alive, Betty thought as tears sprang to her eyes. Kathleen and Helen were standing beside her, and as if they were sharing another silent summons, their hands reached out for hers at the same moment.

Then Dr. Trimble called them. Even before he finished his sentence, her stomach knotted. "Come, girls. We need to get back to the lab."

CHAPTER TWENTY-NINE

RILEY, PRESENT DAY

I stare at Professor Woods's photograph over his bio on the Marquis University faculty page. *All the girls think he's hot*, Alex had said, and I can see why: He's got that hipster scruff combined with a muscular physique and soulful brown eyes.

Not my type, though. He actually gives me the creeps. There's something calculated in his appearance, from his artfully tousled hair to his thin leather necklace. I continue reading his bio: *Woods is married to Associate Professor Elizabeth Harris, who teaches applied psychology at Marquis.*

So they're in the same field. From the outside, her life looks enviable. But it could explode at any moment, just like mine.

It would've been easy for Josh Woods to replace Alex's picture on the student ID with his own and hold it up for Benjy's half-hearted perusal. He didn't even have to change the androgynous name.

If there's a link between him and one of the four women that drove him to want to possess the files, it can't be Betty. He's less than half her age, and given her isolation, they never would have crossed paths.

I'm still glaring at his photo when a text chimes on my phone. It's from Danny.

Warm relief floods my body. He was the real reason I couldn't sleep last night. I kept imagining what they'd done to him to get my phone number.

I'm sorry for everything, his text reads.

I start to ask how he's doing, like I have every time we've communicated, then I backspace over my words. I stare down at his name and let my mind wander back to our first date two years ago.

It was a Saturday morning, and I had absolutely nothing to do. All my friends were married and doing cute couple things like going to a farmer's market or brunch. I thought about hitting the gym or catching up on errands, then impulsively decided to check out the Meetups in my area. Several were taking place that day: a hike, a trivia happy hour at a pub, and a gathering to fix up the home of an elderly couple who'd fallen on hard times.

Bring a rake, wall paint, sponges, and cleaning supplies—or just a willingness to help. Let's give back to this decorated Vietnam veteran and his bride of fifty years, the notice read.

When I showed up at the dilapidated house with a can of neutral paint and two brushes, volunteers were already cutting the lawn and clearing away brush. Danny stood on the rickety front porch, matching people with jobs. Within ten seconds of meeting him, I felt my gaze drifting down to his left hand to check for a ring.

"The plumbing repairs in the kitchen should be done soon," Danny told me. "After we scrub the walls, it'll need fresh paint."

He looked down at the two brushes in my hand and plucked one for himself.

"Mind if I borrow this?"

We spent the day side by side, transforming the old, stained walls with a creamy ivory hue, then went out for Thai food afterward. Six months later, I awoke to find Danny staring down at me. He asked what kind of engagement ring I wanted, as if our marriage were a given. I tried to match his casual tone, but I couldn't stop smiling. *A cushion-cut stone on a classic gold band,* I told him. *Nothing big or flashy.* But when he knelt down on one of our favorite walking trails, in his outstretched palm was a vintage ring featuring a huge teardrop sapphire.

My ring is the one thing of value I've never sold. I told myself it was my last-ditch safety net in case of a catastrophic medical issue or other crisis.

But if I'm going to help Danny, I need the money. I type a response to my ex-husband: I need to sell my engagement ring. Where did you buy it?

Three dots appear, then vanish.

I think the store shut down, sorry. You won't be able to return it. You could try to pawn it if you want.

What a strange reply, I think. Why would he suggest a pawn shop?

Then the realization hits me: The store didn't close down. It probably never existed.

Danny worked as a real estate agent. He had access to lots of houses. Because I did our laundry and always checked pockets, I discovered a few things he must have pilfered: a dozen oxycodone pills wrapped in a tissue, a valuable old coin, a TAG Heuer watch. None of these items were in a case or original packaging, but Danny always had an explanation: He'd lost the watch before we'd met and had just discovered it in his gym bag; the coin had been mixed in with others he'd gotten from a convenience store clerk; the pills belonged to a friend who was trying to kick his addiction and had relinquished them to Danny.

Of course he stole them, probably to fund his growing gambling addiction.

Just like he stole the sapphire engagement ring with a few tiny scratches on the band that I told myself added to the vintage charm.

Was anything about our marriage real?

CHAPTER THIRTY

During the Cold War years, the USA and Soviet Union were known to have been spying on each other using the services of psychic remote viewers.

—*Strategic Analysis Journal*

BETTY 1964

Betty stood in the doorway of Ivy's hospital room clutching a bouquet of pink carnations, with Kathleen and Helen beside her.

Ivy was writing in her diary, and the look on her face was so unlike her usual cheerful countenance. Then Ivy looked up and smiled weakly, and the momentary shadow in her expression passed.

"Did you see the baby?" Ivy asked in a hoarse voice as she set aside the diary.

"Not yet," Betty said, hurrying to Ivy's side. "Viewing hours at the nursery aren't until ten AM."

She reached for Ivy's hand, cradling it gently. The other women squeezed in close in the small space, mindful not to press against the privacy curtain separating Ivy from her roommates. The room smelled vaguely of antiseptic, and a monitor beeped rhythmically in the distance.

"We were so worried for you," Helen whispered. "Did it hurt terribly?"

Ivy shook her head. "They put me to sleep right after I got here. I didn't feel a thing. And I slept through the entire night. They had to wake me to give little Sandra a bottle this morning. Only five and a half pounds, but perfectly healthy. She has a headful of dark curls already."

"I can't wait to meet the little angel," Betty said.

Kathleen was rummaging through her purse. She pulled out a hairbrush and cosmetics case. "You'll feel better when your face is made up," she said.

"Oh, thank goodness," Ivy replied. "I left my purse in Dr. Trimble's car so I didn't have my things. One of the nurses promised to do my makeup before David came to see me . . ." Her voice trailed off, as if she'd revealed more than she'd intended.

Kathleen paused in dusting powder on Ivy's face: "David hasn't been here yet?"

"No, but he will be soon," Ivy said in a tone that made Betty think Ivy was reassuring herself more than the others.

Betty hid her surprise. Of course no husband would be in the delivery room, but wouldn't a loving father come as soon as he could to see his new baby?

"It's for the best, really," Ivy said, as if she could discern Betty's thoughts. "I needed the rest. The doctor said my iron is low. And the nurses fed Sandra her bottle last night. David wouldn't have had the slightest idea how to do it!"

"I'm glad you're giving your baby formula," Kathleen commented. "They say it's the finest nutrition."

"And it means we can help you feed her," Helen added.

"I would love that." Ivy's voice was tremulous. "I want you girls to visit me as much as you can once I'm home."

Everyone fell quiet. Betty could feel the hitch of tension in the air. Helen's gaze dropped to the ground. Kathleen smoothed blush so gently onto Ivy's cheekbones it was like a soothing caress.

Someone had to say it.

Betty cleared her throat. "After we finished with Dr. Trimble last night, he said . . ." She paused. Looking at her pale, fragile friend, it seemed cruel to go on. But she had to.

"He wants you back volunteering in a week."

Ivy's eyes looked shattered. "A week? But that'll be right after I get out of the hospital."

"I know," Betty blurted. "He kept repeating he was so close to gathering the data he needs. We tried to convince him that you had to rest, but he was adamant. He said all of his work would be in vain if the four of us didn't resume."

Kathleen closed her compact with a snap. "I think you should just quit," she said. "What's the worst he could do to you?"

Ivy closed her eyes. "It's not me he would harm," she finally said. "But what if he got David fired?"

The Marquis Wolves football team hadn't performed especially well this season. David, the newest coach, would be an easy target for that disappointment. And if Dr. Trimble, who had such influence at the university, weighed in—

"Could your mother come and help care for little Sandra?" Kathleen's question interrupted Betty's spiraling thoughts.

"Oh, no. My mother is very religious. She carries a small bible in her purse everywhere she goes. She wouldn't approve of my volunteering at the Trimble Institute."

"What about David's mother?" Helen asked.

"That old battle-ax would be the end of me."

With every dead end, Ivy seemed to deflate a little more. Betty had always thought of her friend as buoyant and robust, but now, lying in the metal-framed bed, she seemed a mere husk of her former self.

Betty looked up and caught Kathleen's eye, then Helen's. She understood they were completely in sync.

"So we'll be your family," Betty said as the others nodded. It felt as solemn a vow as the one she'd given at the wedding altar.

"You rest this week and let the nurses take care of little Sandra," Kathleen said. "Get as strong as you can. We'll stock your freezer with dinners."

"And when I grocery shop, it'll be simple enough to get the things on your list," Helen added.

"If you lend us your key we can dash over to your house and make it spick-and-span," Betty said. "And when you come back to the institute, you'll bring Sandra and we'll all help you care for her."

"What would I do without you?" Ivy asked.

"Wipe away those tears, you'll ruin your makeup," Kathleen mock scolded.

A moment later, a nurse in a crisp uniform and white cap entered the room.

"How are you feeling today, Mrs. Lennox?" she asked.

"I'm better now," Ivy said.

The nurse's low-heeled pumps landed briskly on the tile floor as she approached the bed. "I'm going to need to check your pulse and blood pressure."

"We should go," Helen said.

"But we'll come back tomorrow to see you and little Sandra," Betty promised.

"Try to keep up with your facial saving exercises at night," Kathleen advised. "You don't want your jawline to start sagging."

"I will," Ivy promised.

Maybe her dream had been all wrong, Betty thought. Ivy had said the baby was perfectly fine. Perhaps the strange setting of sleeping at the institute had conjured the disturbing image of the destroyed yellow blanket.

Don't think about it, she told herself.

CHAPTER THIRTY-ONE

RILEY, PRESENT DAY

Sandra Lennox was right—Dr. Trimble's grandson is named Sam—and his phone number is listed. After I call him and explain I'm hoping to learn more about the Trimble Institute, he tells me my timing is uncanny.

"I run a group called the Seekers Collective," he says. "We meet every two weeks, and our next gathering is this afternoon. Our mission is to discuss topics like the ones that so obsessed my grandfather. So if you'd like to catch me after the meeting today, I'll be near campus."

He names a local community center and tells me to come to room 102 at 4 PM. I arrive a couple of minutes early. Inside the main entrance of the building, several orange couches with hard plastic cushions are grouped together. A woman with a pierced lip is typing on a computer behind the reception desk. In the adjacent gym someone is shooting hoops, the thuds of the ball amplified in the cavernous space.

"Which way is room 201?" I ask the woman, and she points down a hallway.

I recognize Sam's voice just before I reach the doorway.

"Of course we're all part of the same energy. We're just manifesting physical forms until we return to our source," he is saying. He looks up and spots me hovering there, then gives me a wave.

The high-ceilinged room is utilitarian and holds the lingering smell of coffee and paint from activities that must have taken place earlier today. Seven people—ranging from a woman in her twenties in an outfit that looks eclectically assembled from a vintage store to a gaunt, grizzled man in a T-shirt that says *All who wander are not lost*—are seated on folding chairs in the middle of the room.

"You must be Riley. Come on in, we're just wrapping up. I'm Sam Trimble." He rises from his seat and extends his hand. He's tall and broad-shouldered, with a head full of salt and pepper hair.

"Riley Bell," I reply. "Thanks for seeing me."

He turns to the group. "See you all in two weeks."

Rustling sounds fill the room as the others gather their things and trickle out. Two women who look strikingly similar—they're both tall and thin, with straw-straight blond hair to their shoulders—continue talking. They're discussing a center in Charlottesville that investigates cases of children who seem to have inexplicable knowledge of past lives.

"Our souls are on journeys," says the louder of the two. "We're not hapless beings, stumbling through our existences. With each reincarnation, we're connecting the dots between different parts of our selves. The lessons learned in each of our lives, the failures and successes . . . it's all part of becoming enlightened."

"The point you're missing is the great unknowing," the second woman responds. "We could just be the first step in a much more advanced evolution."

"Why don't we head to the lobby?" Sam suggests. "Debate gets spirited in our group at times. Especially with those two. They're sisters, in case you didn't notice the resemblance."

When we reach the cluster of orange couches, Sam sits down, puts his hands on his knees, and leans forward. "So, Riley, what can I tell you?"

"Sandra Lennox suggested I get in touch. She said if anyone knew about the people involved with the Trimble Institute, it would be you."

Sam chuckles. "I guess my last name is a clue."

"I'd love to hear more about your grandfather's work. I'm trying to locate some of the women who volunteered for him in the sixties."

"Well, Riley, Grandpa was an intense guy," Sam says. "He and Grandma came to live with my family shortly after I was born. He'd stopped working and started drinking, but he was still focused on proving psi exists. He even tried some of his experiments on me, but I didn't have the secret sauce."

"Psi?" I question.

"The Greek letter psi is the first in the word *psyche*, which means mind or soul. I actually tried to write a book about the institute a few years ago. Grandpa had some seriously cool stories. But it was hard to verify everything. I got an agent who was into the idea, but the book never came together. Between you and me, Riley, I wondered if the drinking made my grandfather exaggerate. I'm still thinking about turning it into a screenplay, though."

On the surface, Sam's an amiable guy, but a couple of things make me uneasy: He seems needy, always bringing the conversation back to himself. And I'm picking up the faint scent of booze on his breath. I'm also not a fan of the way he keeps saying my name; it sounds unnatural. Like it's a social tip he read about to appear engaged.

Still, if Sam Trimble knows that much about his grandfather's work, he'll probably be able to give me more than leads to Betty's missing friends. He may know some of Betty's story, too.

I try to redirect him. "Sandra said there were four main volunteers in the 1960s. Young women who became friends."

Sam's body visibly tightens. "Yeah, before we get into that—why do you want to know about them?"

Betty's warning floats back to me. *Be careful.*

My gut is urging me to provide a shield for not just Betty, but for myself. I'm going to keep my vow to start trusting it.

"I'm compiling my family's history and Kathleen Moore is a distant relative. We're not directly related; I think her mother married into my family."

Sam nods. "Kathleen was a stunner. My grandpa kept some pictures, and she could've given Charlize Theron a run for her money."

We're interrupted by a loud voice: "Don't you two look cozy!" I glance up to see the blond sisters approaching.

"Sam, you didn't tell us you had a date!" one calls out playfully.

"Don't mind us, we're just passing through!" adds the other.

"It's not a date," I say quickly.

"Are you thinking about joining our group?" one asks.

"You should!" the other chimes in.

"Riley and I are discussing my grandfather's work at Marquis," Sam explains.

"It's fascinating, isn't it?"

"Are you a reporter, Riley?"

I shake my head but don't elaborate.

"Well, we don't want to interrupt."

"We're testing a new recipe tonight for stuffed cabbage. If it's good, we'll have you over for dinner soon, Sam. Toodles!" Both sisters wiggle their fingers as they continue to the exit.

"They're characters. Exceptionally intelligent," Sam tells me. "They both earned PhDs from Ivy Leagues, Heidi from Yale and Irma from Harvard. And they're foodies—you wouldn't believe how well they cook."

They're not the women I want to know about. "Do you know how I can reach Kathleen?" I redirect him. "Or anyone in her immediate family?"

"Oh, Kathleen died young. Way back in the sixties," Sam tells me.

My heart sinks. I'm not looking forward to breaking the news to Betty that not only have two of her friends passed away, but they died a long time ago.

"It gets worse," Sam continues. "She murdered her husband, then killed herself."

I rear back. "That's terrible!"

"Yeah, Kathleen was asleep on the couch one night and he came in from playing softball and having a few drinks with the guys. He apparently woke her up, and I guess he still had the bat in his hand. Anyway, she got hold of it and swung it. It hit him in the head and that was it, lights out. The theory is she thought he was an intruder and she was trying to defend herself. But we'll never know."

I can't bring myself to ask why. But I don't have to, because in the next breath, Sam tells me.

"When she saw what she'd done, she killed herself. The university kept it quiet. Back then, before the Internet, it was easier to bury those things."

"Wait, this happened on campus?" My voice sounds shrill. "At Marquis, in the 1960s?"

He nods. "Sixty-four, to be exact. My grandfather left shortly after that. Or was asked to leave, if you want to get technical about it."

A chill runs down my spine. That's the same window of time Betty is frozen inside.

"If you're a conspiracy theorist, which I'm not, you'd find plenty to chew on, Riley," Sam says. "Because Helen Hopkins committed suicide the same day. Witnesses saw her jumping off a bridge."

My chest tightens. I can't speak.

Sam must take my shock for interest, because he leans even closer, dropping his voice to a near whisper, like he's confiding a delicious secret.

"Here's the craziest part: Kathleen kills her husband then offs herself one morning. Ivy gets committed to a psychiatric hospital for schizophrenia a few hours later. And then Helen"—he snaps his fingers—"commits suicide that same day."

He shakes his head. "That was the part that got my agent all jazzed. What are the odds that these young women linked by friendship and psychic gifts would all be erased on the same day?"

"There was a fourth," I manage to say.

"Betty Sadler. I'm glad you didn't say you were related to her. I tried to contact Betty when I was starting my book, but I could never find her either. She disappeared in that same twenty-four-hour period, too. She didn't even come back for her friends' funerals, my grandpa said. No one at the college ever heard from her again. But you know what?"

His eyes are dark and intense. I want to look away, but his gaze is locked on mine, ensnaring it.

"I sometimes wonder if Betty had a hand in it all. Think about it: Why run and hide if you're not guilty of something?"

CHAPTER THIRTY-TWO

HELEN, 1964

Helen had a terrible secret. It gnawed at the lining of her stomach much of the time, and sharpened its bite whenever she was around Betty.

If only she hadn't written that note a few weeks earlier. She'd never intended to give it to Douglas; she just wanted to know what it would feel like to see her feelings captured on paper. She should have destroyed it immediately. Now she couldn't find it. She'd torn apart all her belongings, searching for that scrap of paper with her initials and Douglas's entwined in a heart.

Helen's cheeks turned hot every time she considered the fact that Douglas might have found it. But he never acted any differently around her, so she gradually began to believe it might have gotten swept into the trash after she'd accidentally dropped it.

She was trying so hard to fall out of love with him. If only she'd met Betty first, she never would have allowed herself to develop feelings. But the first time Douglas administered the card test, his voice deep and gentle as he told her to relax and have fun, her heart had fluttered. Another time, their fingers brushed and she'd felt a tingle low in her belly. At night, she built fantasies starring the two of them. She even collected magazine tips on ways to be a good wife: *On cold nights, light a fire before he comes home from work so your house feels like a cozy haven. Let him talk first, even if you have a dozen things to tell him.* Helen's soft, romantic heart had always yearned for a man exactly like Douglas.

But then she met Betty, who'd become like a sister to her. Yes, she'd fallen in love with Douglas. But now she loved Betty more.

For the past week, Helen had experienced a reprieve from her relentless guilt. With the birth of Sandra requiring Ivy's hospitalization, Professor Trimble had less use for the women. He'd gone on a business trip to London, which meant they were granted a deliciously free stretch of time. They'd made the most of their break, squeezing in housecleaning, cooking, grocery shopping, trips to the beautician, and most of all, glorious sleep.

They hadn't replenished their deep deficits of rest, but they all felt a bit more refreshed. At least, Kathleen and Helen and Betty did.

Ivy was another story.

She hadn't had any relaxation at all, not with the physical toll of labor and delivery and the demands of a newborn. Even though she'd received good care in the hospital, she didn't look like herself. She seemed subdued, her vitality drained away.

Today Ivy was being released from the hospital. It was also Betty's twentieth birthday. Kathleen had urged Ivy to skip the dinner party she was hosting, but Ivy insisted: "I wouldn't miss it for the world."

"We need to make a promise to end by nine PM," Kathleen told Helen, who'd arrived early to help. "And let's all take turns holding Sandra so Ivy can sip a cocktail in peace."

Helen nodded vigorously. She wanted to please Kathleen. No—she wanted to *be* Kathleen. Who wouldn't?

Tonight would be a challenge for Helen, even though the occasion was festive. Douglas would be here. She'd have a chance to see if the resolution she'd made would stick.

Helen set the dining table with a floral cloth and trimmed the stems of a dozen pink and white carnations before arranging them in a vase. She defrosted frozen shrimp for the appetizer before placing them in a neat circle on a bed of iceberg lettuce leaves. Meanwhile,

Kathleen prepared the roast and Jell-O salad studded with marshmallows and cut-up apples. Dessert would be Betty's favorite pineapple upside-down cake.

The bar was stocked with ingredients for the usuals—Tom Collinses, Manhattans, daiquiris—and candles were waiting to be lit.

Everything was nearly ready when Kathleen clapped her hands together. "Come with me." She led Helen into her bathroom. The walls were tiled in teal to match the tub and commode, and a makeup bag was open on the sink top.

"I love a good makeover," Kathleen said. "Now, close your eyes. I'm going to tweeze your brows first."

Helen flinched at the sharp little bursts of pain, but then Kathleen smoothed a cool, soothing lotion over her eyebrows. She felt soft brushes tickle her skin and the press of Kathleen's fingertips against her cheekbones. While she worked, Kathleen kept up a running commentary. "You really need to buy Suzy Parker's *Guide to Beauty.* It's my bible . . . Suzy says always use a lip brush for applying lipstick . . . Oh, I love this seafoam green on your eyes! . . . Did you know that if you rub half a lemon on your nails, it'll banish nicotine stains? Not that you have any yet, but we'll all get them someday."

"There!" Kathleen took Helen's shoulders and twisted her to face the mirror. "You're going to knock everyone's socks off!"

Helen stared at a version of herself she'd never met. Her eyes looked wider and her lips fuller and pinker. "I love it!" she cried, throwing her arms around Kathleen's neck.

It was Betty's birthday, but she was the one who'd gotten a present.

"Just in time. Sounds like everyone is here," Kathleen said as the doorbell rang. Helen took one last look in the mirror, then grabbed a tissue and wiped away just enough of the makeup to reveal the pale, plain girl she knew herself to be.

She needed to honor her vow. She wasn't going to be tempted by—or try to tempt—Douglas ever again.

It happened just before 8:30 PM.

The night had been a rousing success. Although baby Sandra

awoke and began to wail while they were cutting the cake, Kathleen was able to soothe her by feeding her a bottle. Helen watched as Kathleen murmured to the baby and Ronald tenderly smoothed back a lock of Kathleen's hair, then leaned over to whisper something that made his wife smile. Ronald seemed utterly in love with Kathleen; Helen had noticed his eyes seeking her out throughout the night.

Helen felt a pang of loneliness, as she often did when she lay alone in her twin bed or watched couples strolling hand in hand on the campus lawn.

At least she had friends now. Ivy seemed subdued and her big laugh hadn't rung out once, but at least she was here. Kathleen looked like an angel with the angles of her face illuminated by the tapered candles. And Betty, so gracious and competent, was even able to charm David by refilling his drink and serving him generous helpings of food. He seemed content, his sharp edges softened for the evening.

"We'll try for a boy soon," he said when Douglas told him that the baby appeared healthy and alert.

Not too soon, Helen hoped. Ivy needed time to recover.

The first warning sign was Betty's glass crashing against the floor. She'd dropped it and was staring into space, her face draining of color.

An instant later, Helen felt a tightening in her chest. She couldn't catch her breath, even though she wasn't exerting herself.

"Ivy?" she heard David say. "Why are you shaking?"

"What was that?" Kathleen whispered. "I felt it, too."

Betty winced. "I don't know."

"Oh no, you're bleeding!" Ivy said, pointing. A shard of the glass had bounced up from the floor, slicing a tiny cut in the back of Betty's hand.

Douglas was staring at Betty, not even trying to help her. His lips twitched, as if he'd swallowed something distasteful. Douglas didn't like this side of his wife one bit, Helen realized. But he'd still report it to Dr. Trimble. Whatever had happened, it meant their reprieve was over.

Ronald, who was a darling, brought Betty a bandage and actually swept away the broken glass himself, rather than waiting for one of the women to do it.

"Did something startle you girls?" he asked. "You all had a physical reaction to something."

Helen held her breath. Dr. Trimble had forbade them to discuss anything about his work, and this somehow felt related to it.

"I'm not sure why I was so jittery," Betty finally replied. "But I'm fine now. In fact, I'd love a turn holding sweet Sandra."

She reached for the baby and nestled her close. "Doesn't she smell like a dream?"

"I could just gobble her up!" Kathleen chimed in.

"And that dress! Could those ruffles be any more precious?" Helen added.

They were deflecting attention away from what had just happened. Working together, like Dr. Trimble wanted.

David Lennox's chair creaked as he turned toward Douglas and made a comment about a high school kicker the team was scouting, and soon the men were engaged in conversation again.

"Dr. Trimble will want to know about this," Helen said softly.

"We'll tell him as soon as he's back," Ivy replied.

"While we're wearing matching white dresses, of course." Kathleen rolled her eyes and the other girls laughed.

"I hope we find out what caused our reactions," Helen whispered to Betty as they hugged goodbye. "It was so strange!"

They did find out, the very next day.

While on the airplane coming back from London, at a few minutes before 8:30 PM, Dr. Silas Trimble had suffered a heart attack.

CHAPTER THIRTY-THREE

RILEY, PRESENT DAY

I'm halfway back to Betty's, ruminating about how men like Josh Woods leave paths of wrecked women in their wakes. They rarely pay for their crimes, let alone atone for them.

I'm certain Josh seduced Alex—anxious, insecure Alex, who probably never receives much attention from guys when her more glamourous sorority sisters are around. And then, when the professor was done with Alex, he didn't just discard her. He sacrificed her.

The urge rises in me like a fever.

I pull off at an exit and drift to the side of the road. It's easy to obtain Josh's phone number. It's listed. Another way he's embracing the image of the cool prof, I think. Always accessible to his students, just one of the guys.

I punch in the numbers and listen to it ring.

There's no way Josh will be able to find out much about me. I haven't changed my address to Betty's house, and my car is still registered in my brother's name. All he'll have is my name and phone number. And I have a lot more on him.

The phone rings twice, then goes to voicemail.

I deflate. I wanted to make him feel helpless and broken, the way he left Alex feeling. And, okay, if I'm honest—the way Danny left me feeling.

"I know what you did to Alex Finch," I say in my message. "And I know what you stole from the library. Give it back or I'll report you."

This isn't like me. At least the current me. The old me was impulsive and brave, the kind of woman who'd marry a guy after knowing him for less than a year. It feels good to reclaim a piece of my agency.

I make a U-turn to get back on the highway, passing a car parked a dozen yards behind where I was idling. A moment later, as I turn onto the highway, headlights shine in my rearview mirror.

There are lots of cars on the road at this hour. Still, I feel tension rising in my body, sharpening my senses.

I try to keep an eye on the car, but there are so many flooding the highway that it's impossible to say whether the same one is trailing me.

I flinch when my phone shrills. It's Betty.

"I was wondering if you'd be hungry when you got home," she says. "I thought I'd make grilled cheeses."

I tell her it sounds perfect, even though now she's the one who seems to be taking care of me.

I keep an eye on my rearview mirror as I curve around the exit that leads toward Betty's. No one is behind me. I was probably being paranoid because Sam Trimble's stories are still ringing in my head. But it's hard to relax when I'm dreading telling Betty what happened to her friends.

Betty's street is quiet. Lights glow in a few of the neighbors' windows, but no one is outside.

I pull up in front of the house, then grab my things and head for the porch, shivering as the chill of the night air hits me.

As I climb the first step, a car roars past. I whip around, but it's already disappearing into the distance. All I can tell is that it's a dark-colored sedan.

Probably a neighbor rushing out to pick up a kid or do an errand, I decide as I knock on the front door. It's cracked open, so I push through it, calling out a hello to Betty.

"I'm in the kitchen," she answers.

I walk in to see Betty flipping a golden-brown grilled cheese sizzling in a pan. Two glasses containing clear cocktails topped with olives are waiting on the counter.

"What wonderful timing," Betty says.

CHAPTER THIRTY-FOUR

Twelve subjects (nine of them professed 'psychics' . . .) were tested for their ability to cause mice to arouse more quickly from ether anesthesia than normally would be expected. The results were highly significant overall.

—*Journal of Parapsychology*

BETTY, 1964

The heart attack was relatively mild; it hadn't killed Dr. Trimble. There was a nurse aboard the flight who obtained aspirin and kept Dr. Trimble comfortable until the plane landed and he could be taken to the hospital. After two nights he walked out, trailed by a protesting doctor who had wanted to keep him longer.

If Dr. Trimble had been driven before, now he'd tumbled into obsession. He seemed to be rushing to secure his legacy before a clock only he could hear stopped ticking.

"I don't believe each of you girls independently sensed what was happening to me," he told them after he'd summoned them to his office. "My hypothesis is that one of your minds is delightfully porous, and it absorbed my experience and transmitted a message to the other three. So which one of you felt it first?"

"I can't remember," Kathleen said. "It all happened so fast."

Dr. Trimble pointed at Betty. "It was you, wasn't it?"

"It could have been," she admitted, secretly despairing that she could tune into his frequency.

"President Sherman came to see me in the hospital," Dr. Trimble said. "He understands I'm on the cusp of writing what will be my most significant academic paper to date, one that will bring international acclaim to his university. But I told him I need more time. I know we can go a bit further."

Betty took in Ivy's breath catching, and Kathleen's hands twisting in her lap.

"The cots are still in the basement of the library. I've arranged for other necessities to be brought in. We'll stay there, the five of us." He broke into a smile. "Can you imagine the potential that awaits once you girls are isolated from all outside interference?"

Betty glanced over at Ivy holding little Sandra in her arms. "But Ivy's baby—" she began.

Dr. Trimble tapped his finger against his lips, frowning. He appeared to be thinking deeply. "My wife will take care of the infant."

Ivy gave a faint cry. "But she'll be no trouble at all!"

"My wife is a very capable woman." Dr. Trimble's voice was thunderous. "She can certainly feed and change a child."

"I didn't mean—I just—" Ivy seemed unable to form words, as if her throat had closed up.

"I need your full cooperation, Ivy." Dr. Trimble glared at Ivy, and Betty watched as her friend withered under his gaze. Ivy was trapped; if she demurred, her husband would lose his job. Dr. Trimble had all the power, like he always had.

"How long will you need us?" Betty asked, reaching out to hold Ivy's hand. Ivy gripped her so tightly her fingernails dug into Betty's skin.

"A few days, perhaps. But that depends entirely on the four of you."

The library basement had no windows. They'd be sealed inside with Dr. Trimble, breathing the same air, sharing meals and a sleeping space, even if they strung up a sheet for privacy, which Betty was already planning to do. Cut off from everything and everyone, they'd be at his mercy.

"Of course we're always willing to be of service, but our husbands may object," Betty ventured.

"I've already spoken to them. Your husbands understand their sacrifice is necessary," Dr. Trimble said.

"Ronald said that?" Kathleen sounded surprised.

"He questioned it at first," Dr. Trimble admitted. "But when I explained that you were essential to my work and that you wouldn't be away long, he told me he'd always known how special you were, and that the choice was yours."

"What will happen if I don't go?" Kathleen asked.

"I can test my hypothesis with just the other three. It will take much longer, of course."

Ivy released another small cry, holding little Sandra closer to her.

Kathleen looked at Ivy, the baby, then at the other women.

She lifted her chin. "I'll go."

She'd never looked more brave or beautiful, Betty thought, feeling a rush of love for her friend.

"A couple of days only, though," Kathleen repeated firmly. "For all of us."

"Mmhmm," Dr. Trimble said. "Go home and pack your things. My wife will launder your dresses and I'll bring them when I pick you up. We'll begin the experiments tonight."

Would Douglas still love her when she returned? Betty wondered. He could easily find someone new in her absence, like the pretty girl with the English accent who smelled of roses. Betty had seen Emily several more times in the institute, once coming out of the blackout room and another time being administered a questionnaire by Douglas.

The vision of Douglas spending time alone with Emily made Betty's stomach heave. She had barely made it to her bathroom before she retched.

As she rinsed out her mouth in the sink, she caught a glimpse of herself in the mirror. She looked a sight, with her hair frizzing and her lipstick gone. Who could blame Douglas if he left her? She quickly fixed her face, then launched into a frenzy of sweeping and mopping. She hurried to the grocery store while Douglas's clothes spun in the washing machine, then baked two casseroles that promised to stick to his ribs. She moved their wedding picture to the dining table so Douglas could see it while he ate. She wrote a note telling him how much she'd miss him and sprayed it with perfume before propping it on his nightstand.

She barely had any time to pack. She folded clean underthings and her robe into her suitcase along with her toiletries.

She put her coat over her arm and stepped outside to wait for Douglas to come wish her goodbye. The campus looked lovely in the golden fall light. A girl walked past wearing her boyfriend's letterman jacket, a textbook tucked into the crook of her arm, smiling the smile of someone in love. A Ford Falcon drove past, notes of the Beatles song "I Want to Hold Your Hand" trailing in its wake. Then Dr. Trimble's Buick lumbered around the corner and Betty felt tears sting her eyes.

Douglas hadn't bothered to come bid her farewell.

Dr. Trimble opened the trunk and she placed her luggage case inside next to the other girls', then craned her neck to look down the street, futilely searching for a glimpse of her husband's tall, lanky form. She wiped away her tears as she climbed into the back seat next to Ivy.

"I know we'll miss our men and homes," Ivy whispered, misinterpreting Betty's tears. "And I can barely stand to be away from Sandra. But it's only for a day or two. You shouldn't fret. Have you sensed it yet, what's happening to you?"

Betty stared at her, uncomprehending.

"It came to me in the hospital when I saw you. You're pregnant," Ivy whispered. "I just know it."

CHAPTER THIRTY-FIVE

RILEY, PRESENT DAY

The worst dinner of my life occurred the last time I laid eyes on Danny. I'd taken a 7 AM to 3 PM shift at the hospital, which meant I had plenty of time to chop zucchini and puree tomatoes for home-made lasagna and slather butter onto garlic bread. Even before I pulled the dishes out of the oven, our little home smelled like heaven. We never ate a single bite.

The trill of my phone signaled a call from a creditor who'd obtained my number and sent me scrambling into investigative mode. By the time Danny arrived, I'd talked to the bank, pulled my credit report, and was sitting at the dining room table with an untouched glass of wine in front of me, staring into space.

"Hey, baby! Is something burning?" Danny asked as he came through the door, flashing his easy smile.

Dinner was ruined, and so were we.

The next few weeks were a blur—of me yelling and Danny on his knees, just as he'd been when he proposed, and of me throwing him out then calling him crying late at night. I lost chunks of time; I'd leave the house to drive to work, and find myself pulling into the parking lot with no memory of getting there. I couldn't sleep without taking Tylenol PM, and panic attacks plagued me in strange places—like the shower or an elevator.

I'd never known such deep, all-encompassing pain.

But right now, as I sit across from Betty at the dinner table, I witness it again.

"I am so sorry," I tell her after I break the news about Ivy, Kathleen, and Helen, as cleanly and gently as I can.

Betty's lips tremble and she bows her head. When she lifts it, her face has collapsed. I've always thought that her flawless skin—by now I know it's a by-product of her lack of exposure to sunlight—makes her look decades younger than her real age. But right now, she appears to be every one of her eighty-one years.

Her mouth opens and closes but no words come out.

"Oh, no," she finally cries. "My beautiful girlfriends."

I reach out and hold her hand. Her fingers are icy.

"Do you know the exact date this happened?" she asks in a near whisper.

I have to tell her the second part of what I learned from Sam. "The same day you left."

I'm worried the news will break her. But Betty is stronger than I thought. The color slowly returns to her cheeks. Her back straightens.

"He killed them," she whispers. And I see anger blazing in her eyes.

"I was told Helen committed suicide. Kathleen, too," I say.

"But Kathleen murdered her husband with a baseball bat first?" she asks.

I nod. "Though they think it was an accident. She may have believed he was an intruder."

"Kathleen may have held the bat, but she was driven to that terrible act by someone else entirely," Betty says. "As was Helen."

Our grilled cheeses are now cold and greasy on the plates in front of us. Neither of us can eat.

"One night long ago, we were all together," Betty tells me. "We all had such vivid, unsettling dreams. Kathleen's was about a baseball bat, but she didn't understand the context. We never should have gone with him."

"With Dr. Trimble?" I guess.

She flinches. "I haven't heard his name in over sixty years. My husband and I never spoke of him after we left Marquis."

"I learned about the Trimble Institute from Sandra Lennox," I say.

My words are like a transfusion. "Ivy's baby is alive?" Betty cries. Her grip on my hand tightens.

"Alive and well. She still lives in the area," I say. "She became a therapist."

"Oh, I would love to see her again." Betty's eyes soften. "I used to hold her and sing to her so her mama could get a little rest. Sandra was the most precious baby."

"I think she'd love to see you, too. I have her phone number," I tell Betty. "You can reach out to her whenever you'd like."

"I'd like to call her right now," Betty says. I dial Sandra's number and put it on speaker. It goes directly to voicemail.

"She might be with a client," I tell Betty. "But you can leave a message."

Betty's eyes are bright with unshed tears. "That voice. She sounds just like Ivy."

At the beep, Betty looks at me questioningly. She has never encountered voicemail, I realize. So I quickly leave a message, telling Sandra that Betty would love to connect with her and to call me back anytime.

"Would you pour us another cocktail, dear?" Betty asks. "Tonight calls for it."

I'm no mixologist, but I can make a simple gin and tonic. I add a generous squeeze of lime to the drinks and set one in front of Betty. I also find the bag of salted peanuts I bought at the grocery store, pour some into a little china bowl, and set them between us.

"There is one more piece of this," I say once Betty has eaten a few nuts and has a little protein in her. "When I was trying to track down your friends, I went to look for the Trimble Institute archives at the Marquis library. But the files from 1964 were missing."

"Maybe Dr. Trimble kept them for himself."

I shake my head. "I don't think so. The files were labeled and a few of them were stretched out, like they'd held a bunch of papers. I think someone took them recently."

Betty frowns. Then she pushes her wheelchair back from the island. "I'd like to show you something."

She wheels out of the room as I jump up to follow her. Betty is going faster than usual, her strong arms churning the wheels. She stops at the old roll-top desk in the corner of the living room and opens a low drawer.

Inside is an item so shiny and current it's utterly at odds with this room. It's a FedEx envelope.

"Do you know what this is?"

"It's a rush delivery company." I search my mind for an example she can easily grasp. "Like the old telegrams."

Betty pulls out the letter inside and I scan it. It's written on Marquis University letterhead.

"Dear Mrs. Sadler," I read aloud. "It has come to our attention that your husband, at the time of this death, was in possession of academic files belonging to Marquis University. We request the immediate return of all papers and correspondence during the time of his employment with Marquis. You may use the enclosed envelope to return these documents."

But the address isn't the same one on the letterhead. It's a PO box.

I look up and see Betty watching me.

"The archive files from 1964 went missing recently," Betty says slowly. "And I also received this special letter a month ago. Why is there such sudden interest in a program that was stopped sixty years ago?"

I underestimated her, I realize. Her genteel affect, her home that time forgot, even the fact that she doesn't know what FedEx is belie the truth.

Betty's mind is knife-sharp.

"I have no idea," I tell her. "It was so hard to find information about your friends. It's almost as if it was deliberately buried."

"Like they don't want anyone to ever know what happened," Betty says softly. "But someone else is trying to learn about it now. I have no idea who that could be. Do you?"

"It's possible a psychology professor at Marquis took the papers. He may have been the last one to visit the library to look at them before me."

"What's his name?"

"Joshua Woods."

Betty shakes her head. "It doesn't mean anything to me. Why would he want those old folders now? What was inside them?"

"I remember some of the labels," I tell her. "One was *Library Basement*, but there was nothing inside."

"Library basement," Betty echoes.

"Do you know the meaning of that?" I ask.

Her voice is so rough and raw it's almost unrecognizable.

"Inside the library basement, we were laboratory animals."

CHAPTER THIRTY-SIX

Ganzfeld experiments at the University of Edinburgh show strong similarities between the video the 'sender' was watching and the receiver's thoughts at the time. . . . Suddenly, the man falls down in a deep muddy pool (at the same time, the receiver says: 'Falling. Muddy . . .'). The camera zooms in on the man's face (at the same time, the receiver says: 'Blond hair. Seventies hairstyle. Curly-ish. White face . . .'). All the utterances appear to describe exactly what is being shown on the film.

—The British Psychological Society

BETTY, 1964

"The janitor cleaned this up for us," Dr. Trimble informed them as he opened the door leading to the library basement. A heavy, metallic odor lingered in the air. Cracks marred the concrete floor and the walls were covered with old stains. A few bare lightbulbs hung overhead.

"Where should we put our things?" Kathleen asked.

"Pick any cot." Dr. Trimble was already setting up his typewriter and a stack of notebooks on a long table that looked like it had been borrowed from the campus dining room, and probably had been. He'd brought nothing else but a coffee percolator, an ashtray, a small overnight case, and a canvas laundry sack. He held up the sack. "Take your dresses and change into them."

Betty followed the other girls deeper into the basement. It was an eerie combination of unused and aged. Sets of white bedding were folded on the ends of the four identical beds. At least the sheets smelled fresh. The girls made up their bunks and Betty hung up the sheet she'd brought from home so that their sleeping space had a measure of privacy.

Betty's hand touched her stomach as Ivy's words echoed in her mind: *You're pregnant.*

Ivy was right; Betty could sense it now.

Helen's whisper jarred her into the present moment: "Should we make up Dr. Trimble's bed?"

"Yes, then we can move his bunk farther away from ours," Kathleen replied, picking up the final set of bedding. She and Helen quickly made the cot, then lifted it up and carried it a dozen yards away.

Next the women unpacked as best they could. Kathleen had brought a set of pink rollers, which looked woefully out of place on the floor. Ivy had brought the diary she faithfully kept.

"Should we change?" Helen wondered.

Kathleen opened the sack. Inside were their four dresses, neatly folded.

"We might as well. The more obedient we are, the quicker we'll get out of here," Betty said.

Outside, it was growing dark. Betty spotted a giant cobweb stretching between two corners of the wall that the janitor's mop had missed, but she couldn't see the spider. Maybe it was out hunting.

She sat on the edge of a bunk next to Helen and folded her hands, waiting for whatever would come next. She didn't have to wait long.

"Girls?" Dr. Trimble pulled away one side of the sheet. His big frame filled the narrow pathway between rows of cots. "It's time to begin."

"I brought the sheet in case there wasn't a private room to change clothes," Betty said quickly.

"The sheet is wonderful," Dr. Trimble said. "It keeps you four close and contained. Your instincts were correct."

He studied them in their matching white dresses, his eyes roving over them one by one, then nodded. "I need to photograph you for my records. Arrange yourselves in a line, girls."

Betty shuffled next to Helen, then Kathleen and Ivy joined them in a row. Dr. Trimble lifted a point-and-press Kodak camera and snapped a picture.

Next he instructed them to lay down on their bunks.

"The four of you have become very close over these past months," Dr. Trimble told them. "You share something most uncommon. Others may think they know you, but they can never relate to the inner core of your psyche. Not even your families or husbands. And so you've been alone most of your lives. Before you found each other, you felt adrift. Different. As if you had to wear a mask."

Was it true? Betty wondered. At times, maybe. But she'd always felt her innate gift, as Dr. Trimble called it, paled in importance to her marriage to Douglas.

"It has been very, very difficult for you," Dr. Trimble continued. "Suppression always is."

He sounded like a different man. A kinder one. And of course, he was so smart. He instructed them to close their eyes and listen to his words. The longer he talked about the pain and loneliness they'd experienced, the more Betty began to believe he was right. After all, he was the expert in psychology.

A sob broke free from the bunk next to Betty's.

"I'm sorry!" she heard Helen cry.

"No, no, it's good to feel strong emotions here, Helen," Dr. Trimble said. "Let them out. All the fear and worry you've held for so long. You are finally safe in this place. These girls will never, ever betray you."

Betty felt tears form in her own eyes. She'd never seen this side of Dr. Trimble. He was almost fatherly. It was as if he were tenderly reading them a bedtime story, except it was the story of their own buried pain.

His cadence slowed. Betty felt her limbs relax as his sonorous voice drifted over her like a warm blanket.

"Your bond can never be broken. After all, you only have each other to rely on."

From beneath her closed lids, Betty could sense a change in the quality of light in the room. Dr. Trimble must have turned off the bulbs. The mattress didn't feel quite so hard beneath her back now, and the strange metallic odor had become familiar. She was filled with love toward the other women. She wished she could reach out and hold their hands, but her limbs were so heavy she couldn't move them.

"It's perfectly fine to drift off if you're tired," Dr. Trimble told them.

And with that permission, Betty's last defenses crumbled. With Dr. Trimble's low, rumbling voice still filling her ears, she felt herself slip into a heavy sleep.

It felt like it lasted only minutes before bright lights assailed her eyes and a noise that sounded like an air horn jolted her awake.

CHAPTER THIRTY-SEVEN

RILEY, PRESENT DAY

Sandra calls back within the hour, and after I hand my cell phone to Betty, I go to my bedroom to give them privacy. When Betty ends the conversation, she wheels to my doorway and returns my phone.

"Sandra wants to see me, too," Betty says, her cheeks damp from tears. "She wants to hear all about Ivy. She never had the chance to know her mother."

"Would you like to go visit her?" I ask.

Betty hesitates. "She said if it's easier for me, she can come here. Let me think about it a bit."

We head to the kitchen and Betty makes tea, then we chat more about Sandra. Betty also asks me to recount my trip again, this time from start to finish.

"Sometimes the tiniest detail lodges into our minds for a reason. It's a clue to something much bigger," she says. "Don't doubt your intuition."

"I'm not sure I have any," I half joke.

Betty's eyes meet mine over the rim of her china cup. "Remember the first time you came here? Just before you knocked on my door?"

"Sure," I say. "It wasn't that long ago."

"What in particular do you recall about it?"

I frown, thinking back. "It was nice out. Not too sunny . . ."

She shakes her head. "Just before you knocked, you did something."

"I'm not sure what you're talking about," I confess.

"You turned and looked behind you. I saw you from the dining room window."

"Oh." I'm a bit taken aback. "I didn't realize you were watching me arrive."

"I wasn't the only one," Betty informs me. "My nosy neighbor, the one with the dog? She was peering over her fence, staring at you. You sensed her gaze even from a distance. That's why you turned around. You're highly perceptive, Riley. I confirmed it within moments of meeting you."

Despite the warmth of the delicate teacup in my hands, I feel a chill run through me.

"You're holding another clue," she tells me.

This I remember: She knew I wanted tea that day, not coffee.

"How did you know?" I feel myself leaning back, away from her. I'm a little creeped out.

"It could have been a slight change in your expression when I suggested tea versus coffee. Or something in your body language that indicated your preference. Or perhaps the human mind is more mysterious and complex than you're willing to acknowledge."

"Is that why you hired me?"

"Because you prefer tea? No." She smiles. "But there's a time for logic and a time for trust. I've learned how important it is to understand the distinction."

I skirt away from the topic, feeling uncomfortable. A bit exposed, even. I'm still debriefing Betty on my trip when my cell phone buzzes with a text.

My eyes widen as I read it.

"What is it?" Betty asks.

I read her the message: "I have the information you're looking for. Meet me at noon tomorrow at the Starbucks on Pine Street."

"Who is it from?" Betty asks.

"I don't know." I tap my screen to dial the number. An automated voice tells me the number I'm trying to reach is unavailable.

"They must have blocked me right after sending the text."

A gentle rattling sound draws my attention to Betty's hands. They're trembling as she places her teacup on her saucer. I google the Starbucks and realize it's just off Marquis campus.

"It's got to be the professor. Josh Woods. I left him a phone message telling him I knew what he did to Alex and what he took from the library. He could've gotten a burner phone. I guess I'll find out tomorrow. I'll have to drive back to Marquis."

"I think I'll go with you, dear," Betty says. Then she looks toward the door, as if anticipating our trip. Apprehension sweeps across her face.

There's a wooden ramp leading from the porch to the front walk, so she clearly has had access to the outside. Still, something makes me ask, "Betty, when was the last time you left the house?"

"Oh, a long time."

"What about going to see a doctor?" I ask.

"Douglas found one who came to me. Same with a dentist," she says.

"So, a year?" I guess.

She looks up at the ceiling, as if calculating the time. Finally, she says, "Sixteen years."

The next day, we pull up to the coffee shop half an hour early. It doesn't take long to unfold Betty's wheelchair and help her into it. Betty's head keeps swiveling toward objects that must seem alien to her—an angular modern car; a girl's belly ring glinting below the hem of her crop top; a man talking into AirPods as he types on an iPad. Sixteen years ago, she wouldn't have encountered things like Ubers, the facial masks used to prevent the spread of COVID-19, or smartwatches. Fashion and architectural trends have changed countless times. Everything must be a wonder to her.

I find an accessible table, then order a couple of blueberry muffins and two bottles of water. I sit facing the front door so I can see everyone who walks through. There's nothing left to do but wait.

"What does Professor Woods look like?" Betty asks.

"He's handsome. Not that tall, but athletic. He has dark hair and a beard."

"I suppose it's natural for girls to get crushes on their professors," Betty tells me. "My husband had a few admirers, too. After all, a handsome man with a steady job is a real catch."

I just nod. Her point of view is understandable given her circumstances, but sometimes it's hard to relate to her.

By 12:15, the door has opened a dozen times. A frazzled mother with a red-faced toddler, a few teenaged girls including one with bright pink hair that Betty stares at as her jaw drops, and several businesspeople have come and gone. Our muffins are gone, and I can tell Betty is tired. This must be a staggering amount of stimulation for her.

By 12:45, I finally call it. "I don't think he's coming."

Betty nods. "I agree."

Once she's settled in my car, she begins to doze almost immediately. *Maybe this will be the end of it*, I think. Betty finally has answers about her friends. If Josh has the files, he must've lost his nerve. We've done all we can.

I wake her and help her into the house, then I spend the rest of the afternoon performing the job for which I was hired. I chat with Betty while I empty the dishwasher and prep dinner, then we listen to records together in the living room. She's listless, clearly wiped out from our excursion.

She's wheeling herself toward the bathroom when she makes a sharp, surprised sound.

"Riley? Did you try to enter this room?"

I step into the hallway and glance at the door to the locked room. Then I move closer.

The doorknob is broken; it looks like someone knocked it off before jerry-rigging it back into place.

Betty pushes open the door and flicks on the overhead light. It must have been her husband's old study—I see a big wooden desk with a chair, more bookshelves filled with old hardcover volumes, and a large cardboard box in the corner. Betty heads directly for the box and peers inside.

"Betty, we need to call the police!" My heart is pounding. What if Betty hadn't come with me to the coffee shop? She would have been alone with the intruder.

I dial 911 and give the dispatcher Betty's address. Meanwhile, Betty is wheeling back into the living room.

"They're sending someone," I tell Betty. "Was there anything valuable in the box?"

"It's empty. It used to hold Douglas's papers from Marquis. Do me a favor, dear, and hand me that atlas." She points to one on the bookshelves.

I'm bewildered by her lack of concern over the theft, but I do as she asks. I brace myself for the weight of the large hardcover book, but it's surprisingly light.

I hand it to Betty and she opens it.

Inside are several items, including a man's wedding ring—it must have belonged to Douglas—and a thick stack of papers covered in typewritten notes and scribbles.

"The box used to hold Douglas's papers, as I said. I moved them to a safer place the day you moved in."

I'm still absorbing this when Betty's mind leaps several steps ahead of my own.

"I don't think Professor Woods or whoever it was ever intended to meet us. He just wanted to get us out of the house so he could get in to search for the papers."

CHAPTER THIRTY-EIGHT

KATHLEEN, 1964

Kathleen felt so tightly wound she could snap at the slightest touch. Being awoken abruptly in the middle of the night brought back horrific memories, stemming from when she was fourteen years old and her mother had a new boyfriend, one she claimed was the love of her life. The boyfriend—Mac, who worked at the filling station—complimented Kathleen's long, silky hair, and visited her in the middle of the night under the pretext of making sure she was asleep. He had never committed the worst act, but he touched her in the darkness, stroking his fingers up and down her arms and legs.

"Are you awake?" he would whisper. "If you are, that means you're enjoying this as much as I am."

She'd known he was capable of worse, and her gut told her that he wanted her to fight—to struggle while he subdued her. It would excite him. So she lay perfectly still with her eyes closed, enduring the violations until Mac tired of her mother and moved on.

Kathleen shuddered. She hadn't thought about those wretched nights in a long time. She'd believed they were firmly in the past, but right now, she could almost smell the scent of gasoline Mac's skin always carried.

"Quickly, girls, you'll find fresh notebooks and pencils by the sides of your cots. Write down everything you can remember from your dreams," Dr. Trimble instructed them.

Kathleen wasn't a teenager any more. But she felt equally helpless here in the basement of the library.

Blinking against the piercing light shining from the unadorned bulb hung between the bunks, Kathleen did her best. Her hands were shaking, so her cursive wasn't as neat as it could have been, but she captured the essence of her dream before it faded.

It was a terrible dream.

Kathleen was alone in the library basement in her stiff white uniform. The basement of her dream hadn't been cleaned. Dust coated the counters and floors, and a dead mouse lay by the radiator. She could hear Dr. Trimble's disembodied voice repeating: "Four more times." Even through her dream, she felt the grip of terror.

A certain luminescence had distinguished the dream, making it so vivid and realistic. Logically Kathleen knew she was safe, but emotionally, she felt as fragile as her fourteen-year-old self.

"What time is it?" Helen asked, her voice scratchy.

"Time doesn't exist here," Dr. Trimble said. "In this place, you must free your mind from the constraints of your everyday lives."

"Where is my baby?" Ivy whispered, her hands frantically patting her bedsheets.

"Honey, she's with Dr. Trimble's wife," Kathleen replied. "Don't you remember?"

"Oh, of course," Ivy said, blinking.

Dr. Trimble collected the notebooks, reading each of the entries. When he picked up Kathleen's, however, he suddenly grew still.

"Have you had many dreams that foretold the truth?" he asked Kathleen.

Only bad ones, she thought. She'd dreamt about Mac before he arrived—not him exactly, but recurring nightmares of fear and helplessness in her darkened bedroom.

It was hard to tell a fib with Dr. Trimble staring down at her from beneath his heavy brows. "I think so," she replied.

"Marvelous," he breathed. "Girls, you need to go back to sleep now."

He lumbered toward the front of the basement, and after a moment, the aroma of freshly brewed coffee wafted toward Kathleen, filling her nose. She could hear Dr. Trimble pouring a cup from the percolator he'd brought, then settling into a chair that groaned beneath his weight. The *clack-clack* of his typewriter keys. The burnt vanilla aroma of his tobacco. There were four of them and one of him, yet he seemed to fill this entire structure.

Kathleen compulsively tucked in her sheets as tightly as possible, like she had as a teenager, checking and rechecking them.

Finally, she managed to drift off.

What felt like only minutes later, sharp lights and a blaring noise awoke her again. And again. A total of five times throughout the night.

Four more times, Kathleen thought. Did I foretell what was going to happen, or did I give him the idea to wake us up a total of five times tonight and demand we write down our dreams?

When morning finally arrived, the women were bleary-eyed and disoriented.

"I'm more worn out than if I hadn't slept at all," Ivy said, her voice hoarse and scratchy.

"Maybe we can steal a nap today," Betty told her.

Kathleen went to the bathroom and fixed her face the best she could. By the time she finished, she'd banished the demons of the night.

"I'm going to check about breakfast," she told the other women. "We missed dinner. Surely he needs to let us eat."

"Some fresh fall air would be good for all of us," Betty said. "Maybe we can walk to a diner."

"Then we could change out of these uniforms, too," Helen said. "I feel so strange wearing them."

But on the long table in the common room, Kathleen saw five trays that she recognized as coming from the Marquis cafeteria, filled with pancakes and fruit.

Dr. Trimble must have ordered the trays to be delivered here. Perhaps his wife had picked them up and left them outside the door so that she didn't interfere with the pristine conditions of his experiment.

However the food had arrived, it made one thing clear: The girls weren't leaving. They were essentially his prisoners.

CHAPTER THIRTY-NINE

RILEY, PRESENT DAY

Maybe it wasn't a priority call, or maybe Betty's house is in such an isolated area no cruisers were nearby. Whatever the reason, the police take forty-five minutes to arrive.

"Here's the piece that doesn't fit," says the young female cop with the name tag that reads *C. Antonelli*. "You say you arrived home to find this interior door broken. But there's no sign of forced entry from the outside. And there was nothing in the box to steal."

She and her partner—a short, muscular guy who doesn't say much—keep looking around the house. Their training calls for them to notice unusual details, and virtually everything in Betty's place falls into that category.

"Does anyone else have a key?" Officer Antonelli asks. "A neighbor or family member?"

Betty shakes her head. "There's only one key to this house, and I had it with me."

I see the officers exchange looks. It's another weird detail.

"Is anything missing?" the officer asks. "Jewelry, cash, a laptop?"

Betty and I both checked while waiting for the cops. My engagement ring was right where I left it, zipped into a side pocket of my toiletries bag on top of my dresser. The irony didn't escape me that my stolen ring could've been re-stolen.

"Nothing is missing," Betty says.

I see the cops exchange another look.

"Ma'am, could I ask you to step outside the house and show me the back entrance again?" Officer Antonelli asks me.

"Sure." I lead the way through the side yard to the entrance off the kitchen.

But the officer doesn't want to examine the door. She wants to talk to me alone.

"You say you've been working here less than a week. Accidents happen. Maybe you jiggled the handle and it broke?"

I shake my head. "That's not—"

"I could see not wanting to tell a new boss about something like that," she continues. "But if you've got something to get off your chest, now's the time."

"I didn't break the door handle," I tell her. "I was with Betty the whole time. Ask her, she'll tell you."

"How's her memory?"

"Very sharp. She wouldn't have broken the lock and forgotten. Maybe someone climbed in a window."

"Okay," she says, as if she believes me. But I can tell she doesn't.

The officers tell us to call if we discover something missing, then they leave.

Despite the strangeness of the day, I fall asleep quickly. But in the middle of the night, something pulls me awake. Typically I'd scroll through reels or listen to a meditation, but without Wi-Fi, I'm stymied. I finally decide to wander into the living room and borrow a book. I use my phone's flashlight so I don't disturb Betty, whose bedroom door is open.

Old psychology volumes with worn hardcovers are mixed in with classics—Faulkner, Austen, Hemingway, Joyce. I pick a paperback copy of *In Cold Blood* by Truman Capote.

Then my eyes land on the fake atlas. I only got a glimpse of the papers inside before Betty closed the cover. Could they really be worth someone breaking in here?

I slide out the hollow book, wincing as it thumps against the edge of the bookshelf. I ease open the cover, aiming the beam of light inside.

A creak from the direction of Betty's bedroom startles me. *Just the old house settling*, I tell myself.

The papers are slightly brittle from age, and the typewritten words have faded to gray. The top page seems to be an intake form. It lists the name Emily Robinson, age eighteen, and London, England, as the place of birth. The date of her arrival at Marquis is October 21, 1964.

Beneath these statistics is a category—Zener cards—and a long list of numbers that begin with: 12, 8, 11, 14, 10 . . .

A handwritten note in small, straight letters accompanies the scores: *Exceptional.*

The next notations are categorized beneath the heading *Ganzfeld Experiments/Telepathy*. I scan the results: *sun=lemon. Checkerboard=marbles. Blue=water. Monkey=animal in tree.*

The final notation on the page is circled in ink. It says:

Girl 1 for Phase Two.

CHAPTER FORTY

> Between the ages of two and three, [Ravi] kept asking for toys which he claimed he had in the house of his previous life and said he himself had been murdered, giving names and details . . . In a different district a six-year-old boy, was murdered. . . . His father's name and the details of his murder correspond with the account of Ravi Shankar.
>
> —*Journal of Parapsychology*

BETTY, 1964

After consulting with the others to compile a list, Betty volunteered to bring it to Dr. Trimble. "In our haste to pack, we overlooked a few necessities," she told him.

He was hunched over his typewriter, a half-full coffee cup and his breakfast plate littering the table.

"We should add soap and a sponge so we can clean the dishes," she said, laying down the list the women had created.

He picked it up and squinted as he read aloud: "A nail file, eight sets of clean towels and washcloths, Aqua Net hairspray . . . and saltine crackers and ginger ale?"

"My stomach has felt a bit queasy," Betty explained.

He picked up his pipe and inhaled. Ashes scattered onto his stack of typed papers. If the papers burned up, he might make them start all over again, Betty thought. She suppressed a shudder.

"I'll see what I can do," he told her. "But I may have something even better for you."

Dr. Trimble followed her to the back of the basement, where the other women waited in their white dresses. By now they'd washed up as best they could. Ivy was sitting on the bed, staring into space. She looked beyond tired. She seemed absent, somehow.

"Today I'm going to try something new," Dr. Trimble announced. "You've all experienced the Ganzfeld experiment." He held up two sets of the Ping-Pong ball blindfolds and Kathleen flinched.

"This time, I'd like for the four of you to decide who transmits and who receives the messages. Two in each group."

"We get to decide?" Helen echoed.

"The four of you trust each other completely," Dr. Trimble said. It was a statement, not a question. "Therefore, I believe you'll be able to work together to determine the best grouping to enhance your test results. The more quickly you're able to prove my theory that this contained environment engenders unprecedented results, the more quickly you'll be back at home taking care of your husbands. Let me know when you've made your decision."

He turned to go, then paused. "Deep sacrifice is necessary for the greater good. Remember that, girls."

His heavy footsteps grew fainter as he went back to his command post in the kitchen.

As soon as he left, Betty spoke up. "Kathleen needs to be a transmitter. I can receive."

"Thank you, doll." Kathleen sighed.

"I can receive, too," Helen said.

"Okay," Ivy said. Betty looked at her more closely. Her voice and expression were a bit wooden. Being here seemed to be harming her the most. She bore no resemblance to her usual peppy self.

"Do you think we could actually get out of here tonight?" Kathleen wondered.

"I doubt he'd arrange all of this for such a short time," Betty replied. "But if we do well enough, maybe tomorrow or the next day."

"I'm not sure I can handle two more nights of being woken up every hour." Kathleen shook her head. "It took me so long to fall back asleep each time. And poor Ivy. You haven't even recovered from childbirth."

"I'm fine," Ivy said weakly. "It's David I'm worried about. He isn't used to fending for himself. And I hope . . ." Her voice caught. "Do you think Dr. Trimble's wife will be kind to Sandra?"

"Oh, darling, of course she will!" Betty said instantly, even though she feared the opposite. "She always brings us meals, and she sewed our dresses . . . surely she's feeding and burping and changing little Sandra, and you'll see that your baby is as happy as can be!"

Ivy nodded, but she didn't look convinced.

"I'll let Dr. Trimble know we've decided." Helen stood up from her bunk. Then she threw her arms around Betty's neck. Betty felt the dampness of tears against her skin.

"I'm so glad I have you girls," Helen whispered. "Promise me we'll always be friends?"

"Always," Betty promised. "We'll stay as close as sisters forever."

CHAPTER FORTY-ONE

RILEY, PRESENT DAY

Perhaps In Cold Blood *wasn't the best middle-of-the-night reading material,* I think as my phone alarm rouses me. Not surprising, reading about the slaughter of an entire family amplified my unease. I kept thinking about the car speeding past me as I climbed the steps to Betty's porch yesterday, and the broken lock on the door to the strange room. I can't shake Betty's observation that my mind is more mysterious than I gave it credit for. And beneath it all—like a throbbing pulse—is my worry about Danny.

I hate that I still long for my ex-husband. That I yearn to save him, to be with him again.

I haven't heard any sounds to indicate Betty is awake, so I pull on sweats and creep to the bathroom to wash my face and brush my teeth. She doesn't eat much in the morning, so I make tea and set out an English muffin and strawberry jam. The sunlight is streaming in through the window above the sink. I check the window. It has one of those thumb locks that's ridiculously easy to get through, but it's high up enough that someone would need a chair or ladder to gain entry.

Betty doesn't emerge from her bedroom for another two hours, during which time I've swept the floors, deep-cleaned the refrigerator and scrubbed the kitchen, and stared at the hollow atlas for more than a few minutes.

I didn't investigate the contents too closely last night because there were at least a hundred pages, but the ones I saw were a combination of typed and handwritten, with notes scrawled in the margins, lines crossed out and circled, and words underlined and boxed. Annotations that seemed to befit a math problem more than psychology notes.

"Yesterday must have taken more out of me than I thought," Betty says as she enters the kitchen. "I don't know when I've slept so late."

"I'm not surprised," I tell her, flicking on the gas beneath the teakettle. "How about some breakfast?" The kitchen smells fresh and the old appliances are gleaming.

"It's sparkling clean in here," Betty says. "And yes, an English muffin sounds good."

"Is there anything special you need today?" I ask.

Before she can answer, my cell phone rings. It's an unfamiliar number. Betty stares at my phone like it's an object from another planet.

"This is Elizabeth Harris," a woman says after I pick up. "I'm trying to reach Riley."

I recognize her name instantly. Professor Joshua Woods's wife. The woman I met in front of their home.

"This is Riley."

Her tone grows even chillier. "My husband shared the message you left on his cell phone. He played it for me last night."

Betty is staring at me intently. I'm sure she reads the shock on my face. I can't even formulate a sentence.

"You mentioned Alex Finch," Elizabeth says. "I'm assuming you're a friend of hers?"

"Um, yes," I reply.

"I'd urge you to be more circumspect before you take her lies at face value and harass innocent people. And now I have a question for you: What is it you think my husband took of hers?"

"Her student ID." My voice sounds rusty, so I clear my throat. "He used it to get some files from the Marquis library."

"Why would he need her ID when he has a faculty ID of his

own?" She exhales, sounding exasperated. "Did you know that Alex Finch rated my husband five chili peppers?"

I blink. "Chili peppers?"

"It's a thing, apparently. Students rate their professors based on their hotness quotient. Five is the highest. It's easy to verify online; Alex signed her rating. She has since deleted it, but I took a screenshot. Then Alex began dropping by his office hours. And when he rebuffed her advances, she fabricated their relationship. That timeline is indisputable. Apparently she's under the care of a psychiatrist. Part of our decision to not file charges was because Alex agreed to increase her sessions to twice weekly. She is a deeply troubled young woman; my understanding is her best friend from high school committed suicide and that may have affected her mental state. My husband is soft-hearted, which is why she tried to prey on him."

I regain my footing. "Did your husband deny having Alex's student ID? Because I believe Alex. And I think he took those files."

There's a pause. It makes the hairs on my arms stand up.

"You sound familiar," Elizabeth says slowly. "I have a good ear and I know we've talked before . . . Wait a minute, you were in front of my house yesterday, weren't you?"

I can't think of a plausible denial.

"Josh and I are a family. And if you threaten us, we'll push back hard. If you call or come near either of us again, I'm calling the police."

She hangs up and I stare into Betty's eyes.

"You look like you've seen a ghost," Betty says.

CHAPTER FORTY-TWO

[T]he medium said, [Your father] wants you to tell [your mom] that she can get rid of his neckties now. Does that make sense? . . . My mom began to cry even harder and said, 'The only thing that I kept were his neckties. They're still in his closet.'"

—*Huffington Post*

BETTY, 1964

The women silently ate their dinners of lukewarm macaroni and cheese and overly salted peas and carrots while Dr. Trimble's fingers clacked furiously against his typewriter's keys. Their requested supplies had been delivered along with the meal, so they washed the dishes and took turns showering in the cramped bathroom before drying off with fresh towels and changing back into their uniforms.

Dr. Trimble's hypothesis was being proven correct, he'd told them. The long day of testing had yielded their strongest results yet.

"I've never seen him so excited," Kathleen whispered. "He actually almost smiled."

"He tried to light his pipe when it was already lit," Helen chimed in, giggling.

"Oh, I can't wait to get back home and out of this stupid dress," Betty said, sinking down on a bunk. Kathleen was across from her, and they were so close their knees almost touched. Helen and Ivy came to join them.

"What's the first thing you'll do when you get home?" Helen asked.

"Sleep," Ivy moaned. "I feel like I could sleep forever and not be rested."

Kathleen sighed. "Soak in a hot bath."

Tell Douglas about the baby, Betty thought. Once he recovered from the shock, they'd start preparing the nursery. By this time next year, their lives would be so much more content. She lay a hand on her abdomen, trying to convince herself it was true.

Betty had planned to see her doctor for a pregnancy test and tell Douglas the result first, but as she looked around at the faces of her dearest friends, she couldn't hold it back.

"I have some news," she began. "Baby Sandra's going to have a little playmate next year."

Kathleen got it first, squealing softly and hugging Betty. A second later, Helen joined in. Ivy hugged Betty, too, but her expression reminded Betty of someone who was trying to force a smile for a photograph. It didn't feel genuine. Maybe she was coming down with a cold.

"I haven't told Douglas yet, so you must keep it a secret," Betty said.

"He'll be thrilled, won't he?" Kathleen asked.

Betty felt her eyes fill with unexpected tears. "I hope so."

"Oh, sugar, don't cry." Kathleen patted Betty's knee. "It's this strange place. It's making you weepy."

"It's not just that. Douglas wanted to wait a bit longer. I'm worried he'll be upset at first."

"Douglas will come around," Ivy told her. "Sometimes it takes men longer. They're not as emotional as we are."

"I'm sure you're right." Betty pressed her knuckles into her eyes, trying to staunch her tears. "It's just—"

She couldn't hold back the sob that erupted from her throat.

"It's just a bit of the baby blues," Ivy told her. "I think I still have them, too."

"I really do think this place is preying on all of our minds," Kathleen said. "Last night I kept recalling a horrible time from my childhood."

"We need to get out as quickly as we can, so let's keep trying our hardest during testing," Betty said as the others nodded.

"I wonder if . . ." Kathleen's voice trailed off.

"Say it," Helen urged.

"It might be silly. But Dr. Trimble wants us to be as close as possible to prove his hypothesis. And it seems to be working. So maybe we can help with that."

"I don't see how we can be any closer," Helen said. "We're spending all our time together. We're eating the same meals, wearing the same outfits, and sleeping in the same space."

"That's the physical piece. But I meant an emotional connection." Kathleen hesitated. "Do you remember early on when Dr. Trimble told us to share our secrets, the things we hide from everyone? He meant our special abilities. But I wonder what might happen if we shared our other secrets now. If that could connect us even deeper, by knowing one another so intimately."

The women stared at each other for a long moment, but no one spoke. Then Betty's whisper broke the silence. "I have a secret worry. What if Douglas falls in love with someone else?"

"That could never happen!" Kathleen cried.

"That pretty new girl, Emily, the one with the English accent? Douglas must be spending a lot of time working with her this week."

"Oh, Bets, you can't truly be worried about that!" Kathleen sounded indignant. "He's your husband. And you've just told us you're pregnant with his baby!"

"But things between us have been a bit distant. Someone else could swoop in and take my place!"

"Douglas would never cast you aside. You're a wonderful wife,"

Ivy's voice quavered. "But I've always felt like David could do better. I'm plump and homely. Even my father thought so."

"That's not true!" Betty protested. "You're beautiful."

Ivy shrugged. "I'm glad you think so."

"You are, Ivy," Kathleen insisted, reaching for Ivy's hand.

"I think all of your husbands are lucky to have you," Helen said. "You're the loveliest girls I've ever known. But I worry I may end up a spinster."

"No, no, you'll marry and have a houseful of children," Betty reassured her. "You'll see. What about your crush? That handsome, dark-haired man you've mentioned?"

Helen looked down at her hands. "I—I don't think it will work out."

"Don't be in such a rush, Helen. You've still got a little time. Enjoy your single years while you have them. I would have loved to have been a stewardess for another year. The places I would have seen, the people I could have met . . ." Kathleen shook her head. "I know I'm lucky to have Ronald. I'd never tell him, but I wish I'd met him a year or two later."

"I have another secret." Betty looked down at her abdomen. She couldn't quite believe she was uttering the words she'd vowed to never tell a soul.

She squeezed her eyes shut as she blurted it out: "Douglas thinks I'm taking birth control pills. But I've been flushing them down the toilet."

CHAPTER FORTY-THREE

RILEY, PRESENT DAY

I'm still digesting the venom in Elizabeth's voice as Betty finishes her tea and English muffin.

"I don't understand why someone would want Douglas's old papers after all this time," Betty says.

"Can you remember anything in particular from the paperwork?" I ask. "Maybe something stood out?"

"I've never looked at them," Betty tells me. "I already lived through that time. And I've spent the rest of my life trying to forget it."

I press my fingertip into a tiny, sharp crumb on the counter and transfer it to my plate. "I'm starting to wonder if maybe one of us did knock against that door handle accidentally. Or it could've just loosened with age."

Betty's cup clinks sharply against its saucer as she sets it down. "You know perfectly well that isn't true, Riley."

"I just thought—" I begin, but Betty cuts me off.

"Instincts want to help you, to guide you toward the truth. Yet you quash yours. Why would you do that?"

I lift up my empty hands. "I-I'm not sure."

"You know as I well as I do the door handle was tampered with," Betty said. "Because your mind doesn't have an answer for who or why, you've begun to question your initial assumption. To convince yourself that you're unreliable."

I've never seen this side of Betty before.

She exhales, then continues. "I'm sorry I spoke harshly. It's a bit of a touchy subject for me."

"There's nothing to apologize for," I tell her. "You're right."

Betty gazes down at the pattern of pink roses on her plate. "When I was younger, I knew certain things and there was no easy explanation for how or why. Because my mother didn't understand or experience what I did, she thought it was the work of the devil. I suppose that affected me."

"I can see why," I say. I'm about to ask her more when she pushes away from the kitchen island. "I'm going to take a shower, dear. After that, can we go for a drive? I realized during our outing yesterday the world has changed so dramatically. I'd like to see a bit more of it."

"Absolutely," I promise, bringing our dishes to the sink.

As I rinse the plates and cups, I think about how my instincts told me Danny was kind and generous, outgoing and big-hearted. All those things turned out to be true.

But there was one tiny detail from that very first night that snagged me like a splinter. At the Italian restaurant, I offered to pay half when the bill came. He pulled out his wallet. *I've got this.*

But the waiter told him his card had been declined. Danny brushed it off, saying the card had recently been compromised online and he'd forgotten to throw it away. He lay down a blue Visa, but not before I'd gotten a glimpse of the inside of his wallet.

My instinct was a faint vibration in my body, a warning tremble. *Why so many credit cards?* it whispered.

But I suffocated it with explanations: Maybe he enjoyed perks like getting airline miles with new cards. Maybe lots of people had seven or eight credit cards they carried around and I just didn't know it. Maybe I'd overcounted the cards.

The rush of water traveling through pipes tells me Betty is starting her shower. I wipe my hands and head into the living room.

Something is driving me toward the papers again. It's curiosity—or it could be instinct. But I'm not going to deny it.

Betty's darkest memories are contained within these pages, I think. A sense of trepidation fills me as I lift the yellowing pages out of their container and lay them on the coffee table. There's a faint brown ring on one that could be from someone's long-ago coffee cup, and doodles of intersecting triangles in the margins of others.

I flip through pages of charts and numbers before I find a typewritten one with faint pencil corrections. Perhaps the final product is elsewhere and Douglas saved this draft. Ivy's name leaps out at me and I begin to read:

CONFIDENTIAL PSI EXPERIMENTAL REPORT

Date: June 14, 1964

Subject: Ivy Lennox, age 21

Researcher: Dr. Silas Trimble

Assistant researcher: Douglas Sadler

Location: Berkeley, California

Experiment summary: The researcher became aware of the subject through an article in the *Journal of Parapsychology*, which detailed her exceptional psychical abilities. After obtaining approval from the president of Marquis University, the researcher and his assistant flew to California, where they contacted the subject by phone. During the phone call, the research assistant pretended to be on the faculty of the California college where the subject had already undergone many psi tests. The subject agreed to go to a nearby coffee shop for a double-blind variation on the Zener card test. The sum of $40 was offered to lure her to this experiment.

Prior to her arrival at a designated corner booth, a

stack of cards was arranged in a specific order known by the researcher and placed on the table. When the subject arrived, she sat at the table and touched the top card, speaking aloud the symbol that came to her mind, before moving on to the subsequent cards. The research assistant, who was seated at the next booth, wrote down her answers. The researcher and assistant did not look at or interact with the subject. The subject appeared completely unaware of their presence. When she finished the test, she bought a piece of peach pie from the diner. The researcher and assistant continued to observe her as she walked to the college campus and delivered the pie to her husband, David Lennox. Then she was observed returning to her home on Portner Lane.

Results: The subject correctly sensed 12 of the 25 cards. Given that the chances of correctly guessing any of the cards was 20 percent, this is a highly significant result.

Conclusion: The subject is worthy of intensive evaluation at the Marquis campus and should be persuaded to move there by any means necessary.

CHAPTER FORTY-FOUR

IVY, 1964

"I don't believe you're trying hard enough, Ivy." Ivy looked up at Dr. Trimble towering over her. They were alone at one end of the basement; he'd summoned her for a private conversation. He told her to sit down on the single straight-back chair he'd brought into the space, but he remained standing with a bare lightbulb dangling behind him that draped his face in shadows, deepening the grooves around his eyes and mouth and hollowing his cheeks.

"I'm sorry," she whispered, feeling a stab of shame.

Had they been in the basement for two days or three? She'd lost track. Maybe it was day three. An eternity.

"Kathleen and Betty did extremely well in the tests yesterday. The best results I've ever seen. Likely the best *anyone* has ever seen. But your results were . . . subpar."

She bowed her head. She'd come up short, like she had all her life. She wasn't a good enough wife; David had pointed that out in ways big and small. She was a failure as a mother, too. Whenever Sandra cried and Ivy picked her up, Sandra's wailing increased. But Kathleen and Betty had been able to effortlessly calm Sandra the night of the dinner party.

Ivy was nothing like the joyous woman in the advertisement for Ivory soap who pressed her cheek against her happy, plump baby's, saying, "Cheek-to-cheek softness!" *That* was the kind of mother Sandra deserved.

Ivy couldn't summon the strength to feel maternal toward the little girl who looked so much like her. Her natural buoyancy had been suffocated by something heavy and gray.

Dr. Trimble leaned down and looked her in the eye.

"I need to talk to the other girls," he said. His breath smelled sour but she didn't dare pull away. "They will be the ones to decide the consequences. After all, your inadequate performance will affect them, too, because they'll need to stay here longer."

He walked away and after a moment, she could hear the low timbre of his voice interspersed with the higher, crisper ones of her friends. But she couldn't make out any words. She felt a tear roll down her cheek, but her sadness felt removed, as if her emotions had been extracted and placed on the other side of a glass barrier.

"Ivy?" She started at the sound of Dr. Trimble's voice. She hadn't realized he'd come back.

"A decision has been made."

She knew it was bad from his tone, but she deserved it. She'd let down her friends.

"You will stay alone until the girls vote to have you rejoin us."

He held up her overnight bag and a folded sheet and towel. "I've brought your things."

"What?" she asked.

"Pay attention! Come with me."

Ivy stood up, her body feeling as heavy as if it had been filled with sand. The fabric of her white skirt rustled as she followed Dr. Trimble. He opened a door she hadn't noticed before. It groaned loudly, sounding almost human. Inside the small room was a single cot.

"You'll find a candle and matches in your bag. I'll be back in the morning," he told her, then he shut the door, leaving her in darkness.

Ivy didn't have the energy to even light a candle. Her eyes had adjusted enough to allow her to see the shape of the room, so she wrapped the sheet around herself and curled up on the cot, too weary to even remove her shoes.

CHAPTER FORTY-FIVE

RILEY, PRESENT DAY

As soon as the water cuts off in Betty's shower, I put the papers back in their hiding place and start cleaning the already spotless living room.

Betty wheels in a little later. The shower must have refreshed her, because she has more color in her face and her eyes are brighter. "I've been thinking about our drive," she tells me.

"Are you still up for it?" I ask. "It's chilly out, so you'll need a coat in case you'd like to stop somewhere."

"I'll need to bring more than that. I've decided I want to go back."

"Go back?" I echo.

Her lips tremble, but her voice is steady. "I want to see Marquis one last time, dear. I suppose if I'm not going to be with my old friends ever again, this could be a way to feel close to them. And I can visit with Sandra. Will you drive me there?"

"Of course," I say. It's my job, after all. "But it'll be a long trip."

"I don't mind if you don't. We should both bring overnight supplies. I'd like to look around campus for a while."

I text Sandra to tell her Betty will be in town today and we'd love to meet up with her. She immediately texts back, inviting us to dinner. Betty looks nervous, but she tells me to let Sandra know we'd love to.

I make sure Betty has her blood pressure medicine and grab a blanket and pillow in case she wants to nap in the car again.

We're about to head out the door when she pauses. "There's one more thing." She nods toward the bookcase. "Please bring along Douglas's papers. Just in case."

Betty wheels down the ramp as I hurry to my car and pull it as close as I can to the front walk. Once again, I'm surprised by her strength and agility as she uses her arms to swivel her body into the passenger's seat.

"Would you like to listen to the radio?" I ask as we drive off.

She shakes her head. "Thank you, but I think I'd prefer quiet."

I take that as my cue not to talk. She stares out the window the entire way to Marquis. I don't know if she's lost in memories of the past or consumed by the strangeness of her present surroundings. When someone on an electric bike whizzes by, she gasps. And she's shocked by Amazon's ability to deliver anything from ice cube trays to garden huts after she spots a truck and asks me what it's carrying.

When we reach the Marquis campus, Betty takes in a slow, shuddering breath. "Could you park by the psychology building?" she asks. "I'd like to get out and look around."

"No problem." I find a street lined with two-hour parking spots a block away and Betty has her door open before I can bring around her wheelchair and coat. She knows exactly where she's going, and I quicken my step to keep up with her as she spins her wheels faster and faster. We pass college students with backpacks slung over their shoulders and a member of the grounds crew blowing leaves off a lawn before Betty comes to a stop in front of a building that resembles many of the others anchored on campus: two levels of gray stone, tall windows, and a sharply pitched roof.

"It hasn't changed a bit," Betty whispers. "My goodness, I could almost swear Douglas was inside, waiting to come home to me at five o'clock."

I place my hand on her shoulder and even through the thick fabric of her coat, I can feel her shaking.

"It's as if not a day has passed," Betty continues. "I can still hear my friends' voices and see their faces as if they were right in front of me. The four of us would walk home together when Dr. Trimble was finished with us, chatting and laughing, the way young women do. We'd stop at Kathleen's place first, then Ivy would go to the faculty housing, and Helen would see me off before she went to the dorm."

"You must miss them terribly. You were so close," I say gently.

"We were, until the very end," Betty says. "Then everything changed."

Her attention is diverted as several students emerge from the building. She watches them walk deeper into the heart of campus and I swear I see longing in her expression.

"When I was young, I thought everything would be so easy. All I had to do was reach the next step: find a husband, keep house and cook his favorite meals, and make babies. Life would be grand. And it was, at first."

She stares at the building for a long moment. Her face appears sunken now, like this day has drained more from her than she can give.

"I would like to go inside," Betty says.

"Are you sure?" I ask.

"This place has stolen so much from me. I guess I'd finally like to stand up to it."

I'm about to reach for the handles of her wheelchair to help steer her when she abruptly pushes off. But the curb is sloped and one of her wheels catches its edge. Before I can do anything, her wheelchair overturns and she spills out. Her head hits the curb with a sickening crack.

"Betty!" I cry.

She's unmoving on the pavement.

CHAPTER FORTY-SIX

HELEN, 1964

It was the worst morning of Helen's life.

Every time she managed to doze off last night, Dr. Trimble would shout at them to reveal their dreams before the images evaporated from their consciousnesses. Gone was the man who'd lulled them to sleep the first night with soft, kind words. He was now revealing a harsher, more demanding side of himself, one Helen suspected was his true core.

But physical fatigue wasn't Helen's most pressing concern.

What troubled her deeply was how strangely Betty seemed to be acting around her. Betty was avoiding her eyes and hadn't spoken a single word to her. Or maybe Helen was being overly sensitive. It was only breakfast time, after all, and Betty was exhausted, too.

"Girls?" Dr. Trimble called from the kitchen. "Come eat."

Helen stood up from her bunk, feeling as if she had the flu, and followed Kathleen and Betty into the kitchen. Three metal trays awaited them, holding pineapple juice, coffee, French toast, and individual containers of fruit salad, each topped with a bright red maraschino cherry. Dr. Trimble was finishing the meal on the fourth tray.

"Where's Ivy's tray?" Kathleen asked.

Dr. Trimble shoved the last triangle of toast into his mouth and spoke through it: "She's eating breakfast alone."

Dr. Trimble had come to them last night to let them know Ivy had asked to sleep separately, claiming she needed rest. It seemed strange to Helen and the others, but no one had questioned him. Then Dr. Trimble instructed them to go to bed. "We have a full day tomorrow," he'd said before he lumbered away. He seemed to think it was that easy, that no matter how exhausted and disoriented they were, that they'd all fall asleep at his verbal command.

The new day seemed to be infusing Kathleen with a determination to get answers. Her voice was firm, not placating, as if she were nearing the end of her patience.

"How long will Ivy be staying apart?" Kathleen asked.

Helen noticed a blue vein in Kathleen's temple seemed unusually prominent, as if signaling the pressure building in her system.

"Perhaps one more night," Dr. Trimble replied. "It really depends on Ivy's wishes."

"I want to see her," Kathleen said. "I'll go right now and have breakfast with her."

Dr. Trimble glared at her. Helen held her breath when Kathleen didn't duck her head or apologize for her impudence.

"You will not. Ivy specifically asked to be away from you girls so she could rest. Now, come eat before it gets cold."

The three women sat at the table, silently unfolding their napkins and removing their utensils. Helen had no appetite, but she forced herself to take a bite. The French toast was mushy and nearly flavorless in her mouth. She gathered her courage and asked, "Betty, could you pass the butter?"

She held her breath, waiting to see if Betty would ignore or acknowledge her. "Of course," Betty said as she passed it over.

Maybe her guilty conscience was tricking her, Helen thought. She couldn't stop thinking about that foolish note. It wouldn't have been so bad if she hadn't added the heart surrounding her and Douglas's initials. But surely the square of paper had been swept up by a janitor's broom and deposited into a bin long ago, Helen reassured herself.

So why was she suddenly obsessing about it?

Last night she'd even dreamt about watching as Betty unfolded the note and looked at Helen with shock and anger filling her face.

When Dr. Trimble had barked, "What did you dream, Helen?" she'd lied to him. "I-I was a schoolgirl, and I got caught passing a note in class," she'd blurted.

Had she caught a tiny smile tugging his beard upward?

She didn't know; it was impossible to feel certain about anything. She looked down and realized she was buttering the same triangle of French toast twice.

Her napkin slid off her lap onto the floor and she bent over to retrieve it. Kathleen's foot was tapping frantically against the floor. *How did she have the energy to move?* Helen wondered.

"Today we're going to do something different," Dr. Trimble said. "A longer Ganzfeld experiment."

A sharp clatter signaled Kathleen had dropped her silverware onto her plate.

"How long?" Kathleen blurted, her voice shrill.

"A few hours," he said, as offhand as if he were discussing something innocuous, not his plan to seal one or more of them away, their senses extinguished, their minds frantically spinning.

"I'd like for you ladies to vote anonymously on who will be the subject. Come back and talk to me, one by one, and tell me your choice. You are not to discuss this with each other."

He pointed to Betty. "You first."

Kathleen had stopped moving. Now she was frozen in place, like a prey animal sensing an imminent threat.

She won't be able to take it, Helen thought. None of them liked the experiment. And to be in that state for a few hours—a shudder ran down Helen's spine.

"Betty?" Dr. Trimble slapped his hand on the table. "Come with me. I need to know who you are voting for."

Betty stood up from the table and Helen tried to catch her eye. Helen would volunteer to be the receiver; it would be her penance. She needed to convey her decision to Betty.

But Betty didn't—or wouldn't—look her way.

CHAPTER FORTY-SEVEN

RILEY, PRESENT DAY

I pace the ER's waiting room, guilt lying heavily in my gut. I'm supposed to be a caretaker, yet my client got hurt on my watch.

The waiting room is a circus—a toddler is using a couch as a jungle gym while his mother half-heartedly reprimands him, an old man argues with the receptionist about insurance forms, and a woman hunches over, moaning, while her partner rubs her back. At least a dozen others, some in clear distress, are waiting. Yet Betty was rushed back to be evaluated immediately. With every passing second, my imagination creates darker scenarios.

Finally a young nurse with tired eyes comes into the waiting room, calling, "Ms. Bell?"

I hurry toward her.

"Follow me," she says, using her ID to swipe through a door.

"Is Betty okay?" I ask.

"She's conscious. Head injuries can be tricky, especially in the elderly. We're going to do some tests."

The inner chamber of the ER is sterile and chaotic, with nurses in salmon-colored scrubs clicking on computers or treating patients, an aide wheeling a rattling cart down the hall, and the chorus of dozens of conversations. In the distance, a man is yelling that he's going to sue someone if he doesn't get taken to a bathroom. We pass by several exam rooms before the nurse stops at one and pulls back the light blue curtain that serves as a door.

I step inside and see Betty on a narrow gurney. A monitor beeps steadily beside her and an IV line snakes into her wrist. A raised purple bruise, the width of a fist, is already forming on her temple.

When she opens her eyes and I see recognition in her expression, relief pours through me. At least she's alert.

"Riley," she says. "What happened?"

"Your wheelchair caught a curb and you tipped over," I explain. "I didn't have time to catch you. I'm so sorry."

"It wasn't your fault."

It's perhaps the kindest thing she could have said to me. Betty doesn't even remember what happened, yet she's absolving me of blame.

There's a thin white blanket at her feet. I'm reaching for it to tuck it around her when the curtain is yanked back.

"Mrs. Sadler? I'm Dr. Hernandez."

The doctor doesn't look older than twenty-five, and she's barely five feet tall, but she carries an air of competence and authority.

"Track my finger," she instructs Betty as she moves it from side to side, then up and down. "Can you tell me what day it is?"

Betty frowns. Finally, she answers, "I'm not quite sure. Thursday?"

"And who's the president?"

"The president?" Betty echoes.

"Of the United States," the doctor clarifies.

Betty looks lost. "I can almost picture him," she says unconvincingly.

Dr. Hernandez makes a note in her chart. "Hold on a moment." She ducks out of the room.

I wonder if I should explain that Betty's responses are due to her isolation and lack of a TV and smartphone. Before I can do anything, though, a male technician comes into the room.

"I'm taking you for a CAT scan," he tells Betty as he releases the brakes on her gurney.

I know I won't be permitted to go with her, so I tell Betty I'll be here when she gets back. I sit down on the lone chair in the room and wait. When the curtain is pulled back a little later, I look up to see the young nurse again.

"We were having some difficulty getting the CAT scan," she says. "Betty was uncooperative."

It's difficult to imagine; Betty is always so polite. "What happened?" I ask.

"When the technician tried to put on her earphones and eye mask to wear for the scan, she became hysterical. We needed to do the scan, so we sedated her." The nurse looks down at the chart she's holding. "Does she have claustrophobia? Or any other mental health condition we should know about?"

"Not that I know of," I say. "But she just hired me as a caregiver recently. Did she say anything else? It could help me in the future if she has more appointments."

"Yeah, there was one odd thing. She was talking about something called Ganzfeld. The technician said she's the second one this week. Do you know what she meant?"

I shake my head. "The second one?"

A speaker crackles overhead and a woman's voice says, "Dr. Roberts to trauma bay one, Dr. Roberts to trauma bay one."

The nurse turns to leave and I leap to my feet.

"Wait! What do you mean, the second one? It could help me figure out what's going on with Betty."

"A young woman came in earlier this week, I think the victim of a hit-and-run. She had track marks in her arms but she wasn't on anything when we saw her. When the technician tried to put on her earphones and eye shield to scan her for a brain injury, same thing happened. She started screaming about Ganzfeld and ran out of the hospital."

CHAPTER FORTY-EIGHT

KATHLEEN, 1964

Kathleen feared she was going be sick to her stomach. She couldn't stop trembling. Her friends had betrayed her so completely it felt as if they'd used sharp sticks to jab at her insides.

When Dr. Trimble summoned Kathleen to a corner of the basement, she assumed it was to cast her vote. She still hadn't decided whether to choose Betty or Helen, but she knew both women could endure the Ganzfeld test far better than she. Still, she was reluctant to put either of them in that awful situation. She'd decided instead to reason with Dr. Trimble in an effort to get him to shave down the required time. Half an hour would be long enough.

But Dr. Trimble didn't even glance up at her as he continued marking one of his typewritten papers with a lead-tipped pencil.

"Both of the girls chose you," he said. "Wait a minute . . ."

Kathleen stood there, stunned into immobility, while he slashed through a line on his notes.

"There, that's cleaner." He put down his pencil and finally looked at her. "You'll be going into a separate area of the basement for the Ganzfeld experiment."

"Betty voted for me? And Helen, too?" she whispered.

He nodded. "It seems fair, doesn't it, since they were both receivers yesterday?"

Was he lying? Usually she was perceptive about people's motives and intentions, but her sleep-starved brain wasn't operating at a high level. Maybe her friends *had* reasoned it was Kathleen's turn.

Kathleen's mouth was so dry it was impossible to swallow. She watched as Dr. Trimble took one of the hateful blindfolds from atop his pile of belongings.

"Kathleen!" Dr. Trimble's tone was sharp, and it jolted her out of her temporary paralysis.

Somehow she was able to follow Dr. Trimble to the corner of the basement. She tried to suck in a lungful of air. But her chest was too tight; it prevented her from inhaling deeply.

There was a single folding chair in the corner, turned to face the wall. The space was as shadowy and dusty as the attic of a haunted house. It looked like a place where nightmares were born.

"Sit down," he told her.

Kathleen obeyed. Even the air felt suffocating, as if it had laid here thickly for decades, never stirred by even the slightest breeze.

He handed her the blindfold.

"Please," she begged. "I don't think I can do this."

"Nonsense," he told her. "All you need to do is sit there."

He watched as she pulled on the blindfold and tested it to make sure the strap was tight enough. Her mind whirled frantically, wondering if she could loosen it when he left. Just enough to let in a sliver of light so she could see.

"Here are your earplugs," he told her. She inserted one into her left ear. Instantly, everything sounded more muffled.

"You know what to do. Put in the other earplug. You must keep your eyes open. Then just relax and speak aloud the images that come to your mind."

Was she crying? Her nose seemed runny, but she couldn't feel tears on her cheeks. If her eyes were releasing them, they were trapped beneath the halves of the Ping-Pong balls.

"Just one more thing."

Kathleen paused before putting in the second earplug.

"I'm going to secure your hands so that you're not tempted to end the experiment early."

"No! I don't want to do this!" she cried. "I'm going home!"

But it was too late. He'd already tied her down.

She sat in the utter stillness and waited for the awful visions she knew would come. The darkest corners of her mind, where her ugliest secrets and deepest fears were buried, would flourish under these conditions.

Zags of light, like flashes of lightning, seemed to skim across the darkness. She knew it was a trick her eyes were playing on her, but the electric bursts seemed so real.

Was something crawling on her? She swallowed a scream and tried to brush her hands over herself, but she couldn't move them. It felt like fingertips tracing a line down her arm. Nausea rose in her throat. She was desperate to thrash around and dislodge her blindfold, but fear sapped the strength from her body. Dr. Trimble must be watching her as she sat there helplessly, just as Mac had done long ago.

Of all the dangers her mind was capable of exploring, Dr. Trimble was the worst. He had become the thing she feared the most.

CHAPTER FORTY-NINE

RILEY, PRESENT DAY

When I call Sandra to let her know about Betty's accident and apologize for canceling our dinner plans, she's both distraught and reassuring. She offers to come to the hospital, but I tell her Betty had a sedative and will likely sleep through the night.

"That's good. Rest is probably the best thing for her. But please keep me updated," she begs. "I can't lose Betty now that we've finally found each other."

I promise to text her as soon as Betty wakes up in the morning.

"I've got back-to-back appointments all day tomorrow, but I can cancel everything," she tells me.

"Oh, please don't," I said. "If she's up to it, maybe we can meet for dinner tomorrow night."

Once Betty is moved into a private room, I spend the night in the recliner next to her bed, but it's impossible to doze for more than a few minutes at a stretch. Every hour or two, a nurse or aide swings open the door, flicks on the lights, and checks Betty's vitals. Machines beep in the background, and the ambient noises of the hospital—pages crackling over the speaker, bursts of hallway conversations—filter through the door.

Betty, however, sleeps through it all. The sedative they gave her must have been strong.

It's after 8 AM when I finally hear her stir. I jump up and see her open her mouth to speak, but only a raspy sound comes out. I press the button to incline the top half of the bed, then hold the plastic cup of water with a big straw to her lips and she drinks in a long swallow.

"You're okay," I tell her. "You had a fall yesterday."

"I remember." She stares up at me with haunted blue eyes.

I glance at the monitor that registers her pulse. It's hitching higher, from a steady sixty-two beats a minute to seventy. Then seventy-eight.

"We'll be able to go home today." I hope my words reassure Betty. "You didn't break anything in the fall and you don't have a serious head injury."

"I remember," she repeats.

"What do you remember?" I ask.

"Everything." She squeezes her eyes shut briefly. Her pulse hits ninety.

"Try to take a deep breath," I tell her. "Are you in pain?"

I'm about to summon a nurse when Betty reaches out and grabs my arm. Her fingers are ice cold.

"Someone is doing it again," she whispers. She lifts her head and I see the cords in her neck strain with the effort.

"What do you mean?" I ask.

"Last night, the technician tried to make me wear eye and ear coverings for some test. He told me to lie perfectly still for the duration of the test. It reminded me of the old experiments . . . When I resisted, they brought in a nurse and I heard him saying I was the second one talking about Ganzfeld."

Betty's head collapses back onto the pillow. "Someone stole the library papers and tried to get Douglas's old notes. They're trying to learn everything they can about the experiments. I had no idea why. But now I understand."

Her pulse is over 110. A machine begins to beat frantically. I hear footsteps rushing toward us.

"Someone is doing it again," Betty repeats. "They've started up the old experiments that killed my friends."

CHAPTER FIFTY

HELEN, 1964

Why had her friends done this to her?

It was hard to walk; the floor before Helen was shimmying like the rippling surface of a lake. She stumbled and nearly fell.

"Be careful!" Dr. Trimble snapped as he led her back to the cots where the others had gotten to rest while Helen sat alone in a far corner of the basement, her eyes and ears sealed and her hands tied down.

"Kathleen and Betty both voted for you," Dr. Trimble had told her before taking her away.

Helen had grown to hate the Ganzfeld experiment—all the girls did by now—but always before, she'd been comforted by the knowledge that she was physically close to her friends.

But *were* they her friends? It was hard to know what was real.

In one vision brought on by the experiment, Betty had screamed at her, her face red and hard-looking. Helen heard distant laughter, and a chorus of voices telling her she'd done something terrible, that she was a bad girl and needed to be punished. She saw bursts of orange and red so intense they felt like they burned her eyes. *Maybe it was hell*, she'd thought.

Helen shuffled toward her bunk, still not trusting the ground beneath her. She released a small, surprised sound when she saw all the others were there, even Ivy.

Kathleen was sitting on the edge of her bunk, staring at her hands like they were foreign objects. Ivy lay on her cot in her white dress, her eyes open and her face slack. Betty seemed to have twice her normal energy; she was frantically organizing her things, as if she couldn't get them neat enough.

"Betty, you can worry about that later. Sit down," Dr. Trimble ordered.

Betty immediately followed instructions, perching on the edge of her cot with ramrod-straight posture. She kept blinking rapidly, as if trying to clear her vision.

Dr. Trimble sucked on the stem of his pipe. A faint haze of blue smoke hung in the air.

"I have devoted myself to the study of the extraordinary, to what ancient cultures called the Third Eye. In years ahead, my work will be scrutinized. Debated. *Remembered.*" He began to pace around the cots, not looking at any of the women but at a different, imaginary audience. "Consider the possibilities: The human brain could influence physical matter without touch. Communicate across vast distances without speech. Once we can harness its hidden powers, it can transform reality as we know it."

Helen watched as Kathleen tightened her body, tilting her head down and drawing up her knees, as if she were trying to make herself smaller. Betty still seemed fidgety; she smoothed the sheet beside her repeatedly as her eyes kept sweeping the room, as if she were desperate to bring order to it.

Then Betty reached forward and Helen saw her pick up a square of paper from the floor.

"Did you drop this, sir?" she asked.

Betty's voice sounded strange to Helen's ears. It was distorted, as if Helen were listening to her speak underwater.

"I did not," Dr. Trimble replied.

Betty unfolded the paper and gasped. Her eyes rose to meet Helen's. And in that moment, Helen knew Betty had found the note.

Betty held it up and Helen saw the message she knew by heart, the one she would have given anything to erase.

Douglas is so dreamy. And their initials, entwined in a heart: *DS & HH.*

Helen's pulse began to pound in her ears.

"I-I wrote it before I ever met you!" Helen's mouth felt rubbery and her words weren't as nimble as usual. "I didn't mean it . . . It was just a silly thing . . . a passing fancy . . ."

"I told you what I feared most," Betty said slowly. Left unspoken was the rest: *And you were hoping to make it happen.*

Betty tore the note into shreds while she stared at Helen.

"Girls, it's time for more tests," Dr. Trimble said, as if oblivious to the strain in the room.

Kathleen let out a whimper.

"Settle down, it's just the Zener card game," he told them. "Helen and Betty, pair up. Ivy, come on. Pay attention. You'll be paired with Kathleen."

Dr. Trimble handed Betty and Kathleen each a set of the cards.

Helen couldn't look at Betty's face, but she felt Betty's eyes boring into her. Helen could feel Betty's anger; it radiated from her and swirled thickly in the air. Trying to guess the cards was impossible. Helen had no clarity; it was as if her gift had been extinguished.

"Five correct," Dr. Trimble said when she finished. "Exactly the percentage chance would allow."

Was he smiling? It made no sense that he'd be pleased. She'd performed terribly.

"Now Ivy and Kathleen."

The magic had been drained away from each of them. Ivy had to be prompted several times to even make her guesses. Dr. Trimble finally announced Ivy had gotten six cards correct. He made them repeat the experiment a dozen or more times, with similar results.

A crack of thunder announced the imminent arrival of rain. It poured down, heavy and gray, as the tests stretched on. Dr. Trimble paired them up again and again, mixing up the combinations, and told them to focus on sending and receiving images he showed to the sender. Helen's mind felt blank; she couldn't pick up a single image. All she could think about was the look on Betty's face when she discovered Helen's terrible secret.

Every time Helen failed to summon an image, Dr. Trimble smiled and jotted something down in his notebook. "Extraordinary," he breathed, his voice caressing the word.

He *wanted* them to fail, she thought. She couldn't fathom why.

Helen could no longer distinguish day from night. The storm grew angrier, throwing bolts of lightning. Helen jumped at the strongest eruptions of thunder, but Ivy didn't even flinch. She seemed so listless. Perhaps she needed to eat something. Maybe, if the girls were permitted to eat dinner, Helen could beg Betty's forgiveness.

Kathleen had the strongest will, the only one brave enough to challenge Dr. Trimble. Helen leaned forward and put her hand on Kathleen's upper arm, intending to whisper a suggestion that Kathleen ask for a break.

Kathleen whirled around, her face filled with rage. "Don't sneak up on me and touch me like that!"

Helen's hand fell away. She blinked back tears. They all hated her; she'd ruined everything. She hung her head, too ashamed to look at anyone.

"This concludes our time together," Dr. Trimble finally told them. "You're going home first thing in the morning. Go to sleep now."

Instead of relief, Helen felt panic. In here she could try to beg for Betty's forgiveness. In the outside world, Betty could simply avoid her forever. Unless they would be together in the lab all week.

"Will you need us in the lab as usual tomorrow?" Helen asked.

Dr. Trimble looked at her in surprise, as if he'd already forgotten she was there.

"No, I'm finished with you girls," he said.

CHAPTER FIFTY-ONE

RILEY, PRESENT DAY

After Betty's pulse stabilizes, she tells the nurse she was just startled upon waking in a strange setting. "I'd like to go home as soon as possible," she says. "I'll be calmer and rest there."

The nurse agrees, given that none of Betty's medical tests turned up anything concerning. "I'll go get your discharge papers."

Betty crooks her finger and I move closer. "The other young woman who knew about the Ganzfeld tests must have been close to Marquis, too, since she was also brought to this hospital," Betty continues, as if there has been no break in our conversation.

"But why would someone be doing the experiments again?" I ask.

"For the same reason people have done terrible things all over the world throughout history," Betty says. "A desire for power, money, success. For immortality."

She isn't speaking about a hypothetical; her voice is bitter.

"Dr. Trimble used us. He desperately craved all of those things. He thought if he could harness our gifts and exploit them, the world would take notice. He wanted his name written in history books."

"But he failed," I tell her. "The institute was shut down."

"Because my friends died," Betty replies. "It all makes sense now. He went too far and I imagine he disgraced himself. The university tried to hide the evidence. But he was on to something. Apart, we four girls had curious abilities. But together, we were exceptional. Whoever has his papers knows that."

I drop my head into my hands. Betty seems so certain. And I can't come up with a single good reason to counter what she's saying.

The nurse returns and tells us to make sure Betty stays hydrated and to follow up with her primary care doctor. Betty signs a few forms, then the nurse helps her into a wheelchair while I run to the parking lot and bring around my car. I also text Sandra an update.

As soon as Betty is settled in the passenger's seat, she says, "I don't want to go home. Not yet."

I know the answer even before I ask, "Where would you like to go?"

"Back to Marquis. The young woman who had her ID stolen by her professor? I'd like to talk to her. To see what else she knows. She's the link to the person who took Dr. Trimble's papers."

I pull over to the side of the road and flick on my hazard lights so I can face Betty.

"Look, I think you may be right. I'd never heard of the Ganzfeld experiments before I met you, and I'm in the health care field," I tell her. "The fact that a young woman in clear distress mentioned them? It can't be a coincidence."

Betty nods. "It isn't."

"But you hired me to help with your care, and I can't in good conscience tell you I think we should stay here. You need to be home resting."

"Don't you see? I couldn't save my friends." Unshed tears are clogging Betty's voice. "I have to try to do something now."

I lean my head back and exhale. I know too well the compulsion to try to save someone in trouble, even when it seems futile. So I put my Toyota back into drive and head toward the sorority house.

"I keep thinking about odds. Dr. Trimble was obsessed with them. And don't the odds seem quite small that if the experiments were being conducted on only one person, she'd end up at the same hospital within a week of me?" Betty muses.

My thoughts have been traveling down the same track. "Which

means whoever is doing this is experimenting on other young women, too. With a higher pool, the odds that one would end up at the hospital are much stronger."

"Multiple girls as test subjects. Just as Dr. Trimble prescribed in his papers," Betty concludes.

We're about to turn the corner when I see a police cruiser blocking the street. A small crowd is gathered on the lawn of the sorority house. I spot a few police officers with spiral notebooks talking to young women.

I park in the first spot I can find and when Betty and I draw close to the house, we approach a few young women who are clustered together. I recognize a tall brunette as a sorority sister who was sipping coffee the day I came to talk to Alex.

"Excuse me, but what happened?" I ask. "I know someone who lives in this house. I was here just the other day."

The brunette looks at me. "Who do you know?"

"Alex Finch." Trepidation crawls across my skin. My heart is pounding; suddenly I'm seized with the urge to run, to get away from whatever I'm about to learn.

"That's what this is all about." She waves her arm. "Alex is missing. She was supposed to work in the kitchen last night to help make dinner. But she never came home. They found her phone by the side of the road this morning."

CHAPTER FIFTY-TWO

IVY, 1964

The baby was crying in her bassinet again, even though Ivy had just fed and changed her. They arrived home only an hour ago, and Mrs. Trimble had dropped off Sandra shortly thereafter, departing with barely a word. Ivy desperately needed a nap. But how could she rest when the baby was fussing so loudly?

There was a list of things Ivy was supposed to check when the baby fretted. A nurse had recited them to her in the hospital. She thought as hard as she could, and an answer fluttered through her mind, then disappeared. *Like a timid sparrow,* she thought. Maybe if she was very still and quiet it would flutter back.

Ivy picked up the bassinet and put it in the bathtub, then closed the bathroom door. There, that was better.

It seemed she'd only been laying on the bed for a few moments when the front door opened, then slammed shut. "Ivy? Are you here?"

David was home from work already? Ivy leapt up and rushed to greet him.

"Darling, how are you? Let me fix you a drink."

He stepped back from her outstretched arms, distaste filling his expression.

"Have you bathed today?"

"I—oh, there wasn't time today. Dr. Trimble needed us . . . but I was about to step in the shower," Ivy fibbed.

She hurried to the bar cart and fixed him a Manhattan. Her vision turned blurry and she dropped the cherry on the floor instead of in the drink.

"I'm so clumsy!" She tried for a tone of gaiety as she cleaned it up.

"Your voice sounds strange," David observed. He accepted the drink and took a sip. "Why is the baby crying?"

Ivy had forgotten about that. "She must be tired."

"Well, I'm exhausted," David said. "What's for dinner?"

Ivy felt all the blood rush out of her face. She'd forgotten about dinner.

"Ivy? I asked you a question."

"I-I'm sorry," she stuttered. "We just got home . . . I can put together something quickly."

"I've spent the past four days eating slapdash meals," David said. "I was looking forward to home cooking."

"Tomorrow I'll make all your favorites," Ivy said desperately. "And I'll bake a coconut cake for dessert."

David didn't reply. He walked to the couch and looked down at the empty coffee table.

"Where's the afternoon paper?"

Her head was aching. He had so many questions, and Sandra was still screeching. "The paperboy must have tossed it in the yard," she said. "I'll go look."

She stepped outside and realized it was already growing dark. She felt disoriented; surely they'd arrived home only a little while ago, while the morning sun shone brightly. She spotted the paper trapped in the bushes and walked across the lawn to get it. Dampness seeped through her pantyhose onto the soles of her feet and she realized she'd forgotten to put on her shoes.

She stood in the middle of the yard, frozen. Would it be better to go back to the house and get her shoes, or continue walking toward the paper?

It was all too overwhelming. She couldn't decide.

Then she saw a tall woman in a trim blue dress coming up the sidewalk, carrying a suitcase in her right hand. It looked just like David's mother. No, it *was* her.

David's mother turned up their front walk, her eyes meeting Ivy's. Ivy hoped she didn't notice her wet feet and ruined stockings; she was in no state to welcome her mother-in-law.

"Ivy, did you find the paper?"

Ivy whirled around at the sound of David's voice. He was standing in the doorway, frowning.

"Look who's here!" she cried.

"Who? I don't see anyone."

"But it's your mother!" As she spoke the words, Ivy turned around. She blinked hard a few times. What was happening? David's mother had been marching up the front walk, just a dozen feet away. Ivy had definitely seen her.

Was her mother-in-law playing some sort of trick on her?

Ivy ran to the sidewalk and looked in all directions. His mother was gone.

"What is wrong with you?" David asked. "My mother isn't here. I spoke to her over the weekend. She's at home in Des Moines."

Ivy slowly walked back up the front walk. She saw David look down at her wet stockinged feet. She tried to smile, but her facial muscles wouldn't cooperate. She felt as if she were wearing a grotesque parody of a grin, like a clown.

"Maybe I *should* ask my mother to come for a few weeks," David mused. "She'd get things shipshape around here."

Sharp tears pricked Ivy's eyes, but she kept her voice high and bright. "No, no, I'll do it! You don't need to trouble her."

If she could just sleep tonight, things would be so much better in the morning. She'd have the energy to clean the house and make dinner. And she'd find a way to love Sandra, the tiny baby who deserved a better mother.

"Now go put your feet up and read the paper while I make you a good, wholesome dinner," Ivy said.

She followed him inside and hurried into the bedroom to roll on a fresh pair of pantyhose. She went into the bathroom and fixed her hair and brushed her teeth, then lifted Sandra into her arms. Sandra's face was damp with tears, but she stopped crying almost immediately.

Ivy hurried into the kitchen with Sandra still nestled to her neck and opened the freezer with one hand, hoping against hope it would have something she could easily cook—a few chops or a steak.

She couldn't believe her eyes. Her freezer was full of foil-wrapped dishes, all neatly labeled. She touched them to make sure they were real and not another odd vision.

She pulled out one labeled *Tuna Noodle Casserole* and read the instructions: *Pop in the oven at 400 and bake for 30 minutes.*

Her friends had cooked for her while Ivy was in the hospital, just as they'd promised. Even though they'd banished her to a solitary room in the library basement, this was evidence they'd once loved her.

Tears slid down Ivy's cheeks, mingling with the ones on her neck Sandra had shed.

Tomorrow, she thought. *Everything will get better tomorrow. It has to.*

CHAPTER FIFTY-THREE

RILEY, PRESENT DAY

"Alex is missing?" I echo. My knees threaten to buckle and I grab the handles of Betty's wheelchair to steady myself.

The girl turns away and hurries to meet a young woman in a Tri Delt sweatshirt who is running across the grass toward them. "What's happening?" I hear her cry.

"We should probably leave," I tell Betty.

"But don't you need to tell the police what you know?" she asks.

"I don't have any real information. Surely they've learned of Alex's accusation against Professor Woods, and his against her; it's common knowledge."

Betty's brow creases, but she heads for my car, probably because she's still overwhelmed by the changes to the world since she last saw it. Her brain must feel assaulted not just from her fall, but from the barrage of unfamiliar stimuli.

Once we're inside my Toyota, she runs her hand over the inside of the passenger door. "I'd like some air. Where is the window crank handle?"

I show her how to push the small flat lever and she raises and lowers the window several times, gently shaking her head.

"Can we see Sandra before we go home?" she asks.

"I spoke to her last night. She can't wait to see you. She said she has a busy workday, but we can meet up when she's done."

Betty nods. "In the meantime, I guess there's one other person I'd like to visit. Samuel Trimble."

"Are you sure?" He seemed harmless, but it'll be unnerving for Betty to meet the grandson of the man who caused her and her friends so much anguish.

"Douglas took whatever papers he could grab when we ran away from Marquis. Dr. Trimble probably did the same when he was cast out; he was so protective of his work. Maybe someone has been trying to talk to Samuel about his grandfather's experiments or get the papers. That could be the person who's behind all of this."

I avert my eyes from hers. I didn't tell Betty about Sam's accusation that she could have been involved in the deaths of her friends. But when he meets her, he'll have to realize how wrong he is.

I already have his address from researching him, so I pull up directions to his house. I don't call ahead because I'm worried he'll tell us not to come.

As I start to drive, Betty tilts her head against the window and closes her eyes for so long I figure she has fallen asleep. Then her eyes pop open.

"Whoever is doing the new experiments took Alex," Betty says. "I don't know why or how they're linked, but I feel certain of it."

I brake at a red light before replying.

"Alex could've just decided to get away for a day or two, given all the stress she's under," I suggest. "She could've accidentally dropped her phone when she was getting into an Uber."

"You're doing it again." Betty's tone is an accusation.

She's right. I'm trying to talk myself out of what I know in my gut: Alex's disappearance doesn't have an innocent explanation.

Before I can change my mind, I pull over to the side of the road and dial the police non-emergency number, telling them I have some information on Alex Finch. I get transferred to an officer who takes down my name and phone number and asks me what I know. I describe my meeting with Alex and her revelation about her affair with Professor Woods. Then I tell the officer Alex suspected him of stealing her student ID.

When I hang up, Betty reaches over and touches my hand, but doesn't say a word.

A few minutes later, we turn down Samuel Trimble's street. It's a peaceful cul-de-sac, but Samuel's house is bedraggled compared to his neighbors'. The yard is overgrown and the gutters sag. The low concrete front porch holds a few aluminum chairs and a rickety-looking side table.

I get Betty's wheelchair out of the back and she maneuvers into it. When we're almost at the door, she holds up a hand. "Wait! What is that?"

I look around, but don't see anything amiss. It's an overcast morning, and the street is quiet, other than a couple of women out walking.

"That smell," she whispers. "I'd know it anywhere."

I inhale deeply and detect the aroma of vanilla. I look to my right, onto the front porch, and spot a wooden pipe in an ashtray. It looks like someone set it down while it was still burning; a wisp of white smoke rises from the bowl.

Betty cries out and clutches her head. "I need to get out of here! Help me, Riley."

I grab her wheelchair handles and rush her to my car. She's trembling so violently I'm scared she'll fall, so I half lift her into the passenger's seat.

"Is your head hurting?" I blurt. "Should we go back to the hospital?"

"It isn't that," she says in a strangled voice.

We're half a mile from the house before Betty finally speaks again.

"The smell of that tobacco," she whispers. "I swear I still breathe in that scent in my nightmares. That was Dr. Trimble's pipe."

CHAPTER FIFTY-FOUR

KATHLEEN, 1964

Old hands with crepey skin, young and strong hands, hands with wedding rings or bare ones—men's hands always sought a way to touch Kathleen. Businessmen in classy suits on the airplane, pinching her bottom as she leaned forward to serve them. Guys in the elevator who pressed too close to her. The teacher in high school who'd curved his body over hers from behind as he inhaled the scent of her hair and pretended to check her work.

Her mother lay back for any man who'd given her a scrap of attention. *How could she bear it?* Kathleen wondered. She never wanted to be touched again. Except by Ronald, of course. Her gentle, kind husband, who'd looked into her eyes on their wedding night and repeatedly whispered, "Are you okay?" as they consummated their marriage.

Maybe she would feel an aversion to the touch of other men even if she'd never encountered Mac, but right now, he seemed responsible for every unwanted graze, brush, and pinch she'd had to endure during her lifetime. She'd seen a vision of Mac during that wretched final Ganzfeld test, the ones her friends had banished her to endure alone.

First, the aroma of gasoline signaled he was nearby. Then he appeared, looming over her in the darkness. "Such a pretty girl," he whispered in his low, rumbling voice.

Always before, she'd quaked inside but remained perfectly still during his violations. This time it was different. The roar that emerged from her was born of decades-old rage. She wanted to tear Mac apart, to dig her nails into his eyes.

But he'd just laughed at her, knowing Dr. Trimble had tied down her hands.

"We'll play another time," Mac had said. "It's more fun when you put up a fight."

Now Kathleen paused in putting away her pink hair rollers. She lifted her head, listening hard. Was that Mac in her kitchen, making one of the mayonnaise and tomato sandwiches he always devoured?

The sound didn't repeat so she continued tidying up, stowing her suitcase on the floor of the closet and vacuuming the floors.

Kathleen had imagined collapsing into bed as soon as she arrived home this morning, but she felt too jittery to rest, even though Dr. Trimble had woken them several times again last night. Strangely, though, she kept losing pockets of time, as if she were mentally dozing off while still physically moving.

It was late afternoon now, and her chores were done. She looked around her tidy house, then scrubbed her body in a hot shower, trying to erase the smell of Dr. Trimble's vanilla pipe smoke that seemed to seep into her hair and clothes.

She toweled off and fixed her face and hair, then went to check on the casserole she'd put in the oven. It was golden brown, so she lowered the heat to warm. Ronald should be home at any moment.

She mixed a gimlet and sipped it as she sat on the couch, waiting for her husband to come through the door. It was starting to grow dark outside, but her earlier energy had vanished. She couldn't summon the strength to get up and turn on some lights.

She watched as her half-full gimlet glass tumbled out of her hand and fell to the shag carpet. Luckily the liquid was clear. Her body was leaden; she was unable to sponge up the mess.

Exhaustion slammed into her and she fell onto her side, half lying on the couch cushions. She didn't so much fall asleep as tumble into unconsciousness.

She awoke to find a man looming over her in the darkness, his hands outstretched. She couldn't see his face, but she knew it was Mac. He'd come for her again.

This time, she was ready. She wasn't a young girl. Her hands weren't tied down.

Kathleen could finally fight back.

CHAPTER FIFTY-FIVE

RILEY, PRESENT DAY

"I suppose I shouldn't be so shocked," Betty says. "Many men enjoy smoking pipes. The smell just brought me back to a terrible time."

"Actually, it isn't nearly as common today as it was in the sixties," I explain. "And something else seems off to me."

Betty tilts her head. "What is it, dear?"

I pull to the side of the road and slide my gearshift into park so I can devote my full attention to our conversation. "Sam is clearly interested in his grandfather's work. The book, the screenplay, plus those Seekers meetings he holds. But smoking the same flavor of tobacco in what might have been his grandfather's pipe is next level. It makes me wonder what else he could be replicating."

Betty's hands wring together. "For a moment, I had the wild thought Dr. Trimble had stepped into the house right before we arrived, leaving his pipe behind. I felt such terror. All I wanted to do was hide. But do you know what, Riley? I've spent most of my life hiding."

I finally ask the question that's been gnawing at me: "What were you hiding from?"

She doesn't answer for a long moment. I watch as a red pickup truck comes down the street, gliding over a speed bump before passing us by.

"I suppose saying I was being hidden is more accurate. After Douglas learned what Dr. Trimble had done to us, he felt such remorse. You see, I wasn't quite myself when I returned from the library experiments. I was jittery and forgetful. I had terrible nightmares. And there was another physical condition that made me weepy . . ."

Betty's face twists and I wonder what painful memory she's enduring.

"The final step in the experiments . . ." Betty takes a deep breath. "Dr. Trimble wanted to break us girls apart."

"Break you?" I repeat. "Why?"

"He explained it to Douglas. He needed to prove the inverse of his hypothesis, that our gifts were amplified by our connection. He shattered our friendships to document the negative effect it had on our abilities."

"He sounds sadistic."

"Douglas regretted ever getting me involved with the institute. I thought we ran away because Douglas knew Dr. Trimble's paper would bring tremendous attention to me and my friends. He was terrified of what might happen. He thought at the very least, I'd become a curiosity. He also feared the government could claim me, or that someone could kidnap me to exploit my gifts. I suppose he became a bit paranoid. So he bought our little house and tucked me away inside. And somehow the decades slipped by."

Betty looks down at her wedding ring, twisting the old golden circle around her thin finger.

"But I think there was another reason we ran away. Douglas must have found out what happened to my friends. He was so panicked the morning we left—I'd never seen him in such a state. He never breathed a word to me about it, though."

I'm about to reply when I catch sight of another car coming toward us, slowing for the speed bump. It isn't the vehicle that makes me do a double take. It's the passenger and driver I glimpse through the windshield.

My brain registers the information in a flash, sending what feels like an electric current through my body. But it takes my conscious mind an extra beat to identify what I'm seeing: two middle-aged women who look alike. Straw-straight blond hair. The sisters from the Seekers Collective.

They're staring straight ahead and don't appear to notice me. I twist around as they pass us and watch their sedan continue in the direction of Sam Trimble's house. It's a dark, four-door car, just like the one I thought might have been following me the other night.

"What are you thinking?" Betty asks. "Quickly, tell me. Don't censor yourself."

"Sam couldn't do the experiments alone. He isn't disciplined enough. He'd need someone smart and methodical. A partner—or even better, two."

"Two partners," Betty repeats.

I cast my mind back to my brief conversation with the sisters and describe it to her in detail. Sam had told them I wanted to learn about his grandfather's work. Was that seemingly offhand remark a secret signal to them?

They could have followed me home to learn where I live. They could have gotten my phone number from Sam. The anonymous text message to get Betty and I out of the house so someone could search felt deliberately vague: I have the information you're looking for. Meet me at noon tomorrow at the Starbucks on Pine Street.

I'd assumed Josh sent it and didn't want to write anything incriminating. But maybe it could have been from the sisters, dangling bait to get me to leave the house—so they could get in and see what information I might already have collected.

"We're going back to Sam's house," Betty says. It isn't a question. "I can't imagine he's doing experiments there—but just in case. He could have Alex."

"I don't know how he could be connected to Alex, but it's possible. Or maybe her connection was to the sisters."

I start to drive slowly, thinking thorough possibilities. Samuel and the sisters know what I look like but they have no idea I'm with Betty.

Even if they scoured the Internet—and even if they were the ones who invaded Betty's home—they'd never find a single photo of her past the age of twenty-one.

I park a few doors down from Sam's house and turn off the car.

"How can we get inside?" Betty asks.

"I have an idea," I tell her. "How good of an actress are you?"

CHAPTER FIFTY-SIX

A 2001 Gallup poll found that about half of all Americans believe ESP is real and 65 million Americans have personally experienced it.

—*The News-Times* (Danbury, CT)

BETTY, 1964

"Sweetheart, are you napping?"

Betty leapt to her feet at the sound of Douglas's voice. "No, no, just resting my eyes for a moment."

She looked around for something to do to prove she wasn't being idle, but the ground beneath her swayed and she collapsed back onto the couch.

Douglas's face came closer to hers, looking peculiar, as if reflected in a carnival mirror. "Can I get you a drink?"

She rubbed her eyes and tried to think. Her nerves were frayed. A drink might help her settle down, which would be good for the baby. She had to tell Douglas about it soon. Would he know she'd deceived him and thrown out her pills? Would he turn on her, like her friends had?

Helen's betrayal cut the deepest, but all the girls had forsaken her. They'd voted for her to endure the agonizingly long Ganzfeld experiment without so much as an apology. Betty shuddered, remembering being tied down while she heard a wild animal growling, then saw awful visions of Douglas and the pretty new volunteer together, laughing and kissing. She'd thrashed from side to side, trying to dislodge her eye and ear coverings. She didn't discover until the experiment was over that she'd wet herself, leaving her underclothes and the back of her white dress soaked. She bore the humiliation, holding on to Dr. Trimble's arm as he wrinkled his nose and led her to the bathroom.

"Clean yourself up quickly," he'd said, shaking his arm free of her grasp. She prayed he would never tell Douglas how she'd disgraced herself.

The ride back home in Dr. Trimble's car was just awful. None of the girls spoke a single word. The energy filling the car—rage, pain, resentment—pressed in on Betty, making it hard to breathe.

"Betty?" Douglas prompted.

She tried to smile. "You must be hungry, darling, I was just about to start dinner."

His face came close to hers again. He pressed a hand to her forehead and his palm felt so cool and gentle it brought tears to her eyes.

"We had dinner an hour ago. If you're not back to yourself tomorrow, I'll call the doctor. You don't seem to have a fever, but you don't look well."

He stepped away for a moment. When he came back, he tucked a glass of brandy in her hand and she obediently swallowed it, feeling it warm her throat and chest.

"I'm sorry," she said, and began to sob. He encircled her in his arms and she cried harder. She didn't deserve his kindness, not after the way she'd deceived him.

"Whatever for?" he asked. "You haven't done anything wrong. I'm the one who has been acting poorly. But when you were gone, I realized how much I missed you. I could never live without you, Betty."

She couldn't get enough air to reply. Great sobs racked her body. She wept until she finally fell asleep, and when she awoke in the middle of the night, it was to the sound of a woman screaming. It was her.

CHAPTER FIFTY-SEVEN

RILEY, PRESENT DAY

Someone is moving in front of Sam Trimble's house. I lean forward and peer through my windshield.

"What's happening?" Betty asks.

"Sam is getting in the sisters' car and they're driving off. That's going to make this a lot easier. Now we don't have to wait for him to leave."

I take out Betty's wheelchair and help her into it. With the white gauze bandage still on her head, she appears to be the furthest thing from a threat. At least that's what I'm counting on.

"Ready?" I ask, and she nods.

I once read that confidence is the best camouflage. Act like you belong, and people will buy into it. In case any neighbors are watching, I make sure to stride up to Sam's front door with my shoulders back and my steps unhurried. When I twist the handle, I can't believe my luck. It's open.

I glance back at Betty, who's still on the sidewalk in her wheelchair. A wild thought hits me: Maybe this is a trap. The sisters could have recognized my car and known I was coming.

I dismiss the fear; they didn't even glance my way. I step inside, leaving the door a few inches ajar. I need sound to carry into the house in case Sam comes back soon.

The curtains are open, affording me plenty of natural light to look around. Sam's place is a mess. Books are scattered everywhere—on the couch, table, and floors—layered with mail, old newspapers, kicked-off shoes, and a few crumpled bags from fast-food restaurants. A nearly empty bottle of bourbon sits on the coffee table next to a glass holding a watery brown liquid. In the kitchen, dirty dishes clutter the sink and it smells sour.

I step deeper into the house, toward the rooms in the back. The first door I open is a study. It's a disaster. Papers and books in precarious stacks top the desk, crumpled tissues that didn't make it into the trash can litter the floor, and the carpet looks like it hasn't been cleaned in decades.

My heart skips a beat when I glimpse a man out of the corner of my eye. But it's just a large framed portrait on a wall. I step closer, studying the broad-shouldered man with dark, heavy eyebrows wearing a tweed jacket with big brown patches on the elbows. He's unsmiling beneath his beard. It's Betty's tormenter, Silas Trimble. Captured on canvas, he still gives off a malevolent energy.

In the distance, I hear a high, faint cry. Is Betty calling out a warning? I hurry to the kitchen window. Betty is still on the sidewalk alone, looking like a sweet, helpless grandma in her pearls and sweater set.

The sound could have come from a bird. Or maybe it originated from inside the house. There are two doors in the kitchen. One has clear panes of glass on the top half and leads to the backyard. Anxiety ripples through me like a current as I reach for the handle of the second door.

It creaks when I open it, revealing a staircase descending into a dark space.

"Hello?" I call. There's no answer.

I need to see what's down there. But fear is immobilizing me. Who would notice if I disappeared? My family wouldn't think anything of it if they didn't hear from me for a week or so. And no one at all would be alarmed if Betty went missing.

I force myself to take the first step. My legs feel like jelly and my chest is tight. I don't want to see whatever might be down there.

Then I hear Betty yelling.

CHAPTER FIFTY-EIGHT

HELEN, 1964

Dr. Trimble didn't even look up from his typewriter as he told Helen that she could stay in the dorms through the end of the semester. After that, he said, she was on her own.

"Get a ring on your finger," he suggested. "Campus is full of eligible bachelors."

His fingers resumed clacking his typewriter's keys. She stood there for an embarrassingly long moment until she realized she'd been dismissed.

She walked outside and stood in front of the psych building, blinking in the sharp morning sunlight. Three girls with their arms linked walked by, singing the Chiffons' hit "He's So Fine." A boy carrying a girl's books kept up an animated conversation while she smiled serenely. Another group of boys tossed around a football on the lawn across from the building.

"Are you alright?"

Helen blinked at the girl who'd materialized in front of her. She was well put-together, with a glossy dark bob and green eyeshadow beneath her thin dark brows. She'd been one of the singers; her two friends were waiting farther up on the sidewalk, watching.

"You must be frozen. Did you forget your coat?"

Helen looked down at her arms, bare in her short-sleeved dress.

"Oh, yes," she said, trying to smile.

The girl frowned. "Well, hurry and get inside where it's warm!" She skipped away in her saddle shoes to catch up with the other girls, linking arms with them again.

How many times had Helen walked the exact same way with her friends? Her throat constricted with sobs, but she couldn't shed a single tear.

If anyone could help, she finally thought, it would be Kathleen. Helen walked the familiar path to Kathleen's house, propelled by a spark of energy.

The curtains were still drawn and the house appeared oddly still. Helen stepped over a pair of dirt-caked men's sneakers on the doorstop and rang the bell. There were no onrushing footsteps, no call from Kathleen that she was coming.

She rang the bell again, holding her finger against it for a long moment.

The sound that came from inside made her rear backward. It was a guttural moan that didn't sound human.

"Kathleen?" she called, banging on the door. "Are you okay?"

"Go away!" she heard Kathleen scream.

Helen flinched as if she'd been slapped. Kathleen was finished with her. They all were.

She turned and started to walk. After a while, she became aware there was something wrong with her shoes. One of her kitten heels had broken off, causing her to lurch with every step. Helen took off the other shoe and continued in her stockinged feet.

When cars honked at her, she veered out of the street. A person in a doorway called out to her but she kept her head low and continued to walk.

When she looked up again, the sky was streaked with scarlet and the beautiful bridge that had so captivated her when she first arrived in town was right in front of her. When Dr. Trimble had driven her over it, she'd imagined it was the entrance to a magical new life—and for a while, it was.

There was a narrow pathway between the car lanes and guardrail, just wide enough for a slim girl to traverse. Her legs wobbled and nearly gave out when she was halfway over the bridge, so she decided to stop and rest.

Helen waited until the road was clear of cars, then climbed over the guardrail and perched on a steel beam, dangling her legs. She'd never been up so high; the boats below looked like toys. But she couldn't wring any joy from the moment. Everything in her ached, down to her soul.

Cars continued to pass by, but no one could see her behind the thick gray beam. She was invisible again.

She'd been trying so desperately to hold on to her new life. But after a while, it seemed easier to simply let go and float through the air.

CHAPTER FIFTY-NINE

RILEY, PRESENT DAY

I run to the living room window and see Sam Trimble standing beside Betty as the sisters' car pulls away from the curb. Betty's talking, fluttering her hands through the air as if describing something. Whatever Sam did with the sisters certainly didn't take long.

I ease the front door shut, sealing myself in silence.

Betty is doing her part; she alerted me to Sam's presence by yelling out "Hello!" when he approached, and now she's stalling him. All I need to do is slip out the back door off the kitchen.

But when I twist the handle and pull, it doesn't budge. The deadbolt is engaged, and there's no key in it. I sweep my fingertips over the top of the frame, but they only touch dust. I move aside stacks of mail and look beneath dishes. It isn't anywhere.

I don't have much time. Betty was going to ask Sam for directions to a street just around the corner, pretending she's visiting a friend.

I'm taking my first step out of the kitchen to find a window to climb through when I hear the front door open. I stop moving and hold my breath.

"Thank you again!" I hear Betty call.

"My pleasure," Sam replies, his voice much closer to me than hers.

I duck back into the kitchen. There's nowhere for me to hide except the basement.

I can't risk flicking on a light, so I use my phone's flashlight as I ease down the wooden stairs, wincing as the second one creaks. The air feels thin and drafty. It's much colder down here beneath the house.

The basement is unfinished, with exposed pipes and a cement floor. But the long, rectangular space isn't empty.

Bookshelves are stuffed with volumes, and boxes are everywhere. I move closer to a bookshelf and read the titles: They're old parapsychology journals from Marquis and other universities. Next to the bins is an ancient armchair, covered in dust. The cushions are dented from the weight of someone who must have rested in it long ago.

Voices erupt just over my head. I duck down, then realize Sam has blasted the television.

I move toward an antique-looking desk that holds strange objects beneath a clear plastic dome: a notepad filled with tight, blocky letters, the ink faded to gray. A deck of cards. And a strange pair of goggles made out of halves of Ping-Pong balls.

A framed photo on one corner of the desk draws my eye. It's of four young women lying on a row of cots in a shadowy space. They look asleep—or unconscious. Written on the bottom of the photograph in the same faded gray handwriting is *Girls 1–4*.

If I hadn't seen her wedding picture, I might not have recognized her at that age. Betty is on one of the cots.

This entire basement is an homage to Dr. Trimble's experiments. It's more than creepy. It's next-level obsession.

Goosebumps prickle my skin. This environment seems steeped in an aura of evil.

I look around for an exit. There's one high window, but even if it were big enough for me to squeeze through, I can't. It's covered by security bars and a spider has woven its gauzy web through them.

My chest constricts. I need to get out of here.

I do the only thing I can think of: I pull out my phone and call the one person I know who lives relatively nearby—Sandra. I get her voicemail so I leave a quick, desperate message, asking her to pick up

Betty and come up with an excuse to get Sam out of the house so I can escape.

I feel weak, but there's no way I'm going to sit down in what I'm sure is Dr. Trimble's old chair.

Instead, I kneel on the floor, hiding behind a stack of boxes, and I wait.

CHAPTER SIXTY

IVY, 1964

The new issue of *Ladies' Home Journal* had an important cover headline: "10 Secrets to a Happy Marriage."

This was exactly what Ivy needed. She opened the magazine and read the first rule. *Keep dinner hot and your voice soft.*

"This isn't a library, hon," said the man behind the cash register.

"Forgive me!" She lay the magazine on the counter next to the box of Shake 'n Bake and the russet potatoes she planned to make for dinner.

"It's a lovely day, isn't it?" Ivy commented.

The man in the blue smock stopped ringing up her glass bottles of Coca-Cola and gave her a strange look.

Ivy glanced through the clear panes of the door. Rain was coming down. Had it been raining all morning? She didn't think so; on her way to the grocery, she'd stopped by Betty's house to drop off the gift she'd secretly worked on, but no one had answered the door, so she'd left it on the stoop. Surely the sky had been clear then!

"I mean, it will be a nice day, once this weather settles." Ivy tried for a laugh, but the man merely grunted and handed her the paper sack. She paid with a ten-dollar bill and tried to tuck the change in her coin purse but she couldn't find it, so she dumped it in her purse and went out to her car.

Groceries in the trunk, the key twisted in the ignition . . . what had she forgotten? She turned on the windshield wipers. There, now she was all set. She pressed the gas pedal and the car bucked forward, smashing into the side of the building. The impact snapped her head forward into the steering wheel and rattled her teeth. She sat there, stunned, until a knock on her window roused her.

Ivy stepped out of the car, holding onto the frame. A high, tinny noise filled her head.

"Are you crazy?" It was the checkout man in the blue smock.

"I'm so sorry . . . there must be something wrong with the car."

"I'm going to call your husband. You're not fit to drive!"

"No, it's just slippery out, you see," Ivy tried to explain. "The tires skidded."

Another woman in a blue smock exited the store, stopped short, and stared.

"I'll pay for repairs and everything will be as good as new, I promise!" Ivy called to her.

"Did you take too many mother's helpers this morning?" the male clerk asked.

The female employee spun around and hurried back into the store.

"I don't take pills," Ivy cried. "I swear it. I'm just feeling a little scattered today."

She held a hand to her ear, trying to stop the high, whining noise.

"You're getting soaked! Come here, under the awning. And give me your keys."

No matter how much she protested, the man wouldn't let her leave. Then a police car pulled into the lot and the officer stepped out, walking directly toward Ivy. She began to tremble and sank down onto the sidewalk.

The police officer squatted next to her, holding out a paper towel. "You've cut yourself."

Belatedly, she became aware of wetness on her face. She dabbed the white square to her forehead and it came away with a few dots of bright red blood. Nausea filled her gut and her stomach heaved, but nothing came up.

The officer stepped away and then there was blessed silence.

She wasn't sure how much time had passed, but after a little while, David appeared in his athletic jacket with the Marquis Lions logo, holding a black umbrella. Someone must have called him, maybe the police officer. Relief poured through her—David would fix this; he was a man so they'd listen to him!—until she saw the thunderous look on her husband's face. He didn't speak a single word to her.

"I thought she might be filling her purse," said the man in the blue smock. "She was wandering through the aisles for at least thirty minutes."

This, Ivy could refute.

She opened her purse and let the contents spill to the ground, coins tumbling across the pavement. "See? There's nothing here but my belongings."

David opened the car door and peered inside. "Where's the baby?"

"The baby?" Ivy wished they'd stop asking her questions so she could think. "She's sleeping at home. I just ran out for a minute."

"At least thirty minutes," the store clerk repeated.

Next an ambulance pulled up in front of the store, its siren wailing. Two men stepped out.

"No, no," Ivy cried. "Please don't take me to the hospital. I need to go home!" She remembered the magazine's rule and softened her voice. "I'll keep dinner hot for you, David."

"Look at yourself!" he snapped. She became aware of how she must have appeared—splayed on the wet sidewalk, her hair damp and scraggly, a thin trickle of blood running down her forehead.

The men grasped Ivy's arms and hoisted her up and led her to the back of the ambulance. By now a small crowd of housewives had gathered, whispering as they watched.

"The coconut cake!" Ivy yelled to David, trying to wrench free of the men's grasp. "I promised I'd make it for dessert!"

The men pushed her into the ambulance and closed the back doors. Ivy stared out the small back window. David was watching, his arms folded. Their eyes met. *Please*, she mouthed, putting her palm to the glass.

He turned his back on her.

CHAPTER SIXTY-ONE

RILEY, PRESENT DAY

I'm on my way. Sandra's reply lands on my phone five minutes later, just as heavy footsteps thud on the floor above me. The clatter of dishes tells me Sam is in the kitchen. I moved things around in my search for the key, but surely he won't notice in that mess. I can't stop the horrifying thought: Unless he already knows I'm here and he's toying with me.

I'm still crouched down behind a stack of boxes, my thighs straining, trying to find a connection for all the strange threads I've encountered: Alex's disappearance, the apparent resurrection of the Ganzfeld experiments, the theft of Alex's student ID, her affair with her professor Josh Woods, and the break-in at Betty's house. I have edges of the puzzle, but not the inner connecting piece.

Maybe I've got it all wrong; the sisters could just be friendly acquaintances of Sam's. Josh could be behind everything—and perhaps his wife, Elizabeth, is an accomplice. I reassure myself that at least the police must be looking at him carefully.

Suddenly the television cuts off and I hear Sandra's voice. Relief weakens my body; she got here so quickly it feels like a miracle.

"I know it's out of the blue, but I've been thinking about it, and I've decided I can share a few pages of my mother's diary with you," she says. "But just a few pages for now."

"Amazing! Where is it?" Sam replies, so loudly it's as if he's next to me.

"In my car."

I hear the front door close and I stand up, wincing, and hurry to the stairs. I climb them as quietly as I can, skipping over the creaky second step, and open the door to the kitchen.

It's now or never. I walk into the living room and peer out the window. Sandra is leading Sam down the sidewalk. If he's wondering why she didn't park in front of the house, his body language doesn't show it. He's hurrying, seemingly eager to get his hands on another piece of his grandfather's dark legacy.

I reach for the front door and open it, then slip across the porch and run in the opposite direction, praying Sam doesn't look back.

When I turn the corner, I see Betty waiting, her face creased with worry.

"What happened?" she cries.

Another fifteen minutes later, we're in Sandra's sedan as she drives out of Sam's neighborhood.

"What were you looking for in his house?" she asks.

I start to tell her about Alex's disappearance, but she interrupts. "I think I heard about it on social media. She's the girl who lives in a sorority house, right?"

I nod. "Anyway, for one crazy minute I thought she might be there."

"Why would Sam take Alex?"

Betty and I explain everything to her, our words tumbling out as we each share pieces of the story. Sandra is silent. She's a good listener—either by nature or by training.

Finally, she says, "I'm glad you called me for help." She reaches for Betty's hand. "If things had been different—if my mother had lived—you'd be like my aunt."

"I feel that way, too," Betty replies.

"What happened to the four of you . . . my mother wrote about the experiments in her diary. If someone is doing that to young women again . . ." She shudders. "Should we call the police and tell them we think Sam is involved in Alex's disappearance?"

"We don't have any proof," I say. "It could be someone else. Josh, or even his wife. She seemed to have it in for Alex. She thought Alex made up the affair, but I believe it happened."

Sandra nods. "So what's next?"

Betty speaks up. "If it isn't too much of an imposition, could we go to your house? My head is aching. I wouldn't mind resting for a bit. And then we can talk more."

"Of course." Sandra makes a left, turning onto a main artery. "We can circle back for your car later."

"But don't you have a busy day?" I ask, remembering her back-to-back appointments.

"Not anymore. I canceled everything when I got your message."

We pull up to Sandra's house a few minutes later. Since Sandra doesn't have a ramp, we lift Betty into our arms and carry her inside together. Once she's settled on the living room couch I go back out for her chair. Sandra disappears into the kitchen, returning with glasses of lemonade and a plate of banana bread.

Betty takes a bite. "Oh, this is delicious! What is it?"

"You've never had banana bread?" Sandra asks, feeding a bite to Hank, who wags his tail in glee.

"There are so many things I've never tried." Betty says it without a hint of self-pity. I notice her gaping at the flat-screen TV and modern sculpture atop a marble stand.

"What is this?" She points to an object that's positioned on the big wooden bookshelf to face the front door.

"It's a Ring camera," Sandra explains. "Since I live alone and Hank would make best friends with an intruder, it provides a layer of security. I get notified if someone is coming in through the front door. I can even see through the camera if I'm not home."

"How marvelous!" Betty cries as Sandra shows her the app on her cell phone. "Look, there we are coming in a moment ago, just like you said!"

"Technology is a mixed blessing," Sandra replies. "But at least with cameras everywhere, the police must have leads about Alex."

"I hope so." I take a sip of my lemonade. It's tart and sweet, just how I like it.

"Tell me more about yourself," Betty prompts Sandra. "Do you have children?"

Sandra shakes her head. "I've never married. I guess it just wasn't in the cards for me." Sorrow crosses her face.

"But you're seeing someone special," I say.

She cocks her head to the side. "I am?"

"The carpenter," I prompt.

"Oh, *him.*" Sandra shakes her head. "Turns out he's married. He said he and his wife are having a trial separation, but there's no way I'm getting in the middle of that mess."

She sounds so resolute. Sandra isn't willing to settle; she's honoring her instincts. Once again, I feel like there's so much I can learn from her.

"You've had a rough few days," Sandra says. "Why don't you two rest a bit? I have some emails to take care of. Then we'll figure out what to do next."

I exhale and lean back, feeling some of the tension melting from my limbs. Whatever is happening—and whatever is going to happen—at least there are three of us now.

CHAPTER SIXTY-TWO

KATHLEEN, 1964

Kathleen was dreaming about a watermelon hitting the floor and exploding. That dull, wet thump echoed in her brain.

When she finally opened her eyes, she screamed. Ronald lay crumpled on the floor next to the couch.

"No!" she yelled, dropping to her knees beside him. What had happened? The baseball bat he must have been carrying home from practice lay next to his head.

Someone had hit him with it.

Ronald's sweet brown eyes were still open, but glassy now. Blood was on his face. On the rug. On her hands.

"No, no, no, no," she wailed. This couldn't be happening; it must still be a dream.

What had she done? She remembered a man's hands reaching for her in the night; she'd fought back. She must have grabbed the bat. She'd wanted to kill—but she'd meant to kill Mac.

She opened her mouth and a horrible sound filled the room.

His family would hate her. Everyone would hate her. She couldn't call anyone, not her friends, not her mother, certainly not the police. They'd put her in jail, then they'd put a needle in her arm.

She became aware of someone pounding on the door.

"Go away!" she roared. She gathered Ronald in her arms and rocked back and forth, her tears falling on his face.

"Come back to me," she begged.

When he didn't, she lay him down gently. Then she walked into the bathroom and grabbed Ronald's razor and held it to her wrist.

She still didn't understand what had happened, or how she could've done this. But she knew one thing: She could no longer live without him. Or with herself.

CHAPTER SIXTY-THREE

RILEY, PRESENT DAY

Betty is asleep on the couch, her features slack, her head tilted back on a cushion. Sandra headed upstairs to her small office a little while ago, trailed by Hank. As tired as I am, I can't rest.

I scroll through my phone and see Alex's disappearance has made national news. "Police reportedly have no solid leads in the case," a reporter says in a reel shared to Instagram as she stands in front of the sorority house. "Alex Finch was last seen buying an energy drink at the CVS on Kinwood Street, then getting into her car and heading back toward this Tri Delt sorority house on Marquis's campus. She disappeared somewhere along the way."

I've seen enough true crime shows to know the stats for abductions. With every passing hour, survival becomes less likely.

I stare at Alex's photo on the screen, remembering how she'd stood in front of Josh's house, demanding to be seen. The world can swallow up young women; it happens all too often. It claimed Betty's friends, too.

My body is too jittery to remain still, so I stand up and walk over to the bookshelf, looking at the titles. Sandra and I have overlapping tastes—she also likes mysteries, nonfiction, and self-help books. For a moment I wonder how it would feel to live in this big, beautiful home surrounded by trees. Lonely, I decide. But Sandra had loneliness as a companion all during her early life; she must have made peace with isolation.

I squat down to look at the knickknacks on the lowest shelf. They're whimsical pieces of art—a pink polka-dotted snake coiling up into a reverse funnel, a calico cat unspooling a ball of yarn, and a yellow ceramic dog lifting his leg against a mini fire hydrant.

My thighs are straining again so I reach out to hold onto the smooth, sturdy wood composing the side of the bookshelf, preparing to hoist myself up. And then I see something that makes no sense at all—a small brass plaque affixed to an inside shelf.

I'm frozen for a long moment. When I finally rise, I'm looking directly into the Ring camera. The one Sandra could be watching from upstairs right now.

I'm being paranoid again, I tell myself—just like when I imagined the sisters had set a trap for me, and that Sam knew I was in his basement. Sandra is a busy professional; she's answering emails, not monitoring Betty and me.

I turn around and walk back to the couch, easing down next to Betty. *I must've gotten something wrong*, I think. The brass plaque doesn't mean anything—if I even did see it. I'm so tired I don't trust my own eyes. There could be so many simple explanations.

Betty fidgets in her sleep. "Please don't," she breathes.

I pat her arm, whispering, "You're safe." I know she must be in the throes of a nightmare. But it feels as if she's speaking directly to me, telling me once again to stop talking myself out of what my primal brain suspects. Even if it makes no sense.

The hair rises on my arms as I stand up and walk to the bookshelf again.

I bend down and this time I look more closely, forcing myself to see it clearly. Before I couldn't glimpse the words on a small metal plate on the inside wall of the lowest cubby; I only knew the object shouldn't be there. Now I see the logo clearly.

The bookshelf isn't custom-made. The name of the furniture store Ethan Allen is branded onto the plate.

I straighten up again, this time swiveling so I don't face the camera. I hurry to Betty's side. I'm reaching for her shoulder to rouse her when Sandra's voice comes from behind me.

"Did you two have a nice rest?"

CHAPTER SIXTY-FOUR

"'Children at the Brandon Indian Residential School were test subjects of extrasensory perception experiments during the Second World War,' states a science journal recovered from a university archive . . . Among those discoveries were that milk rations were halved for years at schools across the country, and essential vitamins were withheld. At the Cecilia Jeffrey School in Kenora, students were subject to test trials of TB vaccines as well as a series of experimental antibiotics for ear infections: 'Some students subsequently lost their hearing, according to one news report,' Mosby said."

—Source: an article in *The Brandon Sun* [Brandon, Manitoba], by Alexandra Paul, published January 12, 2015

BETTY, 1964

The front door swung open that afternoon as Betty was arranging magazines in a fan on the coffee table. She'd been working on it awhile; she couldn't seem to get the edges perfectly straight.

Douglas stood there, holding his briefcase and a small wrapped present, his face white.

"You're home early!" Betty cried. And he'd brought her a present, which was so sweet.

He looked around the living room as if he'd never seen it. Then he began pulling his favorite books off the shelves, piling them in stacks on the floor.

"We need to leave. Get your things quickly."

"Leave?" Betty echoed.

"Betty." He crossed the room and grasped her shoulders. "Things have happened . . . we're not safe. *You're* not safe."

"But I—"

"That's enough!" Douglas had never before used such a harsh tone with her, but she knew some husbands did. She had no choice but to obey him.

"What should I pack?" she asked.

"Anything important."

She hurried to the bedroom and took down her suitcase and filled it with clothes and toiletries again. She was wearing her pearls and wedding and engagement rings, her only valuable pieces.

She brought her bag to the living room, where Douglas was stuffing his books into her grocery shopping cart.

"We're not safe?" she echoed his words.

He lifted his head and opened his mouth to answer. A knock on the door interrupted whatever he'd been about to say.

He lifted his finger to his lips, shaking his head.

"Douglas?" Dr. Trimble's voice called from outside.

Betty stared at Douglas as he crept closer to her, whispering into her ear, "Don't utter a word."

Douglas couldn't defy his boss. Unless . . . could this be a new experiment?

Dr. Trimble knocked again, louder. "Douglas, I need to speak with you. If you're in there, it's imperative you come with me. President Sherman has called me in for an emergency meeting."

There was silence for a few moments, then Douglas walked quietly to the door and peered out the peephole.

"He's gone. We don't have much time."

Douglas began carrying their things to the car, filling the trunk and back seat. He grabbed armfuls of clothes and shoes and their coats out of the closet and packed those in, too. The last thing he took was a box containing their checkbook and other important documents.

"When will we be coming home again?" Betty asked.

Douglas looked around the living room, then lifted up Betty's bag and took her arm.

"Never," he said, leading her to the Impala.

He drove too quickly, steering the car onto the highway, his expression grim.

"I don't understand," Betty finally said. "I need to say goodbye to my friends."

Douglas shook his head. "They're all gone."

Betty swallowed hard. "They left, too? But David's coaching job . . . and Ronald is in law school. Are we meeting them somewhere?"

"Oh, Betty." At the unexpected sorrow filling his voice, she fell silent.

When they reached the highway, they passed a police car racing in the opposite direction, its siren wailing.

Douglas swore under his breath and tapped his brakes; he'd been speeding. But the policeman tore by, heading toward campus. As soon as it passed, Douglas pressed the gas pedal harder, until their surroundings blurred. He was in a state. Perhaps he was ill? Douglas had never been prone to anxiety, but right now, she could see it in every line of his body. Betty looked around for something to distract him.

"Is this for me?" Betty asked, reaching for the gift wrapped in light blue paper. It was small and soft, perhaps a new nightgown for their surprise trip. Douglas must have been joking about leaving for good; their record console and Sears dining set and wedding china were all in the house. Surely they'd come back.

"May I open it?" Betty asked, trying to inject a playful tone in her voice. Did he nod ever so slightly? She couldn't be sure. But she slid her fingernail beneath the tape on one end and pulled out the gift.

"I—I don't understand."

It was a knitted yellow blanket, a bit smaller than the one Ivy had made for baby Sandra, with a ribbon of blue in one corner.

"Why did you give me this?" she asked.

Douglas shook his head. "It's not from me. I found it on the front stoop."

"No!" Betty yelled, putting a hand to her stomach. "Douglas, we must go back. Something terrible is going to happen."

"Something terrible did happen, my darling," he told her. "It's too late."

He sped faster. She grabbed the sides of her seat and held on tightly. "You're frightening me. Please slow down."

Douglas turned to look at her. "Don't you see? I have to protect you."

A traffic light was a few dozen yards ahead; it was the same intersection she'd seen in her dream with a ruined baby blanket in the road.

The light flicked to yellow. Douglas didn't slow down.

Out of the corner of her eye, she could see a truck barreling toward the intersection.

She'd misinterpreted one detail of the dream. The ruined blanket wasn't to symbolize the loss of Ivy's baby. It was for hers.

"Stop, Douglas!" she cried.

But Douglas was right about one thing. It was too late.

The vehicles sounded like wild animals fighting as they mangled together. Betty's vision blurred briefly, then darkness closed in, muffling her last sliver of awareness.

CHAPTER SIXTY-FIVE

RILEY, PRESENT DAY

I straighten up at the sound of Sandra's voice, trying to smooth the fear from my expression before I turn around.

When I do, I don't just look at Sandra. I finally face all the warnings I've dismissed.

I've got back-to-back appointments all day, Sandra had said. Yet five minutes after my text, she'd been en route to Sam's house. It was no miracle she'd arrived so quickly; she must have been nearby. Maybe even following us in her dark sedan. A chill runs through me as I realize her car could have been the same one I saw roar by Betty's house after I got home from my first trip to Marquis.

There's also the Ring camera *inside* her house—not on the front door, where they're typically placed. Could Sandra have positioned it to monitor anyone trying to get *out*?

There's a man I've been seeing . . . He's a carpenter and I met him when I hired him to build this bookshelf. Why had Sandra lied? Unless it was to get me out of her house quickly because she was hiding something—or someone—here. The staccato chimes that sounded on her phone when she claimed to be getting a text from the carpenter didn't sound like a typical text alert. Maybe it was a different kind of alert.

Betty stirs on the couch.

"We had good naps," I say belatedly. "But there are a couple of medications for Betty we need to pick up today. I just remembered."

I pray Betty doesn't question this.

"Of course," Sandra says. "Do you need to go to CVS? There's one nearby. We can also get your car while we're out."

I can't help it; I flinch at the mention of CVS. The drugstore chain Alex visited just before disappearing. Could it even be the same store?

"That sounds great," I say.

As I look into Sandra's warm eyes, doubt begins to smother some of my questions. Sandra adopted an old rescue dog; she volunteers with the houseless population. How could someone who has devoted her life to helping others be involved in anything criminal?

Plus there's the puzzle piece that still doesn't fit. Sandra would have no way of knowing Alex. How could their worlds have intersected?

"I just have one more client to finish up with," Sandra says. "Give me a moment and we'll go."

I watch her head upstairs again, thinking, *If she canceled everything today, why would she have one more client to finish up with?*

Probably Sandra just meant she needed to send an email or reschedule. Another point I shouldn't discount: Sandra saved us from Sam's house—she didn't lure us here. Betty was the one who asked to come to the house to rest. Plus, a couple of hours ago I thought the sisters might have been the ones following me. Lots of people drive dark sedans; it doesn't mean anything.

I drop my head into my hands, feeling like competing voices are vying for my attention.

Please don't. I hear the echo of Betty's plea.

She's right; I'm doing it again. I force myself to let my thoughts unspool without censorship.

Something about the words Sandra just uttered—before my mind chattered over them—is tugging at me. I breathe in deeply and close my eyes, letting the echo of her voice float back to the forefront of my consciousness.

Sandra just said she has one more client to finish up with. An electric charge runs through my body; her words feel like they're overlaying vital information.

Sandra is a therapist who specializes in loss. I read this on her website.

I suck in a breath as the realization slams into me: Alex, who experienced deep loss when her best friend died in high school, is seeing a therapist twice a week.

Could Alex be Sandra's patient?

Betty is staring at me. "What's wrong?" she asks.

"We've got to leave."

Unlike me, Betty doesn't stall with doubts and questions. I push her wheelchair against the couch and help her into it.

I push her to the front door and twist the handle and pull. Nothing happens. I look up to see a thick deadbolt. It's disengaged, but the door still refuses to open. There must be another, invisible layer of security.

I fumble in my purse for my phone. I dial 911 but the call doesn't connect. I push the green phone icon at the bottom of the screen again, my stomach clenching. The call won't go through.

"You seemed different after your nap, like something spooked you." Sandra's voice comes from the top of the stairs. "So I tested you. You failed."

CHAPTER SIXTY-SIX

"During the Cold War the CIA started researching ways they could turn Americans into CIA-controlled 'superagents.' Under what was known as the MK-ULTRA project, CIA researchers experimented on unsuspecting American (and Canadian) citizens by slipping them psychedelic drugs, including LSD, PCP, and barbiturates, as well as additional—and additionally illegal—methods such as hypnosis, and, possibly, chemical, biological, and radiological agents. Universities participated, mostly as a delivery system, without their knowledge. The US Department of Veterans Affairs estimates seven thousand soldiers were also involved in research, without their consent. The project endured for more than twenty years, during which the agency spent about $20 million."

—Source: Science.HowStuffWorks.com, "10 Outrageous Experiments Conducted on Humans," by Maria Trimarchi, published February 27, 2024

BETTY, 1964

Betty put her index finger into the little hole on the rotary phone that corresponded to the last digit of Kathleen's phone number. She spun the clear plastic dial counterclockwise before taking out her finger to allow the dial to twirl back into place.

"The number you have reached is no longer in service," a recorded voice said in her ear.

Where had her friends gone?

"All done, hon?" asked the nurse named Peggy, who had a blond bouffant and wore light blue eyeshadow.

Betty nodded and hung up the receiver on the desk phone at the nursing station.

"Let's get you back into your room," Peggy said. "Today's a big day. I'm sure you're glad to be going home to that handsome husband of yours."

Betty tried to inject enthusiasm into her voice. "Yes, I am."

Peggy squeezed Betty's shoulder. "As I live and breathe, I've never seen a man as devoted as yours."

"I'm lucky to have Douglas," Betty replied.

In the month Betty had spent at the hospital, so much about her had transformed. She'd come in by ambulance, unconscious and badly injured. Luckily Douglas was only bruised; the truck had rammed into her side of the car.

Once doctors triaged her most serious injuries—her spinal cord injury that resulted in paralysis below the waist and the loss of her baby—she slept so much they ran tests to make sure she had no underlying illness.

"Here we are." Peggy pushed Betty across the threshold of her room.

Douglas stood there, wearing his usual white button-down, dark slacks, and skinny tie. His face filled with relief upon seeing her.

"Where'd you go?" he asked, hurrying to her side. "I was so worried."

"Just down the hall, darling," Betty soothed him. "I'm sorry I wasn't here when you arrived."

Douglas was not the same man she'd been married to at Marquis. His changes were even more dramatic than hers. He'd grown obsessed with Betty's safety; sometimes when she woke up from a nap, she found him standing over her, his hand resting on her chest, staring at her.

"What are you doing?" she'd whispered once.

"Making sure you're breathing," he'd said. It was such a loving gesture, she told herself, even as the fine hairs on her arms stood up.

Every night before Douglas returned to the new home he'd bought for them with money from his trust fund, he checked to make sure the window in her hospital room was securely locked. Betty was never quite sure if he wanted to keep intruders out or make sure she was sealed inside. If he'd been allowed, Betty felt sure he would've remained in the chair next to her bed overnight, watching her.

"You had two narrow escapes," Douglas said once. "I can't risk a third."

It was ungrateful, but Betty couldn't help feeling relief when night fell and she was alone. As she lay in the darkness, she thought about her friends constantly, trying to summon a spark of their old connection. But it felt irrevocably severed. She tried to block out her memories of Dr. Trimble, but she often dreamt about him, waking up panting and sweating from nightmares, the machine beside her beeping wildly.

"Why don't I help you to your car?" Peggy offered now. "There's no reason for you to stay here a minute longer."

"Our home is all ready for you." Douglas leaned down to kiss Betty's cheek. "The kitchen was finished last night. I had to pay the workers overtime to get it done, but I think you'll like it."

As Douglas picked up her bag with her nightgown and toiletries, Peggy whispered, "I know you've had a rough go of it, and not being able to walk is an enormous challenge. But always remember to be grateful for what you still have."

In the hallway, Douglas pressed the button for the elevator, looking all around, as if he was expecting to see someone he knew.

"Betty may feel especially tired tonight," Peggy told Douglas. "She should just rest at home for the next week, before you start going back out to dinner or to run errands."

Douglas nodded. "That's all we want, to be home together. Right, darling?"

CHAPTER SIXTY-SEVEN

RILEY, PRESENT DAY

I expect to see Sandra holding a weapon. But what's actually in her hand is almost worse: Alex's student ID. "Alex is your patient," I blurt, partly so Betty can make the connection.

"She is," Sandra confirms.

At least she's using the present tense. "Where is she?" I ask.

"Alex is safe for now." Sandra crooks her index finger. "Come back to the living room."

As Betty and I slowly return to the couch, Betty tilts her head toward the door. I know what she's telling me: If I get the chance to escape, I should take it.

As we cross the threshold to the living room, my vision blurs briefly and I stagger before regaining my balance.

"It's kicking in," Sandra says. "Good timing."

I look at my empty glass of lemonade. "What did you put in my drink?"

"Nothing dangerous. Just a sedative to keep you calm."

As soon as Betty is on the couch, I collapse next to her. My limbs feel strange—heavy and uncoordinated.

Sandra reaches for my purse, which is on the floor by my feet, and puts it on her lap. Then she takes a napkin off the coffee table and wipes down Alex's student ID before extending it to me, still using the napkin to prevent her fingertips from touching it. "Can you hold this for a second?"

My mind feels as sluggish as my body, but I understand why Sandra wants my fingerprints on the plastic: to pin Alex's disappearance on me. And a half dozen witnesses from the sorority house can place me with Alex shortly before she disappeared.

I shake my head. "No."

That's when I see it, the transformation I've heard survivors describe in interviews. Some say it's like their assailant removed a mask, revealing soulless eyes. Other describe watching the person they thought they knew morph into a complete stranger as the energy shifted in the room, turning dark and intense.

It's happening now with Sandra. Her seemingly natural warmth and kindness have evaporated. She looks emotionless, which feels even more terrifying than rage. She locks eyes with me until I take the ID.

Sandra plucks the ID from my hand, still using the napkin, and drops it into my purse. "Now put your cell phone on the coffee table."

I do as she says. "It doesn't work here anyway."

"My house is in a dead zone," Sandra tells me as she scoops up my phone with the same napkin and puts it in my bag. "That's one reason I bought it—that and the isolation. I have a booster for when I need Wi-Fi."

"Oh, Sandra." Betty's voice is so soft. "Why are you doing this?"

Sandra's head whips toward Betty. "Do you have any idea what my life has been like?"

"I knew your father," Betty says. "So I can imagine."

"I doubt you can. His second wife made him seem like a teddy bear. She wasn't abusive to her own kids—just to me. Which made them turn on me, too. It was a pleasurable game for them."

"I'm so sorry that happened to you." Betty leans forward. "Sandra, your mother loved you so much."

"Don't lie to me!" I flinch at Sandra's roar.

Sandra clears her throat and composes herself. "The only thing that got me through my childhood was imagining I had a mother who'd rescue me someday. When she died—which my father told me as casually as if he were commenting that it was cloudy outside—it still helped to think that at least one person in the world had loved me. Because of that, I was able to resist my . . . impulses. You see, when you endure as much pain and cruelty in life as I have, the temptation to release some of it back onto others is almost irresistible. Then I read my mother's own words and leaned she didn't love me. She wished I'd go away!"

"But she was sick!" The words burst out of me. "Sandra, you said so yourself—your mom must've had postpartum depression and never got proper care."

"Do you know one of my biggest challenges as a therapist?" Sandra says. "Helping clients understand that hurtful things aren't always personal. They're more a reflection of the other person than they are of you. Now I realize it doesn't really matter. Even if my mother couldn't help it, does that make what I had to bear any easier?"

Sandra sweeps her palms across one another, like she's brushing off our conversation. "Betty, I need to secure you in another room, but I promise you'll be comfortable there. I'm going to take Riley outside."

"I'm not going anywhere," I push back.

Sandra reaches down and lifts up the leg of her jeans and pulls a small gun out of an ankle holster. "This is hunting country. An occasional gunshot isn't uncommon—if anyone heard it way out here."

Even if I had the strength to fight, I'd have no chance. I stand up, feeling as if I'm moving underwater. If I get outside, maybe I'll have an opportunity to escape—or maybe Betty can find a way to get free while we're gone.

"Sandra, I loved you from the moment I first saw you," Betty says softly.

My eyes widen. I can hear the sincerity ringing through her voice.

"Oh, that headful of dark curls. And your little dimples. You were the dearest thing."

Sandra shakes her head. "Stop it." But pain raises a jagged edge on the steel in her voice.

"If I'd known what happened to Ivy, I would have tried to adopt you, Sandra," Betty says. "I would have loved nothing more."

"Well, that's too bad for both of us." Sandra's moment of vulnerability has passed. "Come on."

"I know what you're doing, honey," Betty says, so calmly I can't believe it. "After you read your mother's diaries you decided to replicate Dr. Trimble's experiments. That's why you stole Alex's ID, to get the papers. But why did you need to take Alex?"

Sandra ignores her question, gesturing with her gun. "Go through the kitchen."

Betty is wheeling herself much more slowly than usual. Is she stalling, trying to find a way to connect with Sandra, or is she weakening? "I'd really like to understand why you're starting up the old experiments," Betty says.

"Dr. Trimble was on to something." Sandra falls into step just behind me and Betty. I swear I can feel the gun aimed between my shoulder blades. "Marquis did a good job of covering everything up after everyone died. Back in the sixties, it was a lot easier to erase ugly parts of history. But when I started digging, I discovered Trimble's experiments were more than scientifically sound—they were revolutionary."

"But what are you planning to do?" Betty asks, no judgment in her tone. She's paused now, catching her breath. Either her fall and the shock of discovering what Sandra turned into have drained her of strength, or she's doing an excellent job of pretending to be infirm to keep Sandra talking.

"Once I've got a final set of subjects, the right people will be very interested. Our government, probably. Other governments, definitely. It won't be the first time they've spent big money trying to harness these abilities."

"Oh, Sandra. You still want to be seen, don't you? To be important to someone," Betty says.

"Don't try to analyze me." Betty gives a little cry and I realize Sandra has jabbed the barrel of the gun into the soft flesh of Betty's back. My hands clench into fists; anyone who can hurt a helpless old woman is beyond savage.

"I'm incapable of forming a relationship," Sandra says. "Every man I thought I loved left me. I have no children. Those experiments destroyed any chance I might've had at happiness. Don't I deserve to get something out of them?"

Past the kitchen is a small, dark room with a single bed. When Sandra flicks on the overhead light, I see handcuffs are attached to a bar of the metal headboard.

She didn't prepared this for us, I realize. She has kept people here before—like the young woman who ran out of the hospital, and Alex.

But the room is empty. What has she done with Alex?

"Stay in here, Betty," Sandra says. "I'll be back soon." She motions to me, saying: "You come with me."

She wants both of us to leave, but only she will return. It isn't a stretch to imagine what she's planning to do to me.

"You said you wanted extraordinary results, correct?" Betty tells Sandra. "Then don't take Riley away. She and I share the same abilities; she's even more gifted than me. Let us be your subjects."

CHAPTER SIXTY-EIGHT

> I have seen enough to make me believe that our minds are capable of much more than most of us dare to imagine . . . I believe it is our 'left-brained' tendency to analyze, judge, and predict that prevents us from tapping into this wider field of knowledge.
>
> —Jeff Tarrant, PhD, BCN

BETTY, 1964

"Welcome home," Douglas said, wheeling her up the newly installed wooden ramp and opening the front door with the only key, the one that would remain in his pocket at all times.

He brought Betty inside and locked the door while she looked at the furniture he'd chosen. The curtains were too dark a shade of gold, but the striped sofa and matching armchairs were pleasing. She wanted to stay in the living room a bit longer—something was nagging at her—but Douglas was already wheeling her into the kitchen.

"I had workmen lower the counters and sink," he said. "You can still cook, just like always. You'll find the bathroom has been modified as well."

"How wonderful," she replied.

He'd bought a new Impala, a duplicate of the car that was crushed in the accident. Other copies of things they'd left behind filled the new house: the record player and albums. China in the same pink-and-white pattern. CorningWare pots and pans and a bar cart.

"Shall we have something to eat?" Douglas asked.

Betty felt a rush of relief at the thought of occupying herself with a task. Despite the replicas of their old life, everything was disorienting here. Even Douglas seemed like a stranger.

"Would you like a cocktail first?" she offered.

"Wonderful." Douglas's exhale told her how relieved he felt that she was home. It couldn't have been easy for him, living the bachelor life these past weeks. He'd lost weight and his shirt was rumpled. She hoped he'd replaced the iron and board so she could smooth away the wrinkles.

Dinner was simple, but Douglas seemed pleased with the casserole. Afterward, he wheeled her into the living room and she realized what was nagging at her. The television was missing.

They'd always enjoyed watching *The Ed Sullivan Show* on Sunday nights, and *My Three Sons* and *Bewitched* on Thursdays. While she ironed and sewed, Betty also tuned in to *The Price Is Right* or *Truth or Consequences*. And Douglas never missed *CBS Evening News with Walter Cronkite.*

"Will we be getting a television?" she asked.

"We don't need one. Books are far better for the mind." Douglas settled onto the couch with a Hemingway novel. And that was that.

Money wasn't an issue for Douglas, whose family was wealthy. The size of his trust fund meant he could purchase just about anything they needed—or travel anywhere they wanted. But Douglas no longer had an interest in taking trips. The dream they'd once had of renting a camper to drive around the Grand Canyon was tucked away, like a forgotten photo in the back of a drawer.

Douglas never returned to work, but his days still followed the shape of a scholar's. He read voraciously, visiting the library every time he went to the grocery store and checking out books for both of them. He wrote papers, though he never submitted any for publication, and at night, he listened to records or played cards with Betty. Occasionally they went for a drive after dark, but in time, it seemed easier for Betty to just stay inside.

For Betty, after her accident, there could be no children.

There was only this house, and her husband, and her memories. They didn't fade, though. At night, she lay awake next to Douglas, replaying old images and conversations in her mind.

When she finally slept, she dreamt about the girls: Ivy's boisterous laugh; Kathleen making a quip in her cool, throaty voice; Helen shyly linking arms with them while they walked. Her sisters.

Her days fell into a quiet rhythm. She cooked and cleaned and did laundry—slower than usual, given her mobility challenge, but just as thoroughly and well—while Douglas took over the grocery shopping and yardwork. Douglas also taught her how to play chess and was delighted when she showed a knack for strategy. He brought her books every time he went to the library, and although they were the only house on the street that didn't get the newspaper delivered, he occasionally picked up a magazine from the store. Reading helped fill the time, especially because he wouldn't permit their families to visit.

"Even my mother?" Betty asked early on.

"What if she told a friend where we lived? And someone from Marquis or another institution tracked you down?" Douglas countered. His face grew red and he appeared so agitated that Betty never once asked again.

Something horrible must have been happening on that fateful day when Dr. Trimble had knocked on their door. Awful enough to send not only Betty, but all her friends running. Perhaps Dr. Trimble had another experiment planned for them—something even worse, Betty had told herself.

At night, Douglas continued his habit of checking the locks on all the windows, just as he had in the hospital. Sometimes he'd test them dozens or even hundreds of times before he came to bed. Betty grew accustomed to falling asleep to the clicking sound of the lock on their bedroom window engaging and disengaging.

One spring afternoon several years after they'd moved in, as Betty sat on the porch taking in fresh air, their next-door neighbor waved from over the fence and tried to strike up a conversation: "Where are y'all from?"

Before Betty could answer, Douglas stepped onto the porch, grabbed the handles of her chair, and wheeled her into the living room.

"Betty, why were you talking to her? You know you can't trust anyone!" It was the closest he'd ever come to yelling at her. He closed the door and peered through the peephole.

"But darling, she's a neighbor! Surely she means no harm."

"You *assume* she's a neighbor. But she could be anyone," Douglas replied. "Think about it. If someone really wanted to reach you, wouldn't they plant someone your own age nearby to make you let down your guard?"

"Surely Dr. Trimble wouldn't go to all that effort," Betty said lightly. Douglas was fraught; his face was coloring again and he'd begun to pace.

"You have no idea what he's capable of," Douglas replied. "Or the depth of destruction he caused. Besides, it's not only him I'm worried about. If he did publish his paper, everyone knows about your ability. People could be looking for you right now, Betty. The Russians! Other governments! You are not safe!"

That night, Douglas rechecked the locks so many times that his thumb was swollen and red in the morning.

She never spoke to another neighbor again.

The years bled into one another, then formed decades. Betty's hair turned white, and though Douglas's hearing had faded, he remained as handsome as ever, with his angular face and soft brown eyes.

It wasn't the life she'd imagined, but Betty never stopped loving him.

Then one morning, Betty woke up and looked over at Douglas beside her in bed. He'd just turned eighty-five and had been sleeping later in recent days. She started to slip away to fix her hair and face before he awoke, but something made her pause. She reached out to touch his shoulder, her voice catching as she said, "Darling?"

He took in a shuddering breath and his eyelids fluttered. Then his chest stilled.

Betty bowed her head and rested her hand on his cheek for a long time. With tears streaming down her face, she kissed him and whispered, "Goodbye, my love."

CHAPTER SIXTY-NINE

RILEY, PRESENT DAY

There's no way I can participate in whatever experiment Sandra has planned right now. My brain is so fuzzy from the sedative that even forming coherent sentences is difficult. I nod off, then abruptly awaken as my head jerks back up.

"You can sleep for a few hours," Sandra decides. "Then we'll begin. I have a few things to take care of anyway."

She handcuffs one of my wrists to the metal headboard of the bed in the room off the kitchen. The last thing I see before Sandra closes the door is Betty mouthing something to me. But my eyelids are so heavy they drift shut before I can understand her message.

When I awaken, it's like surfacing from a dark, muddy well. My throat is so parched it hurts. I squint as my eyes adjust to the sudden brightness of the lamp on the nightstand next to me. It takes me a beat to remember where I am, then my stomach plummets.

As I inhale a deep breath to try to steady myself, I smell fresh coffee. Sandra walks through the doorway, holding a white mug with *Lennox Grief Counseling* printed on it in flowing blue script.

"Drink this." Sandra puts the mug in my free hand.

When I hesitate, she shakes her head. "Don't be stupid. If I wanted you gone, you'd be gone by now. The only drug that's in it is caffeine."

She walks to the door. "I'll back in a few minutes."

The coffee is lukewarm—maybe because Sandra feared I'd try to throw the mug at her and she'd get scalded—and I gulp it down, feeling more mentally lucid almost instantly. I can't reach the wicker nightstand from my position, so I set the empty mug on the bed. Perhaps I can find a way to break it and use a shard to defend myself.

I study the room, taking in the small table with two straight-back chairs, the high ceiling, the mirror on the wall, and the door that probably leads to a closet. If I get free, I could hide behind the door and hit Sandra with a chair when she comes back. I pull as hard as I can, trying to make the headboard yield.

My wrist is raw and aching and I've made no progress when Sandra returns. This time she has her gun—and Betty. Betty looks as rough as I feel and she's moving so slowly it's as if she has aged a decade. I wince as I shift positions to better see them.

"What's wrong?" Betty asks.

"My arm hurts from being above my head for so long," I answer truthfully.

"Her results may be compromised if she's physically uncomfortable and can't concentrate," Betty tells Sandra.

Sandra digs the handcuff key out of the pocket of her jeans and hands it to Betty. "Secure the handcuffs around both of her wrists." She backs away, training the gun on us.

It takes Betty a minute, but she figures out how to unlock me. I curl onto my side and Betty cuffs my wrists together. "There, dear," she says, gently patting my sore arm. I feel something press against my elbow and realize Betty has moved the coffee mug closer to me. I drape my arm over it, instinctively hiding it.

"Betty tells me you're extremely telepathic," Sandra says. "It's why she hired you."

I nod. I know Betty is stalling to keep me alive, but it's futile. Even if someone were looking for us, they'd never guess we were here.

"We'll start with a basic telepathy test." Sandra walks over to the small door and opens it. Inside the closet is a tall file cabinet. Sandra keeps one eye on us as she selects a file from the top drawer.

"Can Riley transmit first?" Betty asks. "She seems to do better that way."

"Fine," Sandra says. "This is just practice anyway."

I don't have any of the intuition Betty credits me with. And in a few minutes, Sandra's going to know we tricked her.

Sandra instructs Betty to turn her chair around so her back is to me. Any hope I had that I might've been able to convey visual clues to Betty are gone; she won't be able to see my face.

Sandra hands me the folder, then takes one of the straight-backed chairs, angling it so she can see both our faces. She's maybe six feet from us—too far away for me to lunge for the gun.

"Go ahead," Sandra tells us.

I stare at the back of Betty's head.

"Riley, do you remember what I said about a time for logic and a time for trust? I need your trust now," Betty says. "We have to work together to make this successful."

"Enough," Sandra snaps. "Begin."

It's awkward with my hands cuffed together, but I manage to open the folder and look at the first image. It's a simple one of a black pentagon on a white background. I stare at the symbol for a long moment, unsure of what to do. Then Betty begins to speak.

"I'm seeing a color, or perhaps the absence of color. It could be . . . white. There's a shape. It's a very familiar shape, one we see every morning . . ."

My body feels electrified. Is Betty actually able to discern what I'm seeing? Pentagons are everywhere—from street signs to the tile design in Betty's bathroom. From her angle, Sandra can see the paper I'm holding, too. I sense the hitch in her energy.

A moment later, my logical brain takes over. Betty's words seem deliberately vague—a color or absence of color covers the entire spectrum. And doesn't *everything* have a shape?

"Go to the next image," Sandra instructs me after Betty falls silent.

The next picture is of a motorboat cutting through a body of water surrounded by green trees.

"Action," Betty says immediately. "Something is happening . . . I see *movement.* A sweeping motion, like a powerful arc."

Goosebumps rise on my skin. Her words could be stretched to fit the exact image I'm seeing. Either Betty is exceptionally telepathic or she's equally gifted in conjuring visions that sound specific while being deliberately vague, like a sham street corner palm reader.

Out of the corner of my eye, I see Sandra lean forward, the gun in her hand gleaming. Her expression is hungry.

"Speed. Quickness," Betty says, enunciating each word. "That's my vision, Riley."

"Keep going," Sandra breathes, leaning forward. She looks like she's buying it. Betty's plan is actually working—so far. Betty's wheelchair inches forward slowly. Sandra doesn't notice.

I quickly flip to the next image. It's a man and woman who seem to be having an argument in a parking lot, with their arms captured in angry gestures and their faces frowning.

"This one is more complex," Betty says. Then she falls silent. I grow nervous; Betty's streak of luck must be running out.

"Riley, I'm sensing you're blocked," Betty says. "Don't doubt yourself. You can do this. *Use what I've given you.*"

As I absorb her words, time shudders to a stop.

Barely a heartbeat passes, but tiny details come into sharp focus: Betty reaching for the empty chair by the table, her fingers wrapping around its top. The white mug—a shape I see every morning—that *Betty has given me* next to my arm. Sandra's index finger now relaxed, off the trigger of the gun.

Betty is barely finished speaking when she lifts up the chair and swings it around, smashing Sandra in the face with the heavy wood, her movements shockingly nimble and forceful. The second the chair makes contact I scramble out of bed, holding the coffee mug by the handle and swinging it in a powerful arc to connect with Sandra's temple.

Sandra slumps forward and I manage to pull the gun out of her hand. She's dazed and bleeding; she doesn't even put up a fight.

I back away, training the gun on Sandra, breathing hard. I'm not going to make the mistake Sandra did of letting down my guard for a second.

"You received my message," Betty says to me.

CHAPTER SEVENTY

RILEY, PRESENT DAY

Sandra blinks hard as she raises her head. Blood runs down her cheek like slow teardrops from the small cut on her temple.

"Do you know how to use a gun?" I ask Betty.

She nods. "My father kept one over the mantel. He taught all of us to shoot."

"Good." I gingerly pass it to her. "Because I don't."

"Toss me the handcuff key," I instruct Sandra.

She hurls it at my head and I duck to avoid getting hit. Her eyes are narrow and her face has hardened; she looks like she'd love nothing more than to tear me apart. It's hard to believe this is the same woman I found aspirational.

After some fumbling, I manage to uncuff myself.

"Watch her. I need to find the Wi-Fi booster so I can call the police," I instruct Betty as I hurry toward the door.

"Are you sure that's what you want to do?" Sandra asks. A taunting note in her voice pulls me up short.

"You could look for the booster . . . or you could look for Alex," she continues. "Her situation is a little time-sensitive."

My stomach plummets. Alex was here, probably restrained in this very room while I drank wine with Sandra in the kitchen. Perhaps those chimes on Sandra's phone were a warning that Alex was stirring.

"What did you do to her?" I demand.

"Alex is the subject of an experiment right now. I set it up while you were sleeping." Sandra smiles. "Do you know how long someone can endure the Ganzfeld experiment without going insane?"

Betty gasps.

"Neither do I," says Sandra. "But we're going to find out."

"What have you done?" Betty cries.

"You're familiar with it, Betty. Alex is tied down, wearing a special blindfold that Dr. Trimble himself created—the same one you wore in the library basement. I took it from Sam's house a while ago; it has really come in handy these past few months. Anyway, Alex can't see or hear anything. It's been over an hour. Do you think she'll be able to make it to two or will she snap? Oh, and I gave her a little dose of LSD. Our government used to do it to subjects all the time."

I shudder, sickened at the thought of Alex's disorientation and terror. "Where is she?"

"Really?" Sandra laughs.

I can't believe it—she's enjoying this.

My mind whirls, weighing the variables. Sandra's house is huge, and the booster could be anywhere since it's probably not much bigger than my cell phone, but it's a lot harder to hide a person. I think I could find Alex within half an hour if she's in here. The land is a different matter. If Alex is being held outside on this huge property, unable to hear or see, it could take hours to locate her.

"Why are you doing this, Sandra?" Betty cries.

"Maybe you were right when you tried to psychoanalyze me. It's a way to achieve immortality in a cold, lonely world." Sandra's lips tremble; she actually looks vulnerable.

Then she winks and I realize it was only another act. "Or maybe I'm really good at the long game."

Betty keeps the gun aimed at Sandra as she twists toward me. "Find Alex," she says.

I've just come to the opposite conclusion. "If I can get the police here, there will be a lot more of us searching."

Betty shakes her head. "Trust me, Riley."

I meet her eyes and after a beat, I nod.

"One other thing," Betty continues. "Handcuff Sandra to the chair before you go."

I do as she says, cuffing Sandra's hands behind her and linking the chain through the chair slats. As an added precaution, I take the pillowcases off the bed and use them to tie Sandra's legs together.

"Alex isn't in the house," Betty declares.

"Are you sure—"

Betty cuts me off. "Hurry, Riley, search outside! She doesn't have much time!"

So I run.

The woods surrounding Sandra's house are dark and silent. I don't even have my cell phone to use as a flashlight; I bolted from the house without thinking to grab it.

"Alex!" I yell, spinning in a circle.

She could be anywhere—tied to a tree, beneath a shrub, even back in the house. I plunge ahead, branches slapping at my face as I push through them.

Finally I see something glowing just ahead. I trip over a rock, landing hard on my palms as I catch myself against the unyielding ground. I stagger to my feet and push on. With every second that ticks by, Alex's torture is worsening. I reach the bright spot and my heart free-falls. It's just a path of fungi lit by bioluminescence.

"Alex!" I yell every few minutes, even though Sandra said Alex wouldn't be able to hear me. I can't trust a word out of that woman's mouth. I run until my breathing is jagged and my lungs hurt, stumbling over tree roots, my head constantly swiveling. I'm searching for a glimpse of a clue that could lead me to her, like a scrap of clothing or the tip of a shoe sticking out from beneath a bush.

I don't know how many minutes pass, but any one of them could have tipped Alex over the edge. I'm panting and completely disoriented; this patch of trees is so thick I can't even see Sandra's house anymore.

Tears gather in my eyes as I envision Alex tied up with that blindfold that looks straight out of a horror movie. The adults she was supposed to trust—her therapist and her professor—both abused her. I should have done more to help her when we met. Now it's too late.

I squat down and drop my head into my hands, trying to receive whatever message Betty may be sending me, but the only thought that comes through is this one: I've failed Alex.

CHAPTER SEVENTY-ONE

BETTY, PRESENT DAY

Betty's eyes rove over Sandra's springy curls, her creamy, pale skin, the dimples indenting her cheeks. Sandra is achingly familiar on the outside—she is what Ivy would have gradually become. But Sandra possesses none of Ivy's internal goodness. She is a hollow vessel.

"I don't believe you were conducting these experiments for the reasons you said." Betty frowns. "You enjoy the power it gives you over helpless people. You like causing pain. Did your stepmother and stepsiblings really torment you, or was it the other way around?"

Sandra shrugs and Betty hears the clink of her handcuffs from behind the chair. "Does it matter?"

"Yes, it does," Betty replies, feeling her stomach turn. It is difficult to even be in the same room as Sandra. "Why torture Alex like this? You're not going to get any scientific data. It isn't a controlled experiment. Why did you even abduct her in the first place?"

Sandra shifts in her chair. "Alex showed up here the other day for an emergency therapy session. She was a mess—even more so than usual, and that girl can turn on the waterworks. When she went to use the bathroom I decided to slip her ID into her backpack. Just to toy with her; to make her question whether she'd ever lost it at all. Plus I didn't need it any longer. But she came back from the bathroom too quickly."

"She saw you?" Betty prompts.

"I thought she might have."

"So you intercepted her on the road later. What did you do, pretend to just be coincidentally driving by? Or did you act like she'd forgotten something at your house?" Betty watches Sandra's expression carefully.

"Something like that." Sandra shifts again and winces. "These handcuffs really are uncomfortable."

"Tell me where you're keeping Alex," Betty pleads. "Do it for your mother. It would have broken her heart to see you like this."

Sandra gives a little laugh. "I owe that woman nothing."

It takes Betty a moment before she's able to speak. Then she says the worst thing she can think of to Sandra: "You may share her blood, but you are not Ivy's daughter."

For the first time, Betty feels grateful Ivy is no longer alive. It would break her heart to see what her baby has become.

"This isn't the only extended Ganzfeld test I've performed, you know," Sandra says. She fidgets in her seat again, leaning slightly forward, and looks hard at Betty. "Volunteering with the homeless gave me a nice selection of prospects. There are plenty of runaways on drugs. Who would notice if one of them went missing or started acting crazy?"

Betty sucks in a breath as Sandra twists her body again, rolling her shoulders back.

Betty is still holding the gun in her right hand. With her free hand, she suddenly yanks on her chair's left wheel, jerking it sharply backward at an angle, just as Sandra lunges forward.

Sandra's feet are still tied together—Betty mentally thanks Riley for that—so Sandra trips over them and lands on the floor, her hands still outstretched, right where Betty was a split second before.

Betty wheels backward another few yards before she speaks.

"You had a second handcuff key, didn't you? You tried to distract me by talking, but I realized what was going on when you kept fidgeting. You might think you're good at the long game, Sandra. But I'm better."

CHAPTER SEVENTY-TWO

RILEY, PRESENT DAY

The longer I remain still, the more I become aware of the nocturnal noises around me: the chirp of crickets, the rustle in one of the trees overhead, and the faint, high-pitched cry of an animal.

Was it an animal? I listen closely, but the sound doesn't repeat. I can't even tell which direction it came from.

I have no idea which way to go. If Betty's gift is real, she must be trying to guide me toward Alex right now. She sounded so certain Alex was being held outside.

All along, I considered Sandra a good role model. But I was wrong. Betty is the one I should have been looking up to. She never grew bitter, despite everything she had endured. Leaving her house to return to Marquis was an immense act of bravery, and trying to save Alex is nothing short of heroic.

I start to heave myself to my feet, then I hesitate. I owe it to Betty to try things her way.

I sink back onto the ground and close my eyes, trying to calm the chattering of my mind. I do my best to bring forth an image of Alex, down to her worn sneakers and bitten nails. The longer I sit there, the more vividly I see her in my mind's eye. I can almost hear the defiance mingled with pain in her voice.

My breathing slows.

Where are you, Alex? I think over and over again, until the words become almost a mantra.

Then a strange warmth washes over me. I rise to my feet so quickly it's like I'm being helped up. I turn sharply to my right and start walking. No doubt clouds my mind; my steps are steady and sure. As if I'm following a map.

Less than five minutes later, I spot it between two tall trees, like a mirage. If I hadn't almost walked into it, I would never have noticed it. It's a shed, painted black so it blends into the inky night.

I try to yank open the door, but it's locked. The only other entry point is a small window covered by a dark curtain. I look around and spot a good-sized rock. I smash the window and knock away the loose glass, then squeeze through it.

Alex is tied to a chair, wearing leggings and the same coat she had on during our walk. Cushioned headphones are over her ears and the eerie white blindfold covers her eyes. Her chin is resting on her chest and she isn't moving.

I gently touch her shoulder and she jerks violently, thrashing from side to side.

"Make them stop, make them stop," she wails.

I gingerly remove her blindfold and ear coverings first, then untie her. She slumps to the ground, curling into the fetal position and whimpering.

"You're safe, Alex," I keep repeating. "I'm here to help you."

In one corner of the hut are a quilt and a few bottles of water, the bare essentials for survival. I grab the quilt and cover Alex, who is shaking.

"You're going to be okay," I whisper. She opens her eyes and blinks, but her gaze is unfocused. Seeing her so broken brings tears to my eyes.

"I'm Riley, I met you once before. I'm going to get the police now."

She doesn't answer.

"Try to drink some water." I pass her a bottle and am encouraged when her hand closes around it.

I spot a small battery-operated lantern hanging from a hook across the shed. I hurry to it and turn it on, its glow illuminating the space.

"Alex, don't move," I say. "I'll be right back."

I unlock the door and step out, bringing the lantern with me, but instead of taking it, I put it down in front of the shed. It'll give Alex a source of light and be a beacon to lead me back here.

I look around, trying to figure out which way the house is located. A break in the clouds provides a glimmer of moonlight but I can't see anything other than the thicket of trees. I start to plunge ahead, then hesitate. Something is holding me back, whispering that there's a better way.

I take a deep breath, quelling the panicked voice inside me that's urging me to hurry. I scan my surroundings again, this time more slowly, and I spot headlights moving down a distant road.

I'm now certain it wasn't an animal crying in the night that I heard a little while ago. It was the faint squealing of brakes, likely from a truck. Perhaps I subconsciously recognized this and tucked the information into a back corner of my mind, where it could have been buried by my other thoughts and conjectures if I hadn't coaxed it forward. Maybe that's a big piece of what intuition is—the straining out of extraneous noise and the distilling of what our senses pick up into a new kind of knowing.

I hurry toward the road. When I reach it, I only have to wait a few moments before a car comes toward me. I jump into the middle of the street, squinting in the bright headlights as I wave my arms. Brakes squeal and the driver leans out the window, shouting, "Are you okay?"

"Call the police!" I yell. I give the driver Sandra's address and tell him Alex Finch's kidnapper is being restrained there and that Alex is in a shed on the grounds. He repeats everything to the 911 dispatcher who takes his call as his eyes grow wide.

"Send an ambulance, too," I shout. "Alex is still alive! I'll shine a lantern in the woods behind the house—follow the light and they'll find her."

Then I turn around and run as fast as I've ever run in my life.

CHAPTER SEVENTY-THREE

BETTY, PRESENT DAY

A distant siren wails, growing louder with each passing second. Betty hears pounding on the front door of Sandra's house and loud shouts of "Police! Open up!"

A moment later, a tremendous crash announces the door has been breached.

"In here!" Betty cries. "Back by the kitchen!"

Two officers appear in the doorway, their guns drawn. They look at Sandra, still splayed on the floor with her feet tied, then at Betty in her wheelchair. Betty sees surprise flicker across one of the cops' faces.

She lowers her gun to her lap and puts on the safety. "She kidnapped Alex Finch. She's holding Alex somewhere on this property."

"We've already got officers searching, ma'am." The younger cop kneels down and handcuffs Sandra's arms behind her back, then reads her rights.

"I want my lawyer," Sandra declares. "I'm not saying another word."

"Be careful—she has a handcuff key somewhere," Betty warns.

The officer nods. "We'll search her."

"Ma'am, I'm going to take your gun now." The older officer steps toward Betty and retrieves it from her lap, his movements slow and deliberate.

"It's Sandra's gun. We got it away from her. She held young women here," Betty explains. "Alex wasn't the first. She was using them as test subjects in experiments."

A female officer enters the room in time to hear Betty's words. She turns and yells, "I need crime techs in here."

Then she nods at Betty. "Ma'am, please come with me."

She leads Betty toward the front of the house. Outside, a half dozen police cars and an ambulance ring the yard, their blue-and-red lights spinning.

"Did they find Alex yet?" Betty asks.

Before the officer can answer, Betty looks through the open front door and spots Riley walking out of the woods, alongside medics carrying Alex on a stretcher.

"Is she alright?" Betty cries.

"I think so." Riley hurries to Betty's side, wrapping her in a hug. "She's semi-alert and asking for her mother."

Betty's eyes fill. "At least one girl was saved," she whispers.

They hold on to each other until the female police officer speaks up: "I'm going to need you both to move aside for your own safety."

Betty turns to see Sandra being led through the house by a scrum of police officers. Her hair is disheveled, and the blood has dried on her cheek.

"Sure, but she can't hurt us," Riley says loudly enough for Sandra to hear. Betty waits for Sandra to look at them, but she keeps her gaze fixed ahead and her expression blank.

An empty vessel, Betty thinks again.

They watch as Sandra is put into the back of a cruiser and it takes off, its siren blaring, followed closely by another police car.

"I still can't believe I found the hut," Riley says.

Betty looks up at Riley, waiting a beat. When she has Riley's full attention, she says softly, "I can."

CHAPTER SEVENTY-FOUR

RILEY, PRESENT DAY

I know what Betty is thinking, and I need to nip this in the bud. "Look, I know you tried to send me a message to lead me to Alex, but I've never had a psychic experience in my life."

Betty shakes her head. "I didn't send you a message. I was trying to get a sense of where Alex was being held, you're right about that. But I could only pick up that it was away from the house."

I open my mouth to reply, but words fail me. I think about how I walked so surely toward the shed. A dozen yards in either direction and I would've passed it by.

"You did this all on your own, Riley," Betty insists. "I told you that you had abilities."

"I'm chalking it up to luck," I say, but even I can tell my voice is less certain. "I was bound to stumble across the hut at some point, it just happened sooner rather than later."

"Whatever it was, I'm glad. And I'm just as glad that you picked up on my plan to surprise Sandra."

"I'd been thinking about using the coffee mug as a weapon even before you put it by my arm," I tell her.

"Interesting," Betty says. "What about the chair?"

"That, too. I figured if I could get free, I could smash Sandra over the head with it."

"Just like I did." Betty taps her finger against her lips. "Strange how we independently thought about using the same two objects."

"That doesn't mean anything," I insist. "There weren't any other potential weapons in the room!"

Betty frowns. "Of course there were. The heavy lamp on the nightstand. The wall mirror. To name just two."

I can't think of anything to say to refute it.

The female police officer is approaching us again and I know what will happen next: They'll separate me and Betty to get our statements.

Betty gets in the last word: "Lots of luck and coincidence around us tonight, it seems." There's a wink in her voice.

Yet another officer comes by with Hank on a leash. Hank wags his tail when he sees us.

"Where are you taking him?" I ask.

The office bends down and pats Hank on the head, as if to soften his words: "To the pound. It's a no-kill shelter, so maybe someone will adopt him."

Hank looks at me with cloudy, trusting eyes. He's an old dog, and like Sandra said, they have a harder time getting chosen. This sweet boy could spend the rest of his life in the shelter.

Betty sighs, but she's smiling. "Fine. We can take Hank home with us."

CHAPTER SEVENTY-FIVE

"Detailed case reports of 124 dementia patients who experienced an episode of paradoxical lucidity were received. In more than 80 percent of these cases, complete remission with return of memory, orientation, and responsive verbal ability was reported by observers of the lucid episode. The majority of patients died within hours to days after the episode."

—Alexander Batthyány Pázmány Péter, Catholic University Budapest, and Bruce Greyson, University of Virginia Health System

BETTY, PRESENT DAY

It's like gazing at a painting that continually transforms, Betty marvels as she stares out the open window at the red rock country in Sedona, Arizona. The late spring air smells of juniper—piney and crisp—and the setting sun shades the rocks a deep crimson, creating the illusion that they're glowing from within.

Riley turns off the engine and a hush settles over their camper. All Betty can hear is the faint echo of her own breaths.

"I didn't know places like this existed," Betty finally says. "It's out of another world." And to think, she used to believe she'd never see anything beyond her little patch of land in Virginia.

Luckily, Riley had other plans. A few weeks ago, after their testimony had helped Sandra be sentenced to life in prison, Riley looked at Betty across the dinner table.

"How would you feel about taking a road trip?" she asked, her eyes shining.

The prospect made Betty nervous—then exhilarated. After Riley rented the camper, their first stop was the Atlantic Ocean. The salty, humid air kissed Betty's face as she listened to the rhythmic crash of waves and watched Hank race across the sand, acting much younger than his years. Later Riley wheeled her down the boardwalk as Betty ate cotton candy that stained her fingertips pink, just like it had when she was a little girl.

From there, they set off for the Grand Canyon, stopping along the way in Tupelo, Mississippi, where they drove by Elvis Presley's old house and Memphis, Tennessee, where they all ate fried peanut butter and banana sandwiches in his honor—even Hank. Every day welcomed in a wonderland of sights and sounds and tastes: twangy bluegrass music played by a trio at an outdoor restaurant; the prairies of Oklahoma tinted violet by the oncoming winter; a palomino horse running across a field, her muscular, shiny body rippling.

At times Betty missed Douglas acutely, thinking about the giddy, romantic early days of their marriage. How he would have loved taking these adventures with her—at least the young version of Douglas, the one who wasn't so scarred by life.

"Are you ready?" Riley asks now, starting up the engine. "We can make it to the Grand Canyon tonight."

"Wouldn't you rather camp here and go in the morning?" Betty asks. "You must be tired."

The camper has a cozy bed in the back for Betty and a couch that Riley takes at night, insisting it's comfortable.

"I'm feeling energetic," Riley says. "I think I'll drive for a while."

"I'll stay up with you," Betty decides.

They drive for several hours, alternating Riley's favorite country music station with the hits of the early 1960s. At one point, as Patsy

Cline sings about falling to pieces, Betty looks over at Riley's profile, admiring the way her red-gold hair falls over her shoulders. She realizes that although she gave up hope of having a child long ago, Riley has become her granddaughter.

Riley turns to her and smiles as she shuts off the engine. "We're here." She lowers the ramp and wheels Betty out of the camper to the lookout point. Betty feels her heart skip a beat.

The moonlight reveals the surface contours of the endless canyon before them. Betty can't see all the way to the bottom, but she senses a vastness that stretches the limits of her imagination. This place feels holy.

In the distance, a canyon owl hoots, its call faintly echoing. Overhead the sky glitters with more stars than Betty thought possible.

She takes it all in—the magnificent vista that no photograph or painting could capture, the cool desert air rustling the trees, the nearby deer nibbling on a bush, unbothered by their presence.

Then white streaks sear across the sky, one after the other, like a dazzling display of fireworks.

"A meteor shower," Riley whispers.

Tears streak Betty's cheeks as she sits suspended on the edge of time and sky and the great hollow.

She's waited a lifetime for this.

Later, Riley brings Betty a glass of water and her nighttime pills. She makes sure the quilt is tucked around Betty and the moonroof is open so Betty can gaze at the stars as she drifts off to sleep. Hank is curled up by Betty's side.

"Thank you," Betty murmurs. She feels tired down to her old bones, a deeper fatigue than she's ever experienced. As if something within her is yearning to finally rest.

That night she dreams about her sisters again, the four of them young and carefree, linking arms and laughing as they walk through campus. A couple of boys with the moptops the Beatles made popular are tossing around a football, and another guy and his best girl sit on the hood of a red Corvette as its radio blasts "Dancing in the Street" by Martha and the Vandellas.

"Oh, Bets," says Kathleen in her dream, throwing back her head and laughing. "Isn't it grand?"

"I've missed you all so much," Betty replies.

"But we're together now!" Ivy exclaims, squeezing Betty's arm.

On the last night of her life, just before her heart gently gives out, Betty awakes briefly and looks at the stars and experiences one final premonition: She will see her friends again. She's never been so certain of anything.

CHAPTER SEVENTY-SIX

RILEY, PRESENT DAY

It's been over a month, and it's still hard to believe that Betty is gone.

When grief strikes me, I find solace in remembering how she looked when I went to wake her the morning after we arrived at the Grand Canyon. Betty died with a smile on her face.

Sometimes I find myself talking to her out loud, telling her I wish she'd taught me her secret to making daiquiris, because mine never turn out as well, or that the nosy neighbor with the shaggy dog is getting on my last nerve. I tell her that Alex has transferred to a smaller school and is doing much better, especially now that a young woman who graduated two years ago has come forward to accuse Josh of inappropriate sexual contact. The investigation is ongoing, but it doesn't look good for him.

Usually I have these one-sided conversations with Betty in the morning as I drink coffee, since my insomnia has become a thing of the past.

Now I put my empty mug in the sink and turn up the thermostat a couple of degrees, because winter is making itself known today.

I'm about to jump in the shower when my cell phone rings. It's Danny. I hesitate, then decide to answer.

"Oh, babe, you saved my *life*," he practically shouts. "I've screwed up so many things, but the one thing I did right was marry you. Riley, you are the best thing that ever happened to me."

Maybe I'm gullible, but I believe he means it. Danny and I had big problems, but lack of love wasn't one of them.

"I still can't believe what you did for me," he says.

I used most of the money Betty left me in her will, which she'd inherited from her husband, to pay off Danny's debts. I couldn't live with myself knowing Danny was in danger. I used another chunk to pay for the rest of Alex's college expenses and to cover her loans, which I knew would've made Betty happy.

"I've been good for two months," Danny tells me. It's code; he hasn't gambled in that long. "Please hear me out, beautiful. I'm thinking—dinner. I'll come your way. I'll find a Thai restaurant to take you to, like old times. No, better than old times. A fresh start."

I close my eyes and press the phone closer to my ear. My throat is thickening with unshed tears.

"I want to change, Riley. But it's so damn hard. I don't think I can do it without you."

I could fill a notebook with the things I miss about Danny: the way he never seemed to get in a bad mood, the cowlick that made a tuft of his sandy hair stand up in the back, and how even in his sleep, he'd hold me tight.

I gather every bit of strength I possess. Then I say, "I love you, Danny. Please don't ever contact me again. Goodbye."

I hang up on him and, with trembling fingers, block his number.

Something inside me is shrieking a warning, telling me I'm about to destroy both our lives, that I'll never find anyone who will want me again. Panic grips me; I'm suddenly desperate to call him back.

But a deeper, wiser part of me—the one Betty taught me to listen to—takes over. It tells me that Danny needs to change for himself, not me. I can't be responsible for him ever again.

If Danny truly meant it, he'd prove to himself he can control his addiction. He'd go to meetings, get counseling. He wouldn't use me as a crutch. Acknowledging this doesn't erase my pain. But this time when I cry, it feels as if my warm, salty tears are cleansing an old wound.

I've managed to pull myself together and shower by the time someone knocks on the front door later that afternoon. I set aside the information I'm reading on EMT training—I'm intrigued by the possibility of a new career—and open the door. Then I crane my head to look up at the man standing on the front porch.

"I didn't think you'd be so tall," I blurt.

He laughs. "Riley, it's good to meet you. I'm Bill Stevens from *The Atlantic*."

"Come in." I hold open the door and he steps inside. "This is Hank."

Bill bends down and pets Hank, who wags his tail. I watch as Bill straightens and takes it all in: the old stereo console, the gold-and-navy-striped furniture, the 1960s Sears dinette table.

"Wow, what a place," he manages to say.

"It threw me, too, when I first got here. But I've learned to appreciate it."

In the will she wrote a few weeks before her death, Betty also left me her home—gifting me space to breathe and time to plan my next steps. I haven't changed anything in the house yet, because that would feel disrespectful. Plus I've sort of grown to love the kitchen. I'm thinking about settling here for a while. But I'm also considering moving to the city, as long as I can find an apartment that allows dogs.

What a luxury to have choices.

The only thing I've added to the house is a framed picture of Betty, Ivy, Kathleen, and Helen wearing matching white dresses in the library basement. Sam Trimble gave it to me after Betty died, parting with one of his grandfather's prized possessions. Sam is harmless; it turns out he and the blond sisters from the Seekers Collective are just friends, and they were taking him to pick up a prescription, since his car was in the shop, on the day I spotted them. Sam invited me to join him for the sisters' grand opening of their new café—featuring a tarot card reader and mentalist who purportedly can bend spoons with his mind—but I declined. There's only so much you can take of listening to a guy who keeps talking about wanting to write a screenplay.

"Wait till you see the kitchen." I beckon for the reporter to follow me.

"This is fantastic. Can you actually cook in here?" he asks, inspecting the stove.

"You'd be surprised. I can whip up a mean grilled cheese on this stove."

"I haven't had a grilled cheese in forever. I love them," Bill replies.

"With tomato soup for dipping?" I ask.

"Like there's any other way," he shoots back.

I find myself checking his ring finger. It's bare. That doesn't mean anything—he could be one of those guys who doesn't wear a ring. Or he has a girlfriend. Or he's gay.

I can almost hear Betty's voice: *You're doing it again.*

Bill leans forward, resting his forearms on the island. "Mind if I record this?"

I shake my head. He taps his phone a few times and smiles at me. "Ready when you are."

A lot of journalists wanted to talk to Betty and me after everything happened with Sandra. We didn't agree to a single interview, though. Betty wanted to tell her life story, but she wanted to tell it to me first. While we drove across the country, Betty talked for hours about the events that shaped her: the glass candy jar at the carnival, the experiments in the library basement—the very place where I'd discovered the files were missing—and her best friends who'd been destroyed.

After Betty died, I called back the one writer who'd left a different kind of message. He insisted he didn't want to focus on the salacious details about Sandra kidnapping a sorority girl, which the other outlets had fixated on, but the deeper picture. He wanted to know Betty's story—and Helen's, Ivy's, and Kathleen's.

"I don't know where to begin," I confess.

"Just talk to me like you'd talk to a friend who doesn't know anything about this." Bill smiles encouragingly.

I walk over to the wall and take down the picture I had framed, putting it on the island.

These women in white were deliberately broken, then discarded. Their names were scrubbed from history; it's as if they never truly existed. Telling their story to as many people as I can is my way of bringing them back to life.

I begin: "She was called Girl Four. But she wasn't a number. Betty Sadler was the most extraordinary woman I've ever met."

APPENDIX

CHAPTER 2

"The investigation of extra-sensory perception at Duke University has now been going on for more than three years and has come to include well over 90,000 trials."

Source: The book *Extra-Sensory Perception,* written by J.B. Rhine, Ph.D, head of the Duke Parapsychology Laboratory, published in 1936.

CHAPTER 4

"Capt. Edgar D. Mitchell Jr., the astronaut, said today that four persons on earth participated in the extrasensory perception experiment he conducted during the Apollo 14 flight to the moon early in February. He said he had used 25 numbered cards in the experiment, in which he attempted to send a thought message to the four persons as to what the symbol on each card was. He said two of the four got 51 of the 200 correct, and the other two were less successful . . .

'We're much too uninformed, unknowledgeable in this mechanism of telepathy or E.S.P. to project its uses, but I think once we start to understand what the mechanism is, then we can start talking about uses,' Edgar said . . .

The astronaut was in Durham to analyze the results of his tests with Dr. J. B. Rhine."

Source: An article in *The New York Times*, published June 22, 1971

CHAPTER 6

"Project Stargate was a multimillion-dollar program launched by the CIA at the height of the Cold War to try and get ahead of the Soviet Union on powers of the mind . . . Project Stargate explored reading other people's thoughts, telepathy, predicting the future, and the ability to view a place or time remotely, without actually being there . . . By far the most successful case within Project Stargate was one that occurred during Operation Grill Flame, when a young woman named Rosemary Smith tried to locate a Soviet aircraft that had crashed in the Democratic Republic of Congo (then Zaire). Smith was provided with a map and marked a very specific spot where she perceived the aircraft might have gone down. Map technicians then converted her notations into geographical coordinates, which were sent to the CIA station chief in Zaire. Two days later, the Soviet aircraft was discovered where Smith said it would be, allowing the agency to extract valuable enemy technology."

Source: An article in WarHistoryonline.com, written by Madeline Hiltz, published on June 9, 2021

CHAPTER 8

"A typical Ganzfeld experiment involves two participants. Participant 1, known as 'the receiver' is seated in a comfortable chair in an acoustically isolated room. Translucent ping-pong ball halves are taped over their eyes . . . These measures are taken to reduce external noise and place participants in a comfortable 'dreamy state of awareness'. The reasoning behind such procedures is that anecdotal reports of ESP often occur during altered states of consciousness. Participant 2, otherwise known as 'the sender', is located in a different room."

Source: An article in *The British Psychological Society* published in July 2009, written by Eric Robinson

CHAPTER 10

"The Ganzfeld effect happens when your brain is starved of visual stimulation and fills in the blanks on its own. . . . The full effect usually takes 5 to 7 minutes. Longer exposure may produce stranger results. Your brain is frantically seeking outside stimuli. Finding none, the higher visual cortex starts amplifying available information, generating visual and auditory hallucinations . . . You might hear someone speaking to you or telling you to do certain things . . . or hear sounds, like someone walking in the attic or repeated clicking or tapping noises . . . You might feel that bugs are crawling on your skin or that your internal organs are moving around. You might also feel the imagined touch of someone's hands on your body."

Source: An article in Healthline.com, reviewed by Seunggu Han, M.D., Written by Ann Pietrangelo, published on October 15, 2020

CHAPTER 12

"Since the 1960s, more than 2,200 children from across the world have described apparent recollections from a previous life, all documented in a database maintained by the Division of Perceptual Studies within the Department of Psychiatry and Neurobehavioral Sciences at the University of Virginia School of Medicine . . . Certain consistent patterns have emerged: The most pronounced and convincing cases . . . tend to occur in children between the ages of 2 and 6. They might suddenly describe places they have never been, people they have never met, sometimes using words or phrases that seem beyond their vocabulary."

Source: An Article in The Washington Post titled The Children Who Remember Their Past Lives, published May 2, 2024

CHAPTER 13

"Dear Mr. Carrington, I am not one of those who dismiss a priori the study of so-called occult psychic phenomena as unscientific, discreditable or even as dangerous. If I were at the beginning rather than at the end of a scientific career, as I am today, I might possibly choose just this field of research, in spite of all difficulties . . ."

Source: Excerpt from a letter written by Sigmund Freud to Hereward Carrington, dated July 24, 1921

CHAPTER 16

"Some 2 years ago, the Senate Health Subcommittee heard chilling testimony about the human experimentation activities of the Central Intelligence Agency. The Deputy Director of the CIA revealed that over 30 universities and institutions were involved in an 'extensive testing and experimentation' program which included covert drug tests on unwitting citizens at all social levels, high and low, native Americans and foreign . . . [Subsequently discovered] records reveal a far more extensive series of experiments than had previously been thought. Eighty-six universities or institutions were involved."

Source: a U.S. Senate hearing report titled "Project MKULTRA, the CIA's Program of Research in Behavioral Modification,"

August 3, 1977

CHAPTER 20

Shortly before he was assassinated, President Abraham Lincoln was said to have recounted this dream: "'There seemed to be this death-like stillness about me. Then

I heard subdued sobs, as if a number of people were weeping . . . I arrived at the East Room [of the White House], which I entered.' According to the account, he heard a guard say that the president had been assassinated."

"Did Lincoln Predict His Own Death?"-Smithsonian Channel video

CHAPTER 24

"Dorothy Allison of Nutley, N.J. has assisted police in more than 4,000 investigations and has received many letters from law enforcement agencies describing how she helped them. To produce information in a criminal investigation, most psychics like to have an article or photograph of the victim or visit the victim's home or the crime scene. Allison asks only for the person's date and place of birth and the date and location last seen."

Source: U.S. Department of Justice

Law and Order Volume: 41 Issue: 9 September 1993

CHAPTER 26

"In 1974, San Francisco's Randolph Hearst invited [psychic Dorothy Allison] to help find his kidnapped daughter, Patricia. Allison didn't find the young woman but later called the FBI twice to say she felt Patty was hiding in Pennsylvania and then in New York City. Both 'feelings' proved accurate, and Allison also was correct in predicting that the newspaper heiress would join her captors in robbing a bank . . .

Before David Berkowitz's arrest, Allison also was credited with giving an accurate description of the 'Son of Sam' killer to a police artist and correctly predicting that he would be picked up on a traffic violation."

Source: an article in *The Los Angeles Times*, dated Dec 7, 1999

CHAPTER 28

"A woman named Penny Serra disappeared from Connecticut in 1971. Stymied by a lack of clues, the police brought in psychic Pascarella Downey. Downey had a vision of Serra's murder by a mechanic who smelled like oil and was wearing a name tag with the letter "E," but she told the police that the murderer would not be found anytime soon. It took 30 years, but eventually, a mechanic named Edward Grant was connected to the crime and brought to justice."

Source: The Reader's Digest, July 11, 2024

CHAPTER 30

"During the Cold War years, the USA and Soviet Union are known to have been spying on each other using the services of psychic 'remote viewers,' with the specific objective of gathering intelligence information of military significance. In simple terms 'remote viewing' is 'the ability of human participants to acquire information about spatially (and temporally) remote geographical targets otherwise inaccessible by any known sensory means'."

Source: An article in Strategic Analysis journal titled "Clairvoyant Remote Viewing: The US Sponsored Psychic Spying" by M. Srinivasan, Jan-March 2002 issue

CHAPTER 33

"Twelve subjects (nine of them professed 'psychics' or known to be exceptional performers on PK or ESP tests) were tested for their ability to cause mice to arouse more quickly from ether anesthesia than normally would be expected. Pairs of mice (Swiss-Webster) were simultaneously rendered unconscious . . . The pairs were of the same sex, comparable size, and were litter mates. After both mice were unconscious . . . the subject was told to attempt to awaken his or her mouse. The other mouse was used as a control . . . The results were highly significant overall . . . [with} the experimental animal requiring 87% as much time to awaken as the control."

Source: An article by Watkins & Watkins in the Journal of Parapsychology, published Dec. 1971

CHAPTER 35

"The following extract from a paper by Westerlund et al. (2004) reporting Ganzfeld experiments at the University of Edinburgh, shows strong similarities between the video the 'sender' was watching and the receiver's thoughts at the time: 'On this tape, the target video clip is shown and at the same time the mentation of the receiver can be heard. One of the most remarkable excerpts shows a man who is running through a forest; it seems that he is being hunted (at the same time, the receiver says: "Trees. People running. Fleeing . . .") Suddenly, the man falls down in a deep muddy pool (at the same time, the receiver says: "Falling. Muddy . . .") The camera zooms in on the man's face (at the same time, the receiver says: "Blond hair. 70's hairstyle. Curly-ish. White face . . .". All the utterances appear to describe exactly what is being shown on the film. The next thing that happens in the clip is that the man can no longer keep his head above the surface, so he disappears into the mud (at the same time, the receiver says: "Dead man in the water.")

Source: An article in The British Psychological Society titled "Extra-Sensory Perception: A Controversial Debate," published July 6, 2009

CHAPTER 39

"Case 5: Ravi Shankar, Born July 1951.

When between the ages of two and three, [Ravi] kept asking for toys which he claimed he had in the house of his previous life and said he himself had been murdered, giving names and details. His mother said that at three or four months she noticed a mark on his neck resembling a scar from a knife wound . . . In January 1951, in a different district, Munna—a six-year-old boy, was murdered with a knife or razor. His father's name and the details of his murder correspond with the account of Ravi Shankar."

Source: An article in the Journal of Parapsychology, Volume 30, Published in 1966

CHAPTER 41

"A year and a half or two years after my father died I interviewed a medium for a story. After the interview we had lunch and he asked if I wanted a reading . . . [T]he medium said, "There's a man [who] has a message for you. He wants you to tell Ruth that he loves her." Little did the medium know that my mom and dad had been married for 35 years when my dad died and they were the most madly in love people I've ever met or that my mom's middle name is Ruth and he always called her "Ruthie" (and he was the only one-everyone else called her by her first name). I was shocked. With the hairs on my neck already standing on end, the medium said, "There's more. He wants you to tell her that she can get rid of his neckties now. Does that make sense?" And I was stunned. I responded, "Yes. Even though it's been quite some time since he died, she hasn't been able to bring herself to get rid of his clothes yet." I called my mom after the reading and told her what the medium had said about my father (supposedly) saying he loved her. She was crying when I said, "Oh. And you still haven't gotten rid of his clothes have you?" She said, "Well, actually, I didn't tell you but I finally cleaned out his closets and took everything to Goodwill two weeks ago." I said, "That's so weird—the medium said that 'dad' said you could get rid of his neckties now. It was time." My mom began to cry even harder and said, "The only thing that I kept was his neckties. They're still in his closet."

Source: An article in the Huffington Post, published Feb 28, 2016 written by Antonia Blumberg

CHAPTER 57

"A 2001 Gallup poll found that about half of all Americans believe ESP is real and 65 million Americans have personally experienced it. More women than men report ESP experiences, although in lab experiments men and women perform equally on tests indicating ESP ability . . . So-called 'gut feelings' are often part of ESP warnings of possible danger. One story in the book, submitted by an uncle, centers on his niece who was a teenager and living at home with her parents. One day she caught a ride home from a young man named Michael who told her he sold insurance and asked for a dinner date, which she accepted. When he came to her parents' home to pick her up, he got along well with her parents but when she walked in the room to join them, she caught his eye and immediately went back into her bedroom. After her father came to hurry her up after 10 minutes, she told him she would not go out with the man, that there was something wrong with him. Not understanding her sudden distress, he pleaded with her to fulfill her commitment to her date and in the end, made her tell her date directly. Politely, she thanked the man but said while he was probably 'a very nice guy' there was something about him that made her uncomfortable and she couldn't go out with him. He left and never returned. 'Cynthia, who never locked or even closed her bedroom door before, locked the door and windows that night,' her uncle wrote, adding that the young man was Michael Ross, who murdered four women in eastern Connecticut before he was caught.

The Rhine Research Center has a growing database of over 30,000 stories of people's ESP experiences. Researchers there screened out about half to highlight the ones that show enough detail, incorporate a witness or feature foreknowledge that couldn't have been gained through 'normal' sources."

Source: The [Danbury, CT] News-Times book review of *The Gift: ESP the Extraordinary Experiences of Ordinary People*, published

April 28, 2005

CHAPTER 75

"Detailed case reports of 124 dementia patients who experienced an episode of paradoxical lucidity were received. In more than 80 percent of these cases, complete remission with return of memory, orientation, and responsive verbal ability was reported by observers of the lucid episode. The majority of patients died within hours to days after the episode."

-"Spontaneous Remission of Demential Before Death: Results from a Study on Paradoxical Lucidity" by Alexander Batthyány Pázmány Péter, Catholic University Budapest, and

Bruce Greyson, University of Virginia Health System, copyright 2020 American Psychological Association

ACKNOWLEDGMENTS

Jen Enderlin is one of the most beloved and brilliant people in publishing, and it was she who saw a snippet of news about the Duke parapsychology studies that inspired my writing of this book. Jen, thank you doesn't begin to cover my gratitude for you as a human being and as an editor.

It takes a village to get these pages into your hands and my incredible publishing village includes Katie Bassel, Erica Martirano, Brent Janeway, Robert Allen, Alexis Neuville, Steven Seighman, Jeff Dodes, Marta Fleming, Olga Grlic, Tracey Guest, Sara LaCotti, Christina Lopez, Kim Ludlam, Kerry Nordling, Erik Platt, Gisela Ramos, Sally Richarson, Michael Storrings, Tom Thompson, Dori Weintraub, Guy Oldfield, Mary Beth Roche, Emily Dyer, and Drew Kilman.

On the agenting side, I'm grateful to my team at William Morris: Margaret Riley King, Hilary Zaitz Michael, Sylvie Rabineau, Tracy Fisher and Celia Rogers. My thanks also to my manager Robin Budd and entertainment lawyer Darren Trattner.

The eagle-eyed Laurie Prinz helped improve this novel, as did the friends and family who read early drafts and supported me in other ways, including Alex Finlay, Alex's wife Tracey (who secretly says me I'm her favorite author—but don't tell Alex), Dean Koontz, Charlaine Harris, Kim Howe, Lisa Unger, Jud Ashman, Suzy Wagner and Karlee Rockstroh.

Holly Bario of Amblin Entertainment has turned into a good friend—and a generous guide to the world of Hollywood.

I'm so grateful for this writing life, which helped me during the loss of both of my parents this year. And to my extended found family at RRSA India, who inspire me with their heroic commitment to saving street dogs.

Anthony Barbarino came into my life at just the right time. This one is for you, my love.

And last but never least, for my sons Jackson, Will, and Dylan, the best characters I could dream up.

I love hearing from readers. Please find me on Instagram so we can stay connected!

ABOUT THE AUTHOR

[Photo credit text]
Bill Miles

Sarah Pekkanen is the number one *New York Times* bestselling author of sixteen solo and coauthored novels. Her books are sold in thirty-six countries, with several optioned for TV and film. Sarah also cowrote the screenplay for *The Wife Between Us* for Steven Spielberg's Amblin Entertainment. She serves on the board of directors of International Thriller Writers, and is the founder of the nonprofit IndiaStreetPaws.com, which rescues injured and abused street dogs in India. She lives just outside of Washington, DC.